MW01601377

Dear Nastacia

This book is dedicated to you I apologize for not being the nicest to you. From the mental and physical self inflicted wounds, a lot of damage has been done but, now I am doing much better and learning to love you properly. Thank you for being strong willed despite all the years of torment I have unintentionally done to you.

Regardless of how well this book does in terms of sales, I am happy to have written all of your internal emotions. I pray you have many years of peace. love u

Preface

I would like to get this out of the way right now. I am not endorsing sin. Yes, this book has sexual themes and cursing. Yes, the holy trinity, God, the Son (Jesus), and the holy spirit are mentioned throughout this book. I am NOT saying sin is okay or that all the things the characters did were okay. I have characters who are written to be more spiritually intact than others so that I can create relatable and realistic content. Again, if you find yourself living lukewarmly or identify with a character who doesn't necessarily practice everything our lord and savior have called us to do. I advise that you repent fast and pray to God for forgiveness and guidance so that you may lead a better life that is centered on Christ. I do not mean to sound like a hypocrite when I say this, but as men living on this earth, we are all sinners. No one is perfect but Jesus; as followers of Christ, all we can do is try our best to seek a personal relationship with God and allow the words from the bible and the holy spirit to transform us to be more Christlike.

If you are new to this journey of following Christ, let me be the first to say it is not an easy path that you have chosen. Being a follower of Christ means picking up the cross daily, killing your flesh to worldly desires, letting go of who you used to be, and making way for the who God is transforming you into. Living a Christ-filled life means dealing with spiritual ware and consistently Ephesians 6:12. For we wrestle not against flesh and blood, but against principalities, against powers, against the rulers of the darkness of this world, against spiritual wickedness in high places. You will deal with
spiritual warfare once you give your life to Christ because Satan is going to fight to keep you from going down the

righteous path. Please do not read my book thinking because one of my characters sinned, it is okay for you to do it and later ask for forgiveness. I will reiterate again sin is not okay.

Furthermore, this book is a work of fiction for the most part, with a bit of nonfiction scattered throughout the book. Specifically, in the first three chapters, there's a lot of reality of what I experienced mentioned. Some of the experiences mentioned throughout the book are not Christ-like, but we are all human and will make mistakes. I am not proud of the woman I used to be before knowing Christ, but I truly believe that we have to experience the things that we go through so that;

1- We learn to rely on God,

2- Our testimonies will lead those who arestruggling closer to god

3-We learn from our past; we get convicted by the holy spirit, and by repentance and the practice of spiritual obedience, we grow closer to God.

I began writing this book in the fall of 2022. At that time, I was very centered in my relationship with Christ. I read 10 chapters a day from the Bible, fasting once a week, praying consistently, practicing abstinence, and doing all the things I believed a righteous woman should be doing. In 2023, I would then meet a man that I now realize was placed in my life as a sexual temptation that would unknowingly and unintentionally lead me down a path of sin. I learned during this season of my life that committing one sin would only lead to more sin. I went from being sexually immoral, which led to me being abused, to engaging in sexual acts with other men, which alone is a big sin because the bible is clear on not causing others to sin. Every time, before, after, and during my sexual engagements, I understood what I was doing, and that was a sin in the lord's eyes. Instead of educating or advocating against sexual immorality, I led other men to be more involved in the sin, which is wrong in the Lord's eyes.

My sin and a broken heart began to make me feel empty, and I tried feeling that void with wine, sex, worldly men, and other things. Reading Chapter 3, you will discover how I found God again and healed properly. Again, sin is not okay, regardless of the circumstances. If you read your bible and open to the book of 1 Samuel, you will find the story of King Saul and David, who would later become the king of Israel. King Saul wanted to kill David because God chose David as king, amongst other reasons. While on the run from King Saul, David stopped in the city of Gath, where he pretended to be insane so as too not to be recognized. David committed the sin of lying, David was already covered in Gods protection, even if the people did recognize him he didn't have to lie. David's sin led to every priest being murdered in that city, ordered by King Saul. I mention this story as a reminder that no sin is okay and all sin will result in some consequence. To answer your question, yes, I will have to answer for all of my sins one day before the throne of God.

I beg that for any of you who do not know the Lord or have a relationship with God but are struggling, you repent, pray, and turn to him. It took me a while to truly believe this, but God wants you to come to him as you are and let him do the work. The days I struggled to get out of bed, the days I didn't want to live, the days I couldn't open up my bible, I regret not turning to him. Now I understand this verse Psalm 34:18: "The Lord is near to the brokenhearted and saves the crushed in spirit." I would try to only go to God once I fixed myself up, but that's not how it works; only Jesus can help if you choose to seek him.

Lastly, I wrote this book to talk about my past, a bit of my present, and a way to speak on my future, with a mix of razzle-dazzle in there to create an engaging story line. While writing this book, I experienced many waves of doubt, but by putting my faith in God, I was able to publish the book that you are currently reading from your phone or holding in your hands.

Thank you for giving this new author a chance. I pray that you all come to know God if you do not already have a relationship with him. That all of my hopeless romantic readers are led to their wives or husbands who God has waiting for them. And to those who are hurting and wanting to know peace, I pray the next verse over you, Philippians 4:6–7 , "Do not be anxious about anything, but in everything by prayer and supplication with thanksgiving let your requests be made known to God. And the peace of God, which surpasses all understanding, will guard your hearts and minds in Christ Jesus" Thank you, enjoy.

-Nastacia/Hazel

Acknowledgments

I want to thank God first and foremost for blessing me with the creative ability to write and for getting me to where I am today. I pray he continues to guide my steps and bring me closer to him.

Secondly, I would like to thank my mother for giving birth to me and raising me to be the intelligent, strongwilled woman I am today. I love you even if I don't express it enough.

Thirdly, Thank you to that one raggedy ex, you know who you are. Had you not left me with a heavy heart I'm not sure I would've been able to write some of these emotions out.

Listen to the playlist that helped me write this book

SCAN THE QR CODE

Is This Love?

Thursdays were, without a doubt, my favorite days of the week. While I couldn't speak for my coworkers, I always arrived at work with a more positive attitude, knowing it was my Friday and that I had three days off ahead of me. I spent those days off doing yoga, going on hikes, and spending time with my best friend, Nadia. We would binge-watch TV shows without interruptions while sharing stories about our jobs.

I worked as an EMT, which stands for Emergency Medical Technician, and Nadia was a nurse. We would discuss our most extraordinary cases from that week and reminisce about our college days when we lived with two other girls. This made my excitement for the weekend carry over into my last shift of the week.

After grabbing my items from my apartment and locking up, I jumped into my Jeep and put on my oshaped shades before I pulled my faux locs to the top of my head. I had different shades of brown running throughout my hair. The colors brought out my hazel eyes that complimented my caramel sunkissed skin. The day was so warm, making me want every single ray to touch every part of me and turn my light skin into a lovely bronze shade before the night fell. I always loved it when the sun kissed my skin; it cleared up all my acne and made my hazel eyes shine even brighter, making me look like the queen I was.

I smiled, knowing that I wanted to bask in this confidence. I knew this feeling wouldn't last forever. I felt confident now, but later, I would call myself unattractive, unappealing, hideous, grotesque, and many other words that could come to mind. I knew I shouldn't have these self-loathing thoughts, but when you've been told long enough that you are those things by multiple people in many different settings, you begin to believe it.

I went to Spotify and searched for my "on repeat" playlist, and my hot girl music started to play. For me, this included artists like Doechii, Rico Nasty, and Leikeli47. I needed to hype myself up to prepare for my 12-hour shift. My commute was only 10-15 mins, so it was only a short time before I pulled into work. I hop out of my Jeep and go to my backseat, grabbing my ballistic vest, backpack, helmet, and lunch box. I type in the code to access the inside of the station. My shift started late in the evening, so I wasn't surprised to find the station empty. At this time of day, there were a lot of minor car accidents and people out and about, so medical emergencies were bound to happen.

Out front, I could hear the bass of music playing. I grinned as I entered the garage and saw Captain wearing a white muscle shirt with black tactical pants and boots. Captain stood at about 5'10", as Nicki Minaj once said, he had "waves on swim so they hate on him," the smoothest brown skin, mocha brown eyes, a few freckles that dashed across his face, and the most perfect white teeth. He had big, strong arms used to lift the heaviest of our patients and a thick body. He earned the name "Captain" after he broke protocol by jumping into the lake to save a drowning patient. The patient was already deceased upon arrival, and it was against protocol for any medical personnel to do that; it was the fire department's job to get the patient. When our chief arrived on the scene, he said. "Get your Captain Saving America ass back to the station so we can talk." Ever since then, everyone has referred to him as Captain.

Our station was placed in the middle of a neighborhood, and there was a woman across the street "gardening" as Captain was dancing to Temperature by Sean Paul while he washed our ambulance. My grin widened as I grabbed a towel and rolled it up. I sneaked up on him before I smacked his behind with it. He laughed before raising the water hose and threatening to splash me. My smile dropped, and I crossed my arms over my chest. "You wet my hair, and I will make tonight a very long night for you," I said to him very seriously. I spent 30 minutes trying to lay my edges, and I would not let him ruin them with water.

"And if you smack my ass again, I'm drenching you and all of your stuff." I rolled my eyes at his response; I walked over to the shelf where we kept our towels and threw one to him before we both started wiping down the ambulance. "So, are you doing anything fun this weekend?" He asked casually as he let the windshield wipers down and rubbed the window. I shrugged, "Nothing out of the ordinary; my friend and I might drive around and look at the mansions near the lake, get Italian food, and watch movies. That's about it." Excitement dripped onto my tone. We did the same thing every week but, it was still what I looked forward too.

"What about you?" I asked curiously; his weekends were unpredictable. He would hunt with his brothers for whatever was in season or take a random road trip. Knowing him, he would be building a house for a random family in need or going on some massive road trip with his brothers and then arriving back right before we clocked in for our next shift.

"I'm actually just going to..-" Before he could tell me, our tone dropped, and we both quickly put away the materials to wash the ambulance. He put on his red polo shirt and placed our things in the outside side compartment at the back of the ambulance. I got in the passenger side before he hopped in the driver's seat. I typically always took the first call. He knew I was anxious about driving through traffic and wasn't the best navigator. I progressively got better at memorizing these streets throughout the months, but I got it from my mother. Growing up, she had a terrible sense of direction. Unfortunately, that rubbed off on me.

The streets in this city that ran north to south were numerical, and east to west were alphabetical. It was one colossal square, but I still struggled with my directions. Specific neighborhoods and areas of town were grouped by different universities and trees. People in history or cities. So, it was straightforward, but I still struggled. "Medic 22, you've got a 55-year-old female in cardiac arrest secondary to an overdose at the address of 1002 Frankford Ave. "

"I'll grab the airway bags and the suction, and you worry about the stretcher. Once we get in the house, I'll start on ABCs, you can start chest compression, and I'll start getting the drugs ready. Once the fire department is there, they can check the sugar. One of their guys can take over on chest compression. You can start an IO so that I can start pushing drugs." We both agreed on our roles that he had given, and that was the start of our shift. From that point forward, we had one more cardiac arrest, a diabetic emergency, about 4 "sick people," sick people calls were the most annoying ranging from 20-year-olds having anxiety attacks to 60-year-olds having toe pain. Captain and I had a good dynamic on the ambulance; sometimes, we didn't have to communicate what role we would take on a call. We just naturally flowed together, and that's why I loved working with him.

By 10 p.m., we were finally able to chill and stop for some food. After we had ordered from this hole-inthe-wall Mexican place and eaten our food, about 20 minutes had passed without us being dispatched, so I decided to take this moment to relax and enjoy the silence.

I was content as we sat on the steel-stepping stool at the back of the ambulance. My legs were outstretched and propped up on the curb while I looked at the sky. It was one of the things I would miss about this town; no heavy pollution or tall skyscrapers were blocking the view of the stars. I didn't know when I would be leaving, I just knew since I had graduated with my Bachelors of Kinesiology with emphasis on Exercise Sports Science, that soon after I would leave, I just needed to formulate a budget and a plan. What city would I move too? Was I going to move back home to Dallas or try somewhere new? What career would I pick? When would I apply to Physician Assistant school? I had only graduated a month ago In January I was giving myself until May to have a plan ready since my apartment lease would be ending in August.

I momentarily pulled myself from my thoughts as I looked down at my radio to double-check that it was turned on. I have been known to accidentally turn off my radio from my wide hips, squishing into a couch or hitting a door, causing me to unknowingly turn off my radio and not hear a call. Sometimes Captain would have to search for me or call me so we could respond to a scene since I hadn't heard my radio. Going this long without a call was odd, but maybe it was just one of those nights.

I continued stargazing, and eventually, my mind slipped into maladaptive daydreaming. My mind began to replay the same thoughts that had been distracting me from the current events for the last several weeks. I was stuck in a loop replaying how things ended for Terrell and me. Terrell was a situationship that I really enjoyed.

He made the same old routine exciting and any problems that were on my mind dissipated when I was in his presences. I started to go through the same revolving list of all the things I could've done wrong. I didn't understand how we began our relationship with deep conversations, talked about our future together, had intense, passionate sex, just for things to end with him telling me, we shouldn't have sex anymore, and then he decided to just ghost me afterwards.

I still couldn't understand ; I thought I had effectively communicated and expressed my emotions. I thought we had agreed to remain friends and work towards dating, that we would no longer have sex but try and get to know each other on a deeper level, but, instead, the last few times we hung out, he was just dead silent. He went from trying to learn the inner workings of my mind to suddenly Nothing. Our relationship drastically changed; things had become awkward between us. When we would hang out, he only spoke when spoken to as if this was the military and I was his drill sergeant.

I was starting to wonder. Is sex the only way a man can connect with me? Or want to communicate with me? Was I doing something wrong? Maybe my conversations needed to be more intellectual or unique, or he learned all he needed to know about me. And he concluded I wasn't interesting enough to further explore.

I pulled my phone out and went through my messages for the millionth time to see where I may have gone wrong. I reread our last conversations, carefully dissecting each line. The last message sent was me telling Terrell I couldn't watch his cat for two weeks while he went out of town. Then he left me on read, and that was that. I sighed heavily as I had a sudden onset of tiredness. I rubbed my eyes, blinking back the tiredness from staring at my phone for so long.

As I'm lowering my hands from my eyes. I could see Captain from the corner of my eye staring at me. I turned to face him and gave him a questioning glare, immediately becoming defensive. "What?" I say with a hint of aggravation in my tone. I didn't mean to sound so irritated. I never liked anyone staring at me too long, especially in this close proximity. It made me feel like they were judging me. He seemed unfazed by my attitude and chuckled, shaking his head before looking at the stars.

"Lately, you just always seem worried or stressed about something. It's been weeks. Are you going to finally tell me what's wrong, or will I keep catching you having these moments where you're on the verge of tears?" He turned his gaze back to the stars "You don't have to hide from me..you know that, right?" His voice sounded so genuine, but... I couldn't bring myself to believe him...I averted from looking at him, and I could tell he was looking at me again.

I was hesitant to open up. What if he told all of our coworkers how I was humiliated? What if he judged me? What if he used this against me later? I didn't even realize my eyes were tearing up until he grabbed me gently by the chin. He brought my face to look at him, and I immediately snatched my face from his hold, feeling uncomfortable, "Where did you go?" he asked me, his voice filled with concern.

I wanted to tell him so badly that I was hurting and that I was tired of being good enough for sex but never being good enough to date, always good enough to be in the privacy of a man's room and explore each other in the most intimate of ways but never good enough to be out in public on a date. I was tired of being used and left feeling empty. Tired of doing all the things a woman is taught to do to please a man but never receiving the same respect. I was sick of being a man's therapist, sex toy, chef, and safe place but never getting anything back from it.

I felt a squeeze on my thigh and immediately pulled away from his touch as I was again dragged from my thoughts. "Talk to me, Hazey." We held eye contact, my lips quivering as I fought internally to determine if I should tell him how I felt. Feeling a little trapped and backed into a corner, I sighed and finally speak. "It's just that..." As I was about to open up, our tone dropped, "Medic 22, you have a 72-year-old Female who fell standing in the bathtub." I smile and wipe my eyes before going to the driver's seat, "That's all you, baby!" I say with a laugh as I wipe my would-be tears before I hop into the ambulance.

At this time of hour, usually, the older patients who were in the bathroom more than likely defecated on themselves mixed with other bodily fluids, and it was never a scene that was pretty nor smelled the best. "Yeah, yeah, we will finish this conversation later," he says with all seriousness before smiling and getting inside the ambulance. Captain and I flirted a lot and had become close while working together. I even considered him a friend, but I wasn't comfortable opening up about the real stuff.

The rest of the shift had been going well until the last call; we had to back up another unit, and the medic on that particular truck had anger issues like no one's business. He snapped and yelled at everyone on that call, even yelling at our Spanishspeaking patient, who was very close to being in septic shock due to an amputee infection. The patient wouldn't stop grabbing things as we placed him on the stretcher. This caused the unnamed medic to yell at the patient. That led to him and me getting into an argument after we put the patient in the ambulance.

I wanted to advocate for the patient; I didn't like the medic's attitude toward his patient. Captain stepped in, and I watched as they argued, admiring that he was backing me until the 4th medic on the scene reminded us of the family watching. Captain and I walked away. Once in our ambulance, we loosened our clothes, relaxed as we drove away, and updated dispatch with our status so we could be taken out of service.

. . .

I sighed as I changed into gray booty shorts and a white long-sleeve crop top. I sat on my patio and waited for the sun to rise while I sipped my glass of wine. I had my plants sitting out on my patio with me to catch the morning sunlight's first rays. I sat on my chair with my feet up on the rail. After a long week of being degraded, disrespected, and seeing people at their worst, it was these moments I most looked forward to that always made it worthwhile.

My tranquility was disturbed by a black Ford F250 pulling into a parking space in front of my building, blasting loud music. I sighed heavily, putting my glass down. I watched Captain exit his truck and stand on the truck bed before yelling up at me.

"Yoo!! Get yo ass down here we're gonna go on a road trip." I crossed my arms and looked at him like he was crazy. "What are you talking about?" He looked at me like I was the crazy one. As if I was the one who pulled up to his house playing loud music, disturbing his peace. "I'm tired of looking at your sad eyes. I'm adding some fun and adventure to your life. You got 10 minutes to get ready, or I'm dragging you downstairs!" I groan and shake my head. "And If I don't, then what?"

He reached down, grabbed a giant water gun, and started to shoot at me, surprised that the water could reach me all the way on the third floor and even hit my face. I squealed

17 | P a g e

and ran into the house, "FINE!" I yelled back with a giggle before closing the door behind me in case he ran up here.

I didn't even know what to pack. I had no idea where we were going, but adrenaline and excitement flowed through me. This was the most sporadic thing I've ever done. I packed one pair of jeans and two pairs of leggings, took off my favorite gray shorts to pack them, and grabbed a couple of crop tops and two sports bras with some toiletries. I put on some black sweats with my black pullover hoodie before I grab my items and sit them at my door. I brought all of my plants back inside. Aligning them next to the window and leaving the blinds cracked so they could receive the much needed sunlight while I was away.

After locking my door, I smiled and looked down over my rail. He was still standing on the bed of his truck. "Come on, Hazey! Bring that ass down here!" I give him a one-over as I rest my arms on the rails. I was typically argumentative, constantly debating and fighting against anything I didn't want to do. Why did a man as attractive as him, who exuded so much masculine energy, could have any woman at work or in general to go with him on this trip decide to come to my home and take me? Why did he care so much about my happiness?

I continued to examine him; he had his arms crossed over his chest, and with him wearing a white tank top, I could see every defined muscle. My mind started to fill with mixed thoughts of how those strong arms could wrap around my legs and hold me still as he penetrated into the depths of my womanhood. I don't know how long I stare down at him, as my mind ran rampant with fantasies but his voice interrupted my thoughts.

"You're just gonna stand there, or do I need to come and grab you?" I tensed up when I saw him hop down from his truck, and I moved quickly down the stairs. I've seen this man roll over 400 lbs of dead weight (literally) before; lifting me wouldn't have been that hard for him. I threw my duffle bag in his back seat before climbing into the passenger side. I drape my blanket over my lower body and recline in the seat.

Once he gets inside, I look over at him. "You better not drive stupid, and I wanna stop at Starbucks before we leave town."

"Fine by me. I just want you to sit back and relax." I gave him a questioning look, a tiny part of me feeling as if he had something malicious planned, and suddenly, memories of my mom telling me about sex trafficking and women being killed started to haunt my mind. I guess he noticed the hesitation in my eyes and the excuse I was about to produce so that I could escape whatever he was going to do or plan on doing. He locked the doors with a playful sinister grin.

"I'm not going to hurt you. I just want to help you relax. You've been really stressed and sad lately, and I will distract your mind. With that being said, you're stuck with me until Sunday." I smiled at him, and for some reason, whatever doubts or fears I had in my mind disappeared. "Fine... I'm trusting you, so you better not do anything stupid." My tone remained serious, yet I still leaned back in my seat and stared out the window as my eyes became heavy. The vibration of the road beneath us as he started us on our journey.

I was tired from the shift we just had. "I'm going to nap. If you're tired, just let me know, and I'll drive us to wherever it is you are taking me." I don't know if he responded or not. I ended up falling asleep.

...

I don't know what time it was when I woke up, but the sun was beaming bright and hot, hitting my face, and we were driving over a rough dirt path. I groaned as I sat up and looked around at my settings. We passed tall, dark green trees, and the road before us didn't define where we were headed. I finally make eye contact with him. He grinned from ear to ear and smiled at me before nodding towards the windshield. I looked over, and I saw the two-story cabin home. The cabin featured a rustic wooden exterior with a wraparound porch that offered stunning views of the hills and mountains.

I stared in awe at the home before looking towards him and nodding in approval. "Owned by my great grandfather, who passed it down to his sons, and with each generation, it was renewed, refurbished, and upgraded. It's just gonna be the two of us this weekend. That was my original plan for the weekend: to come out here go hiking, swim at the lake, maybe hunt something, and just spend this weekend chilling. I figured you might need all of this, too." He says as he spreads his arms out and spins around in a circle to emphasize the nature surrounding us. "I know you like nature and hiking, so I figured you would love this." My eyes watered as I watched him return to his truck to grab our things.

No one had ever been this considerate of my feelings..it was more profound than that. No one has ever given me a personalized gift like I had for them; No one ever went all out for me. No one ever bought me something simple because I was having a bad day. I was tired of being the chaser but had grown accustomed to that role. I had never had anyone notice my moods before like he did besides Nadia.

He went to his backseat, grabbed our items, and I followed him to his front door. As he shuffled his keys, trying to find the right key to walk inside, my eyes roamed my surroundings, looking up at the sturdy, tall, deep green trees that towered over us.
It made me feel small, hidden away, and even safe. My eyes came back to ground level, and they examined Captain's shoulder blades as they moved and arched as he held our items in one arm. My hand wanted to reach out and run a finger down his spine, wanting to make that physical contact, hoping it would lead to more. But he unlocked the door, and almost immediately, we were hit with a pleasant earthy pine smell mixed with vanilla.

"I had a cleaning lady come in a few days before freshening up the place and ensuring the water was running properly, and everything was working nicely. No one has been here since Christmas." He explained as he put our items on top of an ottoman in the foyer. He started to take off his shoes, so I followed suit, taking off my slides.

The foyer was a good size and had a left and right entrance. The left side led to a kitchen with brown and white marble counters and a flat stainless steel chef-style oven next to a wooden pizza oven. The right entry led to a living room with a sunken conversation pit! The pit was a circle, which made it even more intimate; the couch itself had a velvet texture and was a lovely shade of amber-orange. A fireplace was at the center of the sofa, and a 75-inch flat-screen TV was mounted above it. I look back at Captain, who leaned against the wall with his arms crossed, a proud look on his face.

"My mom has a whole list of renovations. She and my dad plan on living here permanently, and she wanted to get rid of the "cozy family cabin" and replace it with her own personal taste since this is where they will be retiring." He leaned away from the wall and walked around the space a bit, looking at everything. "Me and my brothers renovated this entire house and have a few more projects, but yeah...."

His eyes met mine, and the smile on his face was filled with pride. "So far, so good," he says as he approaches me. He reaches up, and I am a little confused, but I remain still waiting in curiosity. He pulled a tiny fig from my hair.

I smiled at him and couldn't help giving him a oneover from the small interaction. My hazel eyes were met with his honey-brown ones for a brief moment. I usually could read expressions and looks but Captain had a darn good poker face. Part of me felt like he was digging me, and he was feeling what I was feeling ... and let me tell you..the things I was feeling? I wanted him to pick me up and sit me on one of the cabinets he renovated for his mom and slide his hands beneath my sweats and between my thighs and rub my soft little nub. I wanted him to kiss on my neck, where I had a small, barely noticeable dark brown birthmark that rested just below my neck, just above my clavicle bone.

I knew exactly what I wanted, but his eyes...although warm and welcoming, I had no idea if he was feeling what I was feeling. If he wanted to kiss me as badly as I wanted to kiss him, if he wanted to be skin to skin, or if he wanted to be entangled with me in that king-size bed he had mentioned on the way here.

"Let me show you to your room." I saw a twinkle of excitement in his eyes. I raised an eyebrow at him. "Don't worry, you're going to love it." I couldn't tell if he was being serious or sarcastic.

He led me up the large set of wooden stairs. He turned right down a long hallway decorated with family photos. I examined them as we passed by, and my eye was caught by a picture of him and his family. In the picture, there was snow, and his mother was sitting cross-legged, holding a younger Captain, possibly 5-7 years old, about to throw a snowball at one of his brothers, who was also holding a snowball as well. His brother was about to throw one back at him. While his other two brothers were wrestling in the snow to the left of his mother. His uncle was grabbing each boy by his jacket and tried to pull them apart. As I examined the picture, I felt him place his hand on the lower end of my back right above my behind. I moved myself closer to him, laying my head on his firm shoulder.

"My aunt took this picture of us...we were supposed to be taking a family picture, but that didn't go as planned when my brother..." He pointed at the top of his mother's head, where snow lay on her straight brown hair. "He had meant to throw a snowball at me, but it hit my mom, so I was about to wear him down with the snowballs, then my other brothers started to fight and well...you can see the chaos in the picture," I turn to look at him I could hear the nostalgia in his voice, clearly a happy memory for him. I loved a man who loved his family. That was something I wanted to marry into since I didn't have a lot of moments like this with my own family.

We continued down the hall to the room, and I almost gasped. In the center of the room was a queen-sized bed with a lavender-shaded comforter surrounded by a white canopy, which I called a "princess bed" until he corrected me and informed me of its proper word. The window seal was caved in to make a book nook. Decorated with fluffy white blankets and arm pillows. He showed me to my personal bathroom. Inside was a nice walk-in marble shower with a seat inside. And attached to the left side was a nice sunken garden bathtub. I turned to look at him with a hand on my hip. "Okay, I'm officially impressed. This is super nice." I say with a nod of approval.

We head back to the bedroom, and I hop on the bed, laying on my stomach, sighing with happiness. "Thank you for inviting me out to this nice weekend getaway...this is much needed," I say as I allow my body to sink into the bed. I closed my eyes at the thought of enjoying the sunset/sunrise from this cabin's coziness or... getting familiar with Captain in that conversation pit and seeing which seat on the couch had the best window view of the mountains.

"Well, I'll give you some time; I will start the fire and shower quickly. We can link back up in the living room in an hour or so." He goes towards the door to close it before he can shut it behind him. I call out to him. "Hey, Jamal." He stopped and paused, looking back at me with his eyebrows arched curiously, waiting for me to speak. "Thank you for bringing me here. I needed this." He smiled and nodded his head. "I'll remember to extend an invitation to you next time I come out." He gave me another smile before exiting the room and shutting the door behind him.

I stand from the bed, sit in the book nook, and stare out the window, taking in the views and watching nature.

. . .

We had just finished cooking and eating and sat on the back porch. We decided to watch the stars rather than TV. There were many more stars out here than in Lubbock. I found it crazy how certain people in populated cities would never be able to see these views. I felt great. Currently, waves of relaxation reverberated throughout my body as I relaxed on the couch and my head laid on his shoulder. "I was ghosted," I say simply without looking at him. He remained silent, and I took that as an invitation to continue.

"I was messing around with this nigga named Terrell. We met on Bumble, and the connection was almost immediate. You know, normally, when you hook up with someone, you may have a minimal connection solely based on that individual's physical nature and looks. Still, it never goes any further than that, right?" Although a rhetorical question, I still pause to gather my emotions before continuing. I didn't want to cry in front of Captain but also I was ready to finally talk about it and tell him what had been on my mind, needing a male perspective to give me more clarity.

I continued after taking a moment. "Well, the first time we matched, we chatted for a bit, and then we had sex... it was good, but it's the stuff that took place afterward that made me smile. We had deep intellectual conversations; we talked about religion, conspiracy theories, self-care methods, etc. After that, we had sex two more times, and with each encounter, we had sex for an entire shift. I got to his place at 9 or 10 p.m., and then I didn't leave until 5 a.m."

I could feel myself choke up with emotion, and I sat up, creating a fist and slowly kneading into my stomach to remain calm. I felt Captain put a hand on my hair and rubbed my back comfortingly, but I scooted away from him, not wanting his comfort. "It was super intimate, and he felt so good, and I felt safe with him ... but after we had sex, as we were cleaning up and changing, he asked me where I got my sage from."

I finally turned to look at him, and my eyes were burning from blinking the tears back, but I was angry. "Sage?" he asked me with a confused look. "It's supposed to cleanse evil spirits and release bad energy from the space you're in." He smiled as I said that, and in my defensive state, I glared at him. "What!" I yelled at him, and he threw his hands up defensively. "Just never knew you were a crystals and sage type of girl, but that's a wild thing to ask for after sex," He said with a frown on his face."

I shake my head and roll my eyes. "Never really did the crystals, but the sage I used just because I liked the scent," I say with a shrug. "But I agree...which is why I asked him afterward if he had a problem. My woman's intuition was going off like crazy. Still, he insisted that everything was okay and that I had Nothing to worry about."

I take another deep breath. "I knew once Terrell walked me to my car, and I started to drive away; I felt everything wasn't okay.I went to sleep that morning and woke up later in the afternoon. He messaged me something along the lines that he wasn't supposed to be having sex, that God was disappointed in him, and that he wasn't supposed to be doing that."

My eyes blinked back tears again, and I laughed. "I can understand conviction I truly do, but we had agreed to be friends and work our way into a relationship. So, I told him we needed to talk in person. We met up, and long story short, we agreed that we would work on deepening our friendship. We hung out a few times after that, but it was different; he was no longer having deep and meaningful conversations; his default turned into him being dry and quiet. Then, a few weeks ago, he asked me If I could watch his cat for 2 weeks, and after I said no, he just ghosted me."

I let out a breath and sighed, finding my hair super interesting as I saw Captain staring at me from the corner of his eyes. "And how does that make you feel?"

"It makes me feel like he had a scratch that needed to be itched, and once he was satisfied and moisturized... no longer itchy, he just threw me away, and I was no longer useful to him, not even as a friend." It was my first time admitting that out loud.

"So that's why you've been sad." He ran a hand over his waves and nodded his head as he contemplated his next words. "Well, I can't fix what he did, but I definitely can be the nigga to be better than him. You didn't deserve what you received, and in my opinion, I think he just wanted sex and nothing else...which is unfortunate for him because you really are a gem, Hazey,"

"Oh, yeah? And why is that?" I wanted to know what he saw in me that other men didn't see or didn't want to acknowledge. I also just wanted my ego stroked a bit after all the emotions I had experienced over the last few weeks.

"Well, for starters, my love, your beautiful...I can look into those hazel eyes all day and night while you rant about, how the government is full of literal demons and how these new female rappers are industry plants to push thot culture to stray people from God. You are intelligent, self-sufficient, and work well under pressure."

I felt his arm sink beneath my back; his right arm reached over me, and he gripped the side of my shorts and pulled me onto his lap, making me straddle him. He adjusted me on his lap so that our middles were touching, and I moaned softly as I felt his stiffness rub against my womanhood. "You are passionate, empathetic to your patients, even the frequent fliers, your acts of service are admirable, you are very clean, you are mindful, and so many other things men look for in women."

I swallowed hard and listened intently as he listed various things about me. I could feel my heart race, and I became more nervous as we remained in this position. The realization that my earlier fantasies were about to come to life and suddenly I was nervous. I looked down as I played with the end of his shirt. His hands rested on my hips, and he adjusted himself again before he pulled me against his chest. I started to laugh to avert from the things he was saying. "This is such a lame attempt to get into my panties.". His face had a light smile, but he remained chill. I averted my eyes and looked around our surroundings.

He pulled my chin with his pointer finger towards his lips while his other hand was at the low end of my back, pressing my stomach and chest into his. "You laugh, but I know you're hurting, and that can't feel good regardless of how much you may try to laugh and make a joke of it." I pulled away from his chest, and I swallowed hard my heart was pumping so loud, surely he was able to hear it. I had never had someone look at me as intensely as he was looking at me currently. His arm across my waist was even tighter. I felt my chest start to tighten, and I wanted to escape. I never had a man read my emotions or pay so close attention as he was right now. It was so overwhelming. By the way, his hands held me in place. I could tell he wasn't going to allow me to leave. He wasn't gripping me, but his hands were firm and heavy.

"Are you going to trust me? I'm sensing a lot of emotions coming off of you right now" His voice was soothing. I felt his hands start to rub the bareness of my back, and I tense a little bit. It was like my skin was vibrating after every single contact. His continued rubbing up and down my back in a comforting motion, and with each passing touch, I felt myself slowly get used to the motion and what he was doing to me. "What emotions are you sensing?" I asked him as I adjusted myself on his lap, making myself comfortable.

He stared into my eyes as I awaited an answer, searching for the right emotion to express how I may have felt. "You're anxious ... maybe because you're worried about the aftermath of what we're about to do. You're scared because you don't want me to treat you like Terrell did. Irritated that you're in a vulnerable position, And obviously-" He held my hips down as he thrust back and forth, causing me to moan out loud. Even through the clothing, I could feel his dick almost penetrating through my shorts. "Arousal, you want this dick?" His words were overwhelming and I could feel my face heat up.

"Was I that easy to read?" They say a man who paid this much attention to a woman had to like her a lot. Also, theirs no way he planned all of this just to get into my panties. I reasoned to myself.

I didn't want to think anymore. All I could do was nod my head and respond with a moan. I couldn't take the teasing anymore. I finally met his lips with my mine and pulled him into a soft kiss. His arms squeezed around me and I smiled as he rubbed my sides as our lips continued to grow familiar.

...

After a few hours of some of the best sex I've ever had, I felt the alcohol pass its peak, and I was exhausted. We moved from the outdoor seating area. He pulled me up, and I wrapped my legs around his waist. I was starting to slide down, so he removed his arms from my back and placed them under my behind. I wasn't surprised that he could carry me. He was known for lifting some of our heaviest patients by himself and worked out consistently. He walked towards the patio door before we entered. He carried me all the way upstairs before we made a left at the staircase, and we went to his bedroom, where he laid me down on the large bed. I sunk into the softness of the mattress with his added weight on top of me. My eyes were already closing as soon as I hit the sheets, and I could feel him shift my body sideways before he got on the opposite of me. I felt him pull a blanket over us, and pull me into his chest.

...

The following day, I woke up to the smell of lavender tea with a hint of...chamomile? There was a tray of food placed on the bed. I sat up and examined the plate. He had cooked me scrambled eggs, turkey bacon, a bowl of mixed berries, and two pancakes. I looked around the room and could hear a shower going on.

On the nightstand was a cup of the tea I had smelled and a glass of water. I grabbed the water, and my mind was slightly dazed as I consumed more. I leaned against the headboard as I looked out the window, watching birds chase each other. I was pulled from the beautiful scenery to the sound of a camera snapping. I turned my head over and saw a shirtless captain, with tiny droplets of water falling down his body and dripping onto the gray sweat he was wearing. I stared at him, feeling too drained to argue with him like I usually would if someone was taking off-guard pictures of me. I could tell by his stance and how he held the camera that he wouldn't stop, no matter how I reacted.

I ignored him, sat up, and moved the plate of food in front of me. I went straight for the protein, and I started to nibble on the bacon, trying to pace myself to keep from throwing up,

I got up after eating a piece of bacon, some fruit, and some eggs. I was in much need of a shower, a deep cleanse of my skin and face, and just overall a freshen-up. As I stood up and walked past him, I pointed my finger at his chest "Your skin still damp? I know that means you didn't put any lotion on." I shake my head playfully, pretending to be disgusted. "That makes you so dusty." I felt him smack my ass, causing me to whimper, followed by a giggle. I quickly shut the door behind me and locked it in case he got any ideas of coming in here while I worked on my self-care.

I was in no rush to come out and actually talk to him, especially about what we did last night. It's not that I regretted it or anything. I was just nervous about the outcome of our relationship after we left the cabins this weekend. I shake my head at the thoughts of the future. "We will worry about it Sunday night; for now, I'm just going to enjoy his company," I tell myself as I undress. The future will be there, and for now, I want to focus on the positives of this trip. And that's how the rest of the weekend went. We had more intimate moments hiking, fishing, cooking dinner together, and relaxing.

. . .

Seventy two hours later I watched his truck drive off, and I sighed. As I watched his truck disappear. A small amount of dread filled me with each passing moment. While on the way back, we agreed to start dating. He asked me to be his girlfriend, but I couldn't think of the "what ifs" of us breaking up. As much as I wanted to bask in the giddiness of being in a new relationship, I can't help but mourn the thought of us one day treating each other like strangers and not best friends.

I've had that in relationships before; after you get past the newness of sexual intimacy and the freshness is gone, that's when men start to act differently...at least in my experience. I knew the honeymoon stage could last for months and even years. Still, my most prolonged honeymoon phase lasted 3 months. In my experience, men always switched on me once sex was introduced into the relationship. I wanted a serious long-term relationship, but maybe my actions of having sex initially would be my downfall.

I shook my head; I was tired of thinking. Whatever happened would happen, all I knew was that I would do what I always did: remain genuine, consistent, and open to communication. I walked away from my window before I went to my bedroom and grabbed my chair, moving it to the patio. I watched the sunset, enjoying the familiarity of my surroundings. I felt my phone go off. I was expecting a text from Nadia asking me to come over or my mom sending me some kind of article or YouTube video. I was wrong.

I smiled when Captain's name displayed across my screen. I was surprised to receive a text from him this fast. "B shift boys want to go to the lake and drink. I won't be home until much later, but if you want my company or need anything, hit me up." I smiled at that message before responding. "Naw, I'm chilling 'for the rest of the night. Be safe, and don't do anything stupid."

I couldn't help but squeal and be excited as I read that message repeatedly. He was communicating with me and giving me the reassurance I needed. After a couple more rereads, I finally put my phone down face down on my thigh before putting my feet up. My worries dissipated. We would have to see what would happen, but I was basking in this sense of security for now.

I Knew Better than to Think this was Love.

These last five months have been the best of my life. Whenever I wasn't hanging out with my best friend, I was with my boyfriend. This wasn't some idealized version of a dream man, nor was I being delusional, trying to "manifest" a crush into reality. No, this was my actual partner—someone who was truly mine, and I was his. I finally found a piece of own that wasn't just based on physical attraction or settling for a "nice" guy who treated me well despite lacking other qualities I desired. This man had a stable career, a vehicle, a place of his own, paid his bills, and was loyal to me. His name was Jamal Kalula, aka Captain...MY Captain.

Today, we were in the ambulance working together. We had just finished working with a psych patient who liked putting things in every hole their body had to offer....and I mean every hole you can think of. That being said, it left our ambulance a mess. After taking the patient to a room and giving a report to the doctor, we returned to the ambulance bay to disinfect our equipment. While doing so, I debriefed with Captain, telling him what happened while he was driving. Whenever I tell a story or experience, I'm usually very animated, especially when it involves a story with a patient.

As I went through the recap with him, he was seated in the commander's seat, directly behind the stretcher, where the patient would lay. He had his feet propped on the back of the stretcher. I noticed he was smiling as I talked, but his eyes didn't match his smile. His eyes glazed with admiration instead of humor, and I tilt my head at him in confusion. "What? Why are you looking at me like that?" I asked him, curious to hear why he had that look on his face.

He stood up and approached me. He placed his hand on the small of my back and leaned forward, placing his lips upon mine. I was extremely tense at first. Although in the privacy of the back of our ambulance, we were still in public. Our ambulance was parked in the ambulance bay of the hospital. What if another ambulance pulled in? What if it was one of our coworkers who, after dropping off their patient, decided to visit our ambulance? Which wasn't abnormal among the EMS community!

Yet as the kiss deepened, the tension in my back melted away, and I leaned into it, letting my shoulders drop as I placed my hands on his shoulders. After a moment, he pulled his lips away and began to play with the loose curls that had fallen from my bun. "Come over tonight?" he asked, twirling my hair around his finger and looking into my eyes with anticipation. A smile spread across my face, and I just grinned before playfully pushing him away. "We're going to get in trouble," I said, returning to my cleaning.

Despite the kiss, something felt off. It was as if he had something important to tell me. It was unusual for him to act that way, especially not letting me finish my story. He typically asked follow-up questions, particularly after a call like the one we just had. The ride in the back of an ambulance was usually the most eventful part of a shift; patients often shared their life stories or did something that made me laugh. Surely, Captain would want to hear what our "hole plugger" patient had to say while we were en route to the hospital. But after our intense kiss, he got out of the ambulance and made a phone call while I continued cleaning. It was another odd behavior; he usually helped out.

Hmm, his truth would reveal itself.

. . .

After our shift, I went to his place. We were lying in bed together, my back pressed against his bare chest as I sat between his legs. I was wearing one of his shirts. His hands were underneath the shirt, and he just rubbed my stomach as we cuddled post-sex.

I could see his face in the mirror positioned directly in front of his bed, and I was trying to read his expression. He was gazing blankly out the window to the right, his brows furrowed and his eyes distant. I sat up and turned to straddle his lap, wanting to understand what was bothering him. I placed my fingertips against his scalp and began to knead in slow, deep circles. This had always helped him relax in the past, so I continued in hopes of easing his tension. "What's wrong?" I asked, my tone filled with concern as I awaited his response.

He didn't say anything for a while, and my heart ached. My womanly intuition was buzzing. I could feel it in my navel that he was about to tell me the last thing I wanted to hear. He still wasn't looking at me; it took all my will power not to grab his chin and force him to look at me. I continued to massage his scalp, but the silence was making my mind wander into dark territory, "Did he cheat on me? Did he cheat on me and catch something? Is he about to break up with me? What did I do wrong this time?"

I was so lost in my thoughts that I didn't even notice the tears forming in my eyes, rolling down my cheeks and dripping onto him. He pulled me out of my reverie by wrapping his arms around my waist, hugging me tightly and rubbing my back. After a moment, he released me, simply looking at me. I gazed into his eyes, and they seemed to convey an apology. "What's wrong, Jamal?" I asked, my voice laced with anxiety and irritation. What was he not telling me?

He took a deep breath, likely trying to release his own anxiety before speaking. "Amani called me a week ago, asking if we could meet up. She said it was urgent and that we needed to talk soon." Amani was his ex-girlfriend, and they had broken up a month or two before the New Mexico trip he and I took together. He had claimed that part of their breakup was due to her jealousy of our friendship, saying he talked about me frequently when she was around. Later, he confessed to having feelings for me, which ultimately led to their split.

He sighed heavily before dragging his hand down his face. His eyes had bags underneath them, and I could tell he hadn't slept much. I observed this a week ago at work but didn't say anything because I assumed it was work-related, we did have a lot of stress inducing calls that week. Evidently, it was much deeper than that. I remained silent while he gathered himself. I didn't want to be hasty, so I awaited a response.

"We met a few hours later that night, and...well, she was obviously pregnant at least by a couple of months. She told me shortly after we had broken up, she began to experience pregnancy symptoms. Missed period, nausea, tender breast, etc. She went to a doctor and discovered she was pregnant. She hadn't said anything until now because she didn't know if she would keep the baby or not, and she didn't know if she would tell me." He shook his head and let out a breathy disbelief laugh.

I stayed quiet for a few moments, gathering my thoughts and wiping my tears. I felt more angry than hurt; maybe if he had acted differently and not been so animus, I wouldn't have been so defensive. "So where do I fit into this equation, and what will you do?" I asked, my voice barely above a whisper. I shifted off his lap and began to get dressed, fully aware of where this was headed. He stood up as well, pulling on his clothes. "Well, I mean... I'm sorry, Hazel, but you know how important family is to me. I didn't grow up in a two-parent household..." He paused, but I kept getting dressed. I wiped my tears, determined not to show any more emotion in front of him. How could I be vulnerable with someone I was losing?

"I don't know what I'm going to do, honestly..." He stated pathetically as I continued grabbing all my things, ensuring I didn't leave anything behind. "Hazel, stop and talk to me, please." Unlike him, he said it in a desperate voice I had never heard before. It almost made me pause, but I didn't owe him anything. He was playing in my face.

After I had grabbed everything, I finally looked at him and stood by his bedroom door. "I have nothing to say; you're breaking up with me to be with your baby mama." I shrug my shoulders. "I'm not going to fight that, but what I'm not going to do is tell you we can still be friends, and I'll be there for you every step of the way and give you words of wisdom; you can get that from your baby mama, friends, and family." He had me bent out of shape if he thought I was going to lie and say we would always be friends and that nothing would change between us. How were we supposed to be anything outside of each other's soul mates? We are WAY past friendship. I wasn't mature enough to damper my feelings for him.

I took a deep breath as I started to feel myself choke on my words. "Congratulations on fatherhood and getting what you've always wanted." I walked out of his bedroom and rushed out of his house before he could grab me and stop me, but as I got in my car, it finally registered in my mind that I never heard his footsteps behind me. I looked up at his door, and I didn't see him. The tears I was holding back finally released, and I started crying.

I had never felt like someone's first choice in my life. Yet for the last five months of dating him, I felt on top of the world. He did the bare minimum that I had never experienced before: we went on plenty of dates, I spent time with his family. But in the back of my mind, a nagging anxiety lingered while we cuddled, making me wonder when he would disappoint me like the other men in my past. And now, here I was, facing that reality in this very moment.

When I got home, I stripped my clothes and immediately got in the shower to scrub his touch off me. While I was driving home, another realization came upon me, this nigga gave me some break-up sex, and I hadn't even known it was break-up sex. The thought alone sent me into a spiral. I was crying so hard at that point I had to pull over with my eyes watery and my vision so blurry from the tears to the point that I wasn't able to drive straight and see the road. I knew deep down in my heart not every man was the same, but damn, it was getting harder to remain optimistic.

As I continued to undress, I started to take off my shirt, and as I pulled the shirt over my head, I realized this was Jamal's shirt. I stare at it for a while. It was a black shirt with a male lion seated; the lion had dreads and a blunt coming from its mouth. Very corny shirt, but I love Lions, and I always told him I would never give him this shirt back. I shake my head at that thought now. I go out my front door, and from the third floor, I drop it over the rail and watch it drift into the muddy puddle. I go back inside, and I get in the shower.

For the rest of that night, I curled on the couch even though it was hard to focus. I started to make a todo list. It was May, and my lease ended in three months. I was so busy being a girlfriend that I had forgotten the reality of my future. My best friend was the only thing keeping me in this town, but even she was moving to Dallas in January. I loved my job but knew that wasn't enough to keep me in Lubbock. I was tired of this small town and wanted to return to the big city. I've been here for 4 years now, and although I love the short commute, no

lines in most places, and the cheap gas, I was just ready for more and to be closer to my friends and family in Dallas.

After reading my to-do list:

- Find a job
- Find an apartment
- Furniture shop
- Start packing

I started to feel hopeful and immediately applied for jobs.

...

Jamal and I decided to keep everything between us. A month had passed, and we knew if we requested new partners on the ambulance, everyone would know something was wrong, and I didn't want to deal with the gossip. We were no longer flirty at work, but we were still a great team as far as patient care went and being on crazy scenes together. Captain would attempt to have normal conversations, and I would engage a little, but our interactions were different; I was short and monotoned with him. He no longer was a safe space for me. We weren't joking and laughing like we used to, and our debriefings ceased. In the four weeks since his revelation, He never apologized or reassured me that he cared for me or that his feelings for me lingered. I didn't have closure, but the excitement of leaving in a few weeks distracted me from my broken heart, which demanded my attention and insisted on being comforted.

I couldn't handle this type of pain right now. I knew if I opened that door, I would be dealing with not just the recent events but also the residing feelings from Terrell. After things ended with Jamal, I realized I had never truly healed from the initial heartbreak; I had just found a nice distraction. Over the last several weeks, I had fleeting thoughts of heavy rejection weighing heavily on my mind. Now, I had two men I needed to heal from, but instead of feeling my emotions, I compartmentalized and focused on my future rather than harboring on the past. The female rappers and social media that I allowed to influence me taught me that's how a real woman handled her business, not realizing I was only hurting myself and delaying my healing.

On my final night in town, I stood in the middle of my apartment. I had just finished taking videos and pictures for my records in case the staff tried accusing me of anything. When I was finished, I did a final walk-through and sighed as I circled through the apartment. Despite the past several weeks, I had many good memories here. This was my first "big girl" apartment without any roommates. It was the first time I felt independent and on my own. The apartment was only 500 square feet, but it was extremely cozy and spacious despite the lack of square feet. I had a small, cozy bedroom and a home washer and dryer. A decent-sized living room and kitchen. This place will forever live in my heart.

I lock up the apartment, saying goodbye as my eyes water up. I walk down the three flights of stairs. "I'm not going to miss these stupid stairs," I say out loud. I made sure my new apartment was on the first floor. As I got to my car, I could see out of the corner of my eye a black shirt underneath a bush, and I immediately knew it was the shirt I threw from my patio several weeks ago. I sighed, knowing that I didn't want to leave it there. I run towards the bush. I pick up the muddy shirt and throw it in my jeep. "That's the only thing you get to hold onto, Hazel," I stated before pulling out of my paid space for the last time and exiting the apartment complex.

I spent my final night at Nadia's. We had drinks, put on face masks, and watched trashy TV. We reminisced over our college days, and I was genuinely happy. I considered calling Captain so that I could, at the very least, get closure, but Nadia convinced me that nothing good would come from the conversation. She stated all of the facts, he picked his baby's mother over me, he had goodbye sex with me, and he didn't care enough to ever apologize or check to see how I was doing. "You just have to accept those facts, girlie, and move on with your life. Let what happened in Lubbock stay here and create new memories in Austin." We clinked glasses to that, and I downed my drink.

The following day, we hugged each other tightly and expressed how much we loved each other. I was so happy to leave, but the change made me sad. As soon as I got in my vehicle and could no longer see my dear friend waving me goodbye, I started crying. By the time I made it to the outskirts of town, I was blasting some Rico Nasty and ecstatic, thinking about all the new things I would experience.

Bye, Lubbock. Hello Austin.

Welcome to ATX

Austin was the reset I needed. A new career? Check. Friends? Check. New favorite spots? A lovely modern apartment? Check. A new man? Several, none of which left me feeling satisfied mentally, spiritually, or emotionally. I moved to Austin because it was the first place I could find a job. I applied to jobs in Houston, DFW, San Antonio, and Colorado, but Austin offered me the best opportunity, so I took it.

I worked for the marvelous Dr.Johnson when I first moved to Austin. She was an obgyn with her own private practice. She was an eccentric black woman with a natural self-confidence that made people gravitate to her. During my video interview, we hit it off immediately, finding similarities in our style, music choice, and love for God. She hired me and took me under her wing. It was a unique opportunity. I earned so much experience while shadowing her. I witnessed many women give birth. I learned to care for, nurture, and understand the needs of a pregnant woman who is continuing to grow and change with life within her and post-birth needs. It was beautiful, and I knew I had chosen the right path.

My first year in Austin mainly consisted of working and trying to save money. I knew I would attend Physician Assistance school the following year and needed to save as much money as possible since I knew I wouldn't have much time to work. After two years of schooling, I graduated with a Master of Science in Physician Assistant (PA) studies and became a licensed PA. After graduating, I decided to work for a local ER at a major hospital and gain experience there while working part-time at Dr. Johnson's Obgyn Clinic.

While I was in school, I didn't go out much or do much exploring but, Dr.Johnson had a neice, her name was Alameda. She had graduated from medical school and became an OBGYN; in a few years, her aunt would retire and hand the clinic down to her. Alameda was feisty, ratchet, educated, and overall a charm. She was the home girl I called when a nigga did me dirty and I needed a good time or if I wanted to try a new restaurant. She was always down for a good drink along with some good food.

Once I graduated and had a career, I finally started exploring various places in Austin. It was amazing being surrounded by the beautiful town lake/Ladybird Lake and seeing all the consistent greenery this city had to offer. It was a nice change in scenery after living in Lubbock, aka the Dust Bowl, for the last 4 years. I discovered that all the restaurants on the lake had the best views and ambiance, but the food was a 4/10, maybe 5/10.

The best food was scattered throughout central and east Austin. If I wanted to go partying or bar hopping, specifically where the black community was, I only found my people at The Domain, a huge outdoor mall with a section set aside for bars and clubs, at midnight on Fridays and Saturdays that's noticeably when all the black people stepped out. Alternatively, I could venture to Pflugerville, a city about 15 minutes north of Austin, where many African Americans resided.

I'll admit I assumed that by moving to a major city, an increase in black culture would finally surround me, only to be supremely disappointed. Through colleagues,

46 | P a g e

classmates, Facebook groups, and just randomly chatting up black people I would see out and about, I was slowly but surely able to find my community. Although some days were still a struggle. Now and again, I would go to Houston with Alameda or visit friends and family in Dallas if there were any extraordinary black events or places I wanted to try.

Despite the lack of my culture in this city, I loved how Austin is in central Texas, so it was easy for me to travel to different cities. It is almost three hours to Houston, nearly three hours to Dallas, and two hours to San Antonio, San Marcos, and Corpus Christi, so I had a lot of day trip options. There were so many hiking and walking trails everywhere in this city, so that was also something I frequented.

My dating life for the first 3 years was nonexistent. I honestly didn't have time and knew I needed to heal. I knew this because I didn't trust any man who I encountered. I assumed they all were going to treat me the same: Use me for sex and then dispose of me once they fulfilled all of their needs or their ex came back. At some point during my transition from Lubbock to Austin, I opted for hypersexuality instead of love. I didn't think love existed and sought the one thing I knew: I could always receive sex.

Sex only imprinted temporary satisfaction. Once the man expelled his seed, I was left to my thoughts and felt an empty hole in my chest that grew bigger with each interaction that came from being with a man.

In my little free time, I would journal and read my bible; I grew spiritually and deepened my relationship with God, which allowed me to forgive all the men of my past. A pivotal moment in my journey occurred when I was lying in bed one day, crying and ranting to God about Jamal, and I felt a voice speak in my mind that wasn't my own, "Forgive him because I have forgiven you." My spiritual growth increased from that moment.

I read my bible more, and God revealed what I needed to change about myself. I stopped smoking weed and changed my music to things less vulgar, sexual, and violent. I filled my music library with Christian artists. I had become abstinent and learned to experience my emotions now and have healthy coping mechanisms rather than just numbing myself with a substance.

The seclusion and isolation had made me anxious around men. Despite being apprehensive about dating, my self-growth allowed me to grow my selfconfidence. I had always been a plus-size woman, but I learned to love myself, and my newfound confidence wasn't false. I think people could feel that energy exuding from me. Men were approaching me in public, and we would exchange numbers. It was common for me to gain a couple of numbers when I did choose to go out. It never went any further than that. I would schedule dates, but then, in the moments leading up to it, I would just cancel. The thought of being intimate or vulnerable scared me, made me feel physically ill and I ran away from it.

Another year had passed since I had moved to Austin, and I was finally starting to get comfortable in my routine. All ties to my past were officially cut, I was settled into my career, and I was killing it in every aspect of my work.

While working in the hospital, I met a social worker I worked closely with in the ER. His name was Isaiah. He was one of the few black employees in our department, so he stood out when I first saw him in passing. It was almost instant attraction on my end. Until that moment, the men I had been talking to barely held my interest; they were mildly attractive and semi-interesting. So when I saw this mature brown skin dread head with a chest and arm piece that peaked out from beneath his polo shirt, he had a clean aesthetic about himself. I knew I had developed a crush. Immediately I began to ask my coworkers about him, and no one seemed to know much about him, which in my eyes, was a bonus; it meant he wasn't whoring around the ER like the rest of the staff on hand.

From that moment forward, I tried formulating a plan to get to know him. My work besties and I started speaking in code, referring to Isaiah as Jerome or Jermaine since he looked like a 99-cent Jcole.

Isaiah and I always talked to each other, but it was usually just on a professional level. I tried my hardest to be the most professional, serious, and nononsense I could be around him; I wanted to come off as mature to impress him. When trying to figure out more about him, his colleague told me Isaiah's age. There was a 15-year age difference, and I didn't want him to think I was immature; I wanted him to respect me. I was 27 and he was 42.

After our first conversation, it didn't take me long to take my shot. Within the first two weeks of knowing each other, I told him I could do his hair. It was a long shot, but we lived in Austin, and his hair appeared as if he needed some care and a retwist. He accepted my offer, even after I clarified that I didn't know much about locs; we still linked up later that week. I figured that meant he liked me because why else would someone with locs let someone without experience with locs touch their hair?

Before he came over, I spent a lot of time on YouTube looking up tutorials on retwist. During the first meet-up, I deep-conditioned his hair, blowdried it, and attempted my first retwist, which wasn't all that bad. With the first time being successful, we met up a few more times, but things slowed down from there. A month had passed, and he hadn't made a move. I was okay with this pace. It gave me a chance to get to know him. I had never met a man intellectually on the same level or higher than me. I enjoyed listening to him explain his field of psychology expertise and what he knew about human behavior.

I was attracted to how he picked up things about myself that I knew but had never openly expressed. Whenever he revealed a part of me no one else had, it sent tingles running through me. He would never know that because instead of accepting what I knew to be accurate, I would deny it and fight him. It felt good to be seen, but I also didn't like being exposed. It was uncanny and made me wonder what else he knew about me without me having already vocalized it.

My friends told me I needed too just outright say how I felt. The thought made me nauseous; I was intimidated by this man, which made it hard for me to be vulnerable. I would practice expressing myself with my friends before he came over. Which was all time wasted because once he walked through the door, I was quiet as a mouse, and it would take me a moment to warm up to him. After a month had passed, my friends were fed up. They forced two shots down my throat and made me send him a text message expressing my feelings.

The response I received wasn't what I had wanted or expected. After expressing how much I liked him, his text response was, "So you want some dick huh?"

I had grown so close to God and knew I should have ended things right then and there. I was also aware of the fact that I had grown from men treating me this way....or so I thought. I had just been crying to God about how men perceived me as a sexual object, but instead of running away, I allowed my lust, flesh, and sexual curiosity to take control. A lesson God would later teach me a lesson on.

That text message changed the trajectory of our situation forever. In the beginning, we didn't have a lot of sex, but the sex we did have left me feeling intense. I never had a man who got it right with the first stroke. His maturity showed in the best way possible; his experience was evident, and he had good stamina, frequently making me want to tap out. The thrill and excitement of this new man were short-lived.

We weren't having nearly as much sex as I thought we would, and because I had been doing his hair for so long, it started to feel like an expectation rather than a favor or romantic gesture. I was beginning to feel used. It didn't help when he promised me small gifts that were never delivered on his end. He had reasons for the delayed gifts, but I would've been okay with anything as a sign of appreciation as long it wasn't food or something useless.

Each interaction was starting to leave me more depressed than the last. It was draining. I really liked Isaiah, and I thought if I kept doing nice things, maybe the feelings would be reciprocated. I realized I wanted romance, intimacy outside of sex, and a real relationship. He had already told me he wasn't looking for anything serious, so I knew better than to continue seeing him. I didn't know how to end things.

Once he quit his job as a social worker at the hospital for a better opportunity, I started to think of an exit strategy. I planned a meet-up with him, hoping it would be the last time. It ended in lousy sex, animosity, hurt feelings, and more. All on my side.

The no contact only lasted four months. On a random day in March, I had awoken to the typical "How you've been?" text. The timing was unnervingly perfect. I had just ended a situationship and had been thinking about Isaiah. Despite the feelings and curiosity, I knew I needed to stand on business, and I had planned to ignore it, which I did all day. Then he called me, and I was never the type to ignore a call.

I hesitated, inviting him back into my life. I wanted to be abstinent; I promised God and myself I wouldn't spiral again and that I would wait to give it to my husband, but, truthfully, I was weak, overwhelmed with my schedule, and I missed him. I dealt with internal turmoil for a while. I had distanced myself from God while being with Isaiah due to guilt, and I didn't want to do that again.

With everything said above, you would think I just blocked him and went on with my life, but no. After we had spoken on the phone, I decided I wanted to spend the block a second time. I felt a shift in our energy; this was the most playful and flirtatious we had ever been with each other. I wanted to tap into that and see what would happen. I had become a different woman since I last saw him, and I wanted him to see that for some reason.

I went to his home a few days later, and the whole experience changed me. When I saw him, I was still anxious, but not nearly as much as I had been in the past. I had always considered myself a good communicator until that night when I was in his apartment and territory, and he made me speak up.

He was quiet and patient and waited for my response; when I tried pulling an avoidant tactic, he redirected me; it was something I wasn't used to. I knew this sounded similar to something. I'd said this in the past, but this felt different.

He wasn't trying to get me to speak up just to get into my panties; this felt genuine. Although my romantic feelings for him had significantly dissipated, I still liked him enough that

I could never just be his casual friend as long as I was single.

I knew this was wrong to admit, but I was able to explore other relationships without having physical intimacy since I was with Isaiah again. Everything surrounding him was exciting. He was my little secret that no one knew about, and The sex was much different this time around. It was a lot more sensual, and he was a lot more....involved. The foreplay was everything I wanted and needed. It was all very overstimulating and would leave me reminiscing about it days later. I had become so comfortable with him that we stopped using and caring about condoms, and that was extremely unlike me. I was so paranoid about pregnancy that even if a man had only put the tip in before putting on a condom, I would still take a plan b.

These feelings were short-lived. He was starting to fall short; it felt like he was using me again, and my emotional needs weren't being met. I couldn't connect with other men on a fundamental level because I knew I had feelings for him despite how much I tried convincing myself that I didn't.
Conviction was also beginning to eat me up. I knew I wasn't supposed to be having sex with this man, and truthfully, deep down inside, I knew he was keeping me from my husband. The man that was meant for me wouldn't make me feel so empty after we had sex.

Eventually, Isaiah moved to Houston, but he still had a therapy gig that brought him back to Austin twice a month. Despite how he made me feel, we planned to have a sleepover at my place while he was in town for business. Despite the flirty text messages and how nice he was the week leading up to our sleepover, I was still disappointed and left empty when he stayed over. He let me down with mediocre sex, no aftercare, and no conversation. I knew I had to end things. He and I had been in this endless cycle for the past year. He'd give me everything I needed: a gift, foreplay, a long sex session, a little bit of aftercare. Then, the next time he wouldn't do any of those things, he would promise to be striking the next time we linked, and then the next time he came over, it would be amazing. It was a toxic cycle that left me wanting more but left me feeling distant from God and empty.

After lying in bed, crying, and begging God for forgiveness, I finally sent that text message.

"Heyyy

Tbh, I don't wanna see you anymore. I'm tired of sinning; I don't want to have sex anymore. I love making you happy and helping you relax, but I gain nothing from this other than a heavy heart. It's best to cut ties now before we end up with a baby.

Have a good day, and I'll be praying for you and your endeavors."

I finally ended it, and although I was depressed, I was able to appreciate all that came from it. Being with Isaiah taught me I needed to be confident and vocal in the relationships following him. I could set clear boundaries, and I knew exactly what I wanted. That season of my life was the first time I felt my age. Up until now, I still felt like I was seventeen years old.

I would be lying if I said I was happy and immediately ran back to God, and all was merry. Following the breakup, I sought out more men to fill that void. I wasn't even horny; I just really needed a hug, but strange men didn't care about emotions, so I matched their energy. I hardly read my bible, drove fast, listened to loud music God had delivered me from listening to, and didn't handle my responsibilities.

After my finances slowed down, my depression started to feel scary, losing interest in all the things I once loved and conviction sitting on my chest as if God himself was standing on top of me. I finally decided to turn back to God. It didn't happen overnight, but it took several months to heal from the hands of strange men, loneliness, insecurity, and sin overall. Once I gave my healing to God by praying, fasting, repenting, and reading my word, I finally found the peace I once knew before I knew Isaiah. Once I was at peace with God, I decided to be abstinent again, and I didn't care about dating anymore—at least not right now. Isaiah made me realize all of the energy I was putting into him. I could put it into myself, and I did just that.

Fast forward 2 years, and I opened up my own clinic! With my savings, sponsors from local blackowned profit and nonprofit businesses, and some investors. With a hefty donation from Dr.Johnson, I could finally open up my clinic. I had a steady flow of clients and was recently able to hire an obgyn while having three midwives and two doulas. The business was flourishing so much that I even considered hiring an assistant.

I had been slowly creating a social media presence, and I was pretty popular, especially on TikTok, for posting the best black spots. It turns out I wasn't the only one searching for my culture. Trying to manage my schedule, read my DMs, and care for personal matters was becoming overwhelming. Despite the stress, I was grateful for these kinds of problems. ...One year Later...

Today, I was in my office finishing up notes and overlooking things from my previous patients while waiting for my nurse to come and get me. The patient I met with had just moved from Lubbock due to her husband getting a job. I was friends with this patient in undergrad. We were close then but grew distant due to life, but when I received a random phone call from her a month ago, we clicked like old times. She told me her husband had just received a 5-year construction contract to work on something here in Austin; she was 28 weeks pregnant and needed a new doctor. I immediately agreed and fitted her into my schedule.

When my nurse told me my patient was ready, I stood up smiling, grabbing my pink lab coat. I smiled as I entered the room. We both squealed and hugged each other. I pulled away from her, and I rubbed her stomach lightly. "Wow, Mariah, I feel like we were kids pretending to be adults on campus just yesterday, and now here we are. You're growing a baby, and I'll be there every step of the way." I smiled at her warmly, and she smiled back.

Out of the corner of my eye, I saw a male figure who appeared bothered and annoyed. I cross my arms over my chest and give him a one-over while she sits down and prepares for our appointment. "Hello....and you are...?" I ask as my eyes evaluate him. He wasn't her husband. I knew her husband from a Facebook post, and this wasn't him. This man was a bit large yet not fat, but he wasn't skinny or overly muscular. He was a nice in-between thick...like a linebacker. Peaking over the collar of his shirt was a chest piece; bilaterally, his big arms each had a sleeve, and I could tell they told a story, and I wanted to read it. His arms were big, and for a second, I had an image in my mind that I knew I would have to repent about later. My eyes traveled to his face...his handsome face was framed by a perfectly trimmed beard and a chiseled jawline, and despite the moody and irritated vibe I was getting from him, his brown eyes showed a warm curiosity. He was no good.

I felt a lot of red flags run across my mind. "He's a tatted dread head and built like a stud....he has many women, and I would not become one of them," I thought.

Despite the red flags, I felt my heart flutter a bit, and my friend pulled me from my thoughts. "Oh yeah, Hazel, this is my brother Marquis! My husband had to settle some things in Lubbock and couldn't be here with me today. My brother lives here with the rest of our family, but he was the only one free today, so I made him take me to my appointment today." I nodded my head in understanding. I knew she had brothers, but I had never met her family. "Well, it was nice to meet you." He tipped his head in response to me in a southern matter, and I felt my face heat with a blush, "I'm

Hazel." I reached out to shake his, and in return, he clasped my hand, giving me a firm shake. My soft hand in his rough one made me shiver. I couldn't handle this small interaction, so I just turned away from him, feeling his eyes trace my backside. "Yeah, this the last time

his fine self will find himself in my building." I think to myself as I focus my attention back on her. I harden my exterior, frustrated at the thought of being excited about a man I wouldn't even give a chance to. It's been a minute since I felt an instant attraction for a man, but I refused to lose sight of God again; besides, he was my friend/patient brother.

After the appointment, we closed for the day, and I headed home. I stayed in a lovely two-bedroom loftstyle apartment. The inside of the apartment was dark brown industrial. There were three large floor

-to-ceiling windows in my open-concept living room, kitchen, and dining room area. Upstairs, I had a sunroof as well as slanted large windows. Against every window, several plants lined up, varying from different pathos to large snake plants and others.

When decorating my apartment, I wanted a different look but one that was still modern. I also wanted the inside to remain cozy but unique. I loved my apartment and all the fur/fluffy pillows I had throughout it. My walls were covered in different black art, primarily styles of black women and our lovely Afros.

I make my way upstairs to my walk-in closet. I strip my pink scrubs and place them into my laundry basket. My closet had a floor-to-ceiling mirror lined with white dimmed lights. I stared at my body, examining my side profile; my hands rubbed my stomach, squeezing the rounded but solid area. I forced a smile on my face, and instead of squeezing, I began to rub that area gently; it was a constant battle to remind myself to be gentle with myself. I've experienced significant weight loss due to rigorous exercising, stress, and better eating. I still wasn't where I wanted to be, but I promised myself that on this journey of weight loss, I would also learn to love myself in every stage I found myself in. I turned around in the mirror and looked back at my back roll, which was also pretty stubborn.

"You are beautiful inside and out, whether you are 100lbs lighter or heavier. God loves you, sculpted and perfected you, and this body is his temple; you are nothing less ." I finally made eye contact in the mirror, and a genuine smile appeared. "I love you, Hazel," I say softly and heartfelt. I look around my closet, searching for an outfit for dinner with the girls. It was a lovely, warm June evening. I went for a green silk cami blouse with matching green silk with darker green flowers imprinted on a skirt.'

I checked the time. I had about two and a half hours to prepare so I could take my time. I walked into my bathroom, turned off the lights, and grabbed my remote from the counter. I turned on the strip lighting beneath the cabinets and in the shower. I had a walk-in shower with a rainfall shower head. I tilted the shower head back to avoid getting my hair wet.

"Hey Alexa, play...Stay Flo by Solange."

911 What's your emergency?

Yesterday's activities left me feeling drained. After dinner, we decided to go to The Domain and a wine bar. I got home about 5 a.m. I didn't typically enjoy going out like that, but once in a while, it was fun. Since yesterday, I have been eating poorly all evening and night. I decided that today, I would be productive and do something that had more substance to it.

After going to the gym, taking a pleasant nature walk around the lake, deep cleaning my apartment, Bible study, and reading, I ended my night with some self-care. Self-care consisted of taking a hot shower with a scented shower steamer, using one of many body scrubs, doing my skincare routine, burning a candle, and watching a movie on my list or reading a book.

At approximately 1:57 a.m., I was sitting on my couch wrapped in a warm fuzzy blanket, my portable heater was on, and I watched Poetic Justice for the 100th time. It was my comfort movie. I couldn't get enough of Tupac in this movie. I was obsessed with black romance films, especially the '90s films. Back then, there wasn't any social media, social anxiety, or fear of being accused of harassing someone; if a man saw a woman they liked, they approached her and made things happen. I loved how the men had to get creative with flirting and getting a woman's attention.

Like in Love Jones, Darius saw Nina in the record store, and he wouldn't let her get away a second time. Although a bit stalkerish, and I will admit if that happened in today's time, he would probably be in jail, and so would the cashier for aiding him, but also, in today's time, he wouldn't have to do that, he could just post her on TikTok and ask the people to help him find her, and eventually he would find his way in her DMs or the algorithm would put the video on her page. Regardless, none of that is the point. The point is that the men of the 90s were bold and fine. I wish I was in my 20s during that time.

As I watched Justice storm angrily away from the mail truck down the road, I received an alert from my phone. I lazily picked it up and saw that it was a notification from the camera at my clinic. I opened it up, and I gasped as I saw the glass being broken and two individuals going inside. I stood up quickly, ripped off my lavender face mask, grabbed my keys, and put on my fuzzy pink slippers before running out the door.

Once I was in my Jeep, I started to call 911. I steadied my breathing and drove slowly. I knew it would be dangerous to approach the scene alone; after all, they could have weapons. As instructed, I described the individuals to the 911 operator and parked one street from my clinic. Upon arrival, I killed my lights as I sat and waited. I was watching from my phone and saw that the men were in the storage closet, unsure what they would want to take or what they were looking for.

About five minutes later, three marked SUVs pulled into the parking lot, followed by a blacked-out charger. I exited my vehicle, the air hit my legs, and I cursed myself internally. I wore a black silk cami with matching black shorts and my pink silk robe. On self-care days, I wore my expensive yet comfy PJs. I didn't have time to go home and change; besides, I knew from first-hand experience that first responders often saw people at their worst when responding to emergencies, and my current outfit choice wouldn't be shocking to them, especially at this hour.

I approached the officers as they prepared their weapons; I was bombarded with questions. I handed them my phone so they could see the live feed of the suspects, who were now in my office. As I was answering questions, I saw familiar locs pop over the car door of the charger on the scene. I was shocked to see my friend's brother... "Marquis?" I asked, my voice filled with curiosity.

I had no idea he was an officer. Granted, I didn't ask him about his career, and Mariah hadn't told me. He turned around, looking confused, as he searched for the voice that said his name. When his eyes finally landed on me, he smiled and nodded at me, and for a moment, I was lost in analyzing him. His face was warm looking from the smile, very unexpected from when I last saw him in my examination room with that brooding look he had been sporting.

I saw his eyes quickly scan my body, and I felt uneasy. I was unable to read his facial expression. Did he at least like what he was observing, or was he judging me? The feeling annoyed me that I cared about his thoughts on my body. I began to grow more frustrated with myself. It didn't matter if he liked what he saw or not. When I looked in the mirror, I liked what I saw, and that's all that mattered.

He turned from me, drawing his weapon; he and the three other officers began to enter the building. I tensed up as I waited for everything to unfold. The officer outside waiting with me watched what was happening from my phone. The suspects were in my medicine cabinet, attempting to steal drugs. The cameras didn't have sound, but from inside the clinic, I could hear Marquis's voice and the other officers' commands. From the live feed, I can see them aiming at the suspects, and the suspects, knowing they were cornered with nowhere to go, started to follow commands.

They slowly turned around with their hands up and dropped to their knees. Marquis and one of the other officers put away their weapons as they approached each suspect. The other officers had switched to tasers; just as Marquis placed his hand on the shoulder of one of the suspects, the suspect quickly reached for my tiny lion paperweight that was on my desk and shattered it on the ground as Marquis went to pin him the suspect had grabbed a piece of broken ceramic and slashed at his face. One of the officers, standing back, tased the suspect, and Marquis put him in cuffs. The officer standing with me called for an ambulance on his radio.

Everyone came outside, and I took a good look at the suspects. I didn't recognize them; it was a young hispanic male and a young white male. It was later explained to me that they were street pharmacists looking to hit a lick to sell. After speaking to a robbery detective about the process, I opted to proceed with pressing charges; after settling that with the detective, I looked for Marquis. I found him near his vehicle; he was pulling out a first aid kit from his trunk. He had a laceration on his right lower jaw. I gently approached him with his back to me, lightly tapping his shoulder. He turned around, appearing agitated, until he realized it was me, and that warm smile was back on his face; now that I was closer, I could see it was a humorous smile. "Oh, you think I'm funny?" I asked him, trying to figure out why he was smiling at me like that.

As I waited for a response, I took his first aid kit from his hands. I put on gloves and stood close to him; he had a cedar yet clean smell about himself. I pour saline onto some gauze before I press it onto his jaw. "I just imagined you rushing out of the house. Let me guess: You were having some kind of self-care night? Now you're outside in those bougie ass pajamas."

As he painted the picture of my night, it dawned on me it was my first time hearing him speak. His tone was rich and deep. I noticed he had a southern drawl that stretched the vowels. His voice made me think of the rolling, expansive hills Texas had to offer; he had the kind of voice you would hear in a movie. A scene where everyone was gathered on a wrap-around porch, drinking sweet tea and listening to him as he told a story about his days as a young buck, yet his voice didn't match his speech mannerisms. He spoke like any other black man in Texas who spoke using ebonics. I liked it... a lot, actually.

As he spoke, I was completely enamored, unable to take my eyes off him. Standing at 5'7"—or 5'9" in heels—I had to tilt my head to meet his gaze, as he seemed to tower at least 6 feet tall. As we held eye contact, there was this undeniable spark between us, an electric connection that hinted we were both intrigued by one another. Unlike past encounters where the attraction felt unbalanced, our shared energy was vibrant and mutual, making the moment even more special yet unnerving.

We were so close that I was feeling overwhelmed.
It's been a minute since I've been attracted to anyone, and this attraction was powerful. I looked down at his arms and could make out the faces of individuals, bible scriptures, and animal symbolism. I wanted a closer examination of each one...an examination while I sat on his lap. I blush and clear my mind.

"How do you know I was doing self-care? And you're not wrong. I'm a bougie girlie." I say with a smug smile, I was bougie, and that was no secret. I was the kind of woman who spent hundreds every month on pedicures, facials, candles, and skincare." Because your skin has that glassy glow that women get after doing skincare, and you smell like lavender as well as vanilla." His eyes looked at me as if waiting for me to deny it. I didn't think he was as observant as I was of him, leaving me a little speechless.

"Are you a detective?" I asked playfully, unsure of how to respond to his inquisitive nature. "Yeah, actually, I'm a homicide detective," he replied with pride, his passion shining. Of course, he was; I wondered if he could detect

66 | P a g e

the lust that was looming off my body for him. If so, it was time for me to leave.

I was naturally tired at that hour in the morning, so I found my movements more relaxed than usual when treating someone. I listened as he explained his role in the police department and his other duties. After cleaning up his laceration, I examined it more closely. I got lost in thought as I ran my fingers along his jaw. My fingers traced the visible scars that extended down his neck. I didn't realize he had stopped talking until the silence enveloped us. One of my hands rested on his shoulder, while the other held his jaw in my palm, gently rubbing the mark along his jaw with my index finger.

I lifted my eyes to him, and he looked down at me with an unreadable expression. I realized maybe I was being invasive, but he wasn't resisting; he appeared more relaxed and curious. Perhaps he enjoyed what I was doing. Or I was too tired to recognize social cues. Regardless, I stepped back, crossed my arms, and chose not to address what I was doing.

I yawn before speaking, "Well, I bet you can detect I'm tired. Your cut shouldn't need stitches; keep it clean and put antibiotic ointment on the scar. Thank you for tonight." I say as I yawn again. He just chuckled. "I'm detecting many things from you right now, shawty." He pulled his phone out to look at the cut from his camera before putting it away and closing his trunk. "I'll see you tomorrow at the baby shower, right?" I felt a spark run down my spine; my face was warming up at his comment, I was too shy and embarrassed to tap into what he meant by his comment, so I focused on his question instead.

I was invited to Mariah's baby shower. I offered to be in charge of the gender reveal since she could trust me not to reveal the gender to her family members. I was surprised to know he would be at the baby shower. I know he's the brother, but still, I know men typically hate these kinds of events, "You enjoy baby showers?"

We were walking towards my car, and he opened my door for me. "Not at all, but the basketball game will be on, and my sis showed me the menu." He rubbed his stomach, and I smiled as he moaned, thinking about the foods he would be consuming. I rolled my eyes at him before sliding into my driver's seat.

"Just like a man to show up when food is announced." He closed my door and shrugged his shoulders. "What? A nigga gotta eat, right?" He says with that cheeky smile. His smile made me smile, and I looked away from him, shaking my head. "I'll see you tomorrow." He nodded his head before walking back over to his buddies. As I took off, I looked into my rearview mirror, and I saw his buddy giving him crap about something. He was shrugging his shoulders, and I wanted to know what they were discussing. Was it me? I thought curiously as I drove home.

. . .

He wasn't wrong; the baby shower food was hitting!
She had the typical black baby shower foods, meatballs, those little sausage things, deviled eggs, and wings, but

then she also had pasta, tacos, etc. The dessert table had a variety of cupcakes, ice cream, cookies, brownies, whatever you name it.

I was in the corner. I had set up my tripod and set up my phone. I was semi-popular on TikTok, with almost 10k followers. I had gained my following when I first moved to Austin. I was in search of black people and finding my culture in this city that offered a lot for Asians, Hispanics, and white people. I wanted to find bars and spots I knew my people frequented. I also posted nature/hiking spots, cool study spots, etc. Like any influencer, I started off with hardly any views. One fantastic birthday weekend, my friends decided to do the "dapping up 10s" challenge, where you dap up any attractive man you see in public. The video went viral; ever since, my account has become more popular.

I had spent all day gathering the things I would need for the gender reveal. She asked me to keep it simple since it was a bit last minute. Since they both enjoyed hunting, I bought one sizeable black balloon. Since they both owned bows and arrows, they would pop the balloon together with one bow and arrow, and blue confetti would spill out, revealing they were having a little boy.

I looked at the camera, examining myself before I started filming. My curly hair was hanging down to my shoulders, with a right side part. The camera revealed my hair was shrinking, slowly going from my shoulders, working its way up my neck, and reaching my ear, so I pulled it into a messy bun. I wore a lavender short silk dress and tan heels wrapped around white straps up my ankles. Everyone thought the baby was a girl because of what I wore, but I loved this color, which looked good on me.

Just as I was about to start filming, I could see Marquis at the back of my camera; he was wrestling with many kids on the ground. I smiled and shook my head. I removed the camera from my tripod and started recording him. It was about 5 little boys and girls on top of him, and they were hitting him. As the play continued, one of the little girls was knocked to the ground and started crying. He stood up, picked her up, swinging her around. She wrapped her arms around him and hugged him tightly when she calmed down. As he patted her back, he looked up, noticed me recording, and rolled his eyes but continued to comfort her.

As her tears faded, he gently assisted her back to the ground and approached me with a playful smile. "Ma'am, I'm going to have to confiscate your property!" he joked while I set up my tripod again. I rolled my eyes at him. "Not a chance. Now step aside unless you want to join my video." His approach towards me made me tense.

I couldn't help myself. Maybe I just wanted to prove that I wasn't sensitive and could hold my weight. I tried being the soft girl, but it never worked out in my favor, and neither did being mean. At least I wasn't being taken advantage of when I acted the way I was currently. I knew better; he was a cop, an attractive one, too. I would not be falling victim to this. Been there and done that; in the end, all I would end up with is a broken heart and regret. He backed away with his hands up and went to the cooler, grabbing a beer. Then he went to the living room, where the rest of the men were watching the game. I sighed, but it was better this way.

About an hour later, I called everyone over, handed the balloon to the couple, and began recording to capture this moment. Mariah and her husband stood side by side, each holding a bow and arrow aiming for the target. On the count of three, they released their arrows, popping the giant balloon and releasing blue confetti. There was a mixed reaction, but mostly, the parents were happy. I laughed as Mariah yelled, "This is the beginning of our D1 babies!"

After celebrating for a bit, I started to pack up the rest of my belongings so the family could enjoy the moment. I don't know why, but Marquis was on my mind. Maybe I should give him a chance...I mean, it's not fair to categorize all men and then put them into a subcategory of first responders. What if he was cool? At the very least, we could be friends. I was looking for him everywhere, but I couldn't find him.

I figured we would see each other again at some point.

I decided to give up and just go home. I was tired and had a lot of stuff to do to prepare for my work week. As I walked to my car, I saw Marquis leaning against a truck with his arms crossed as a girl stood before him. She was rubbing her hands up and his cloth chest. She was a tiny thing, about 5'2", Hispanic female with long, wavy, dark brown hair that fell to her curvaceous ass. I couldn't hear the context of their conversation, but I didn't need to. Of course, she was his type, and of course, maybe he was just being friendly with me.

My heart high-fived my mind despite the small grief my heart felt. I felt a gentle wave of longing, desiring a partner who would appreciate me for more than just my appearance. I dreamt of a deep and meaningful relationship, one where connection flourishes. I admired those who effortlessly found love and yearned for that same joy. My feelings were short-lived, and it instantly turned into annoyance. I barely knew him, and I would rarely see him.

He made eye contact with me as I passed him. My lips formed into a tight smile, and I just tipped my head off to him and continued walking towards my car. I felt his eyes on me, but when I turned around, I saw her pulling his face to hers, and they kissed. I faced forward again and eventually made it to my car. As I drove past him, I saw him holding her hands to his chest, and I shook my head.

My intuition about him was correct, and I wouldn't doubt it again.

Grey's Anatomy Isn't Real

A couple of times a month, I picked up shifts in the ER; it was a nice change of pace from the clinical setting. I couldn't work full-time due to having my own clinic, but I loved the rush of a weekend spent in the ER occasionally. I was a trauma junkie at heart, and I got my fill-in every so often. Not that every single weekend was crazy, but this weekend in particular was crazy for sure.

Marquis POV

My shift rotated every four weeks; during this rotation, I was off Monday through Wednesday unless it was my turn to be on call. Then, I just responded to any possible homicide city-wide. Lucky me, right? Thursdays were college night, so you had the 18-22-year-old crowd. The young crowd was a bunch of dumb, drunk, and/or high kids pushing their limits. Fridays, everyone getting off their 9-5 decided to drink early and party all night; Saturdays were a mix of it all, and Sundays were typical family-related drama. Not every single weekend was crazy, but it was certainly busier than Monday through Wednesday.

I was exhausted, Alexis and I spent most of yesterday night and early this morning fighting.

Alexis was my ex-girlfriend. We had been dating for about one year, but I decided to break up with her. I met her at a friend's kickback; it started as sex and developed into something more. We broke up after I discovered she had been talking to some firefighter.

That alone wasn't the reason why I ended things. Once I realized I didn't care that she had been entertaining another man, I knew the relationship wouldn't go beyond the point we were at.

She came to the baby shower to drop off a present since she and Mariah had become friends. I knew it was a setup, but I gave her the benefit of the doubt. After she dropped off the present, she asked if we could talk. We had been broken up for at least two or three weeks and hadn't spoken since. I agreed to her coming over, thinking she needed more closure, but man, I was wrong. She begged to get back together and said we should try again.

I was hearing her but not listening. I had already made my decision but wanted to keep this as civil as possible. As she pleaded with me, I saw Hazel walking out of the house. I couldn't help but stare. She had a thick, curvy frame, and her caramel bronze skin was glowing under her light purple dress. My eyes gazed at her glossy legs; I wondered what it would be like to touch them. I just knew she was smoother than butter.

It made me think of her in those silk shorts yesterday, where I had a better visual of her thickass thighs. Her hips were naturally wide and curved up. She had a small pouch of stomach but was still beautiful. My eyes then met her face, which was in a tight grimace. She walked fast past us, and I couldn't help but stare at her ass that jiggled with each step. "Damn, she's so thick I could handle all of that." I thought to myself before Alexis pulled my face to hers and kissed me.

I didn't fight it. My mind had been on sex, and now I wanted to tear into something. I took Alexis back to my place, and we had a rough and while session. I immediately felt terrible and told her we shouldn't do this anymore. She screamed at me and accused me of using her. I didn't argue back because she wasn't wrong.

I had thought of Hazel while hitting it from the back. As bad as I felt, I never wanted to be the reason a girl was hurting. But I couldn't help but imagine Hazel. I didn't know much about Hazel, but from what I knew, she was intelligent, passionate, downright gorgeous, and serious about her business. I wanted to tap into something like that. I'd never been with a woman like her before. The women I usually settled for were popular, sex fiends and just wanted to have fun. This was great until I thought about my future, wanting to have a family who I could trust to be around my family and friends.

Alexis and I had a great time in the bedroom, but the conversations didn't go far, and I think she only liked the idea of being with a detective. Our whole relationship consisted of good sex and her making content on social media that consisted of her filming me. I hated her "Day in the Life of Being a First Responder Girlfriend." Her videos were not consistent with what she was doing in real life. She would record herself setting up my lunch box. In reality, she only prepared my lunch a few times a month, and it wasn't even homemade food, which is what she promoted; it was always from restaurants. She would also record a time-lapse video of herself staying up late waiting for me to get home; truthfully, she was just coming in late from the club. Sometimes, we would walk in simultaneously, and then she would sleep in late with me.

She always filmed me when I was deep in thought or just relaxing. Then, she would edit the sound with some sad music or voice over, making me out to be some sad, moody officer who needed as much empathy as possible. Remembering those pointless arguments helped me make my final decision. I told Alexis we should end things and move on. After getting cussed out, called out of my name, and informed that I was losing the "baddest bitch in the game," She finally packed all of her items and left around 2 a.m. I felt terrible, but the relief was also amazing.

I walked through the ER with my partner Dee. We had just left the scene of a shootout at a bar. It left two deceased and one in critical condition. Our victim was brought to the hospital, and I needed to get a report and see how bad the damage was. As we waited for an update, we flirted with the nurses at the nurse's station. I was mildly interested in these women. They were mostly surfaced level, wanting to know how many times we had drawn our guns that day and what the most dangerous calls we had ever taken. I felt a strong presence just as I contemplated how I would exit the conversation.

I wasn't the only one who felt it. The nurses even straightened up and made themselves appear more busy. I looked around until my eyes landed on Hazel walking over towards us. She had just exited the surgery room with a nurse and the doctor. She was talking to them as if she was the doctor. Her eyebrows were knitted, and she had sweat beading down her forehead. As she approached us, she gave passing nurses orders and instructions regarding my victim's patient. Once at the nurses' station, she immediately started barking orders, making some of the staff tense up and scramble as they did what she asked before finally acknowledging me.

I was surprised to see her here today. I have been a detective for a few years now. While I was quite familiar with several doctors in the city, including all the major hospitals and other medical staff, I had never encountered or seen Hazel until today.

I watched as she grabbed a wad of tissues before patting away the beaded sweat on her forehead; her sandy brown curls were piled on top of her head. Despite her outward attitude, her Hazel eyes shined bright green with passion. I could tell by the dilation of her pupils, high brows, and widened smile she loved the rush and adrenaline of the ER. I found that surprising since her clinic had a calm vibe about it. She had hundreds of plants all over the clinic, water fountains, and a Wax burner. She had a record player in the waiting room who continuously played gospel, neo-soul, or lofi. One of the receptionist's duties was to continue to flip or change the record. According to the yappiest and most flamboyant receptionist I had ever seen, she didn't mind doing it because it helped her get her steps in. She had a very soft aura to her in general, and this intense energy she had right now was unrecognizable, but I loved it.

She opened his chart before showing me the picture of the X-ray. "He experienced a clean entry/exit wound in the left upper quadrant, just nicking the liver a bit. Hemorrhaging is being controlled, and vitals are steady, but it'll be a minute before you all can talk to him." Her voice was professional and monotone. That tone didn't match the look her eyes had just held. It felt like she was holding back and purposely being stiff with me. There was no room for questions. She gave me some papers and turned, leaving as quickly as she came. I watched as she walked away, as if she couldn't stand to talk to me for a second longer. I knew she had seen me kissing my ex, but I didn't think it would result in me getting the cold shoulder. The stiffness in her approach prompted me to consider the possibility that she might have feelings for me. If she was pissed, that only meant she liked me. I smirked to myself, deciding to accept the challenge.

When she left, the nurses relaxed and went back to talking. I watched her until her fine figure disappeared around the corner. Even in scrubs, her body was still banging. I felt my partner Dee hit my shoulder. I looked at him and saw that stupid grin on his face. He always got that look when he knew I was feeling a woman we encountered at work. It was no surprise that he had gotten to know me so well. We first met 10 years ago in the academy as Cadets; since our first sparring match in the ring, we have been close.

"Now, what did you do to piss off Hazel? She's normally cool. The energy between you two was off." He said as we walked to the break room to grab coffee. "She did not wanna talk to yo ass." He cracked up laughing.

I gave him an annoyed glare, "How do you know Hazel?" I asked as I opened the door to the breakroom, letting him walk in first, following behind him. "She's my sister's obgyn; she's also given me several reports." He answered as he poured himself a cup of coffee before walking to the lazy boy recliner, getting comfortable; we would probably be waiting for a while. "You don't know Hazel?" he asked me, his face showing disbelief.

"Naw, man, I met her for the first time last week. She's my sister's obgyn and friend from college. Today was only our 4th time seeing each other ever."

His eyes widen in realization. "Her clinic was the one you responded to the other day for that burglary call!" He nodded his head as if it was all clicking. I shook my head in response, and he smiled. "Did she reject you or something? You must've done something to her." I rolled my eyes. "Naw, man, I think she's just busy, I haven't made a move yet." I didn't feel like talking about my baby shower theory. That meant I would have to tell him about Alexis and me, and I was too mentally exhausted to rehash that entire exchange.

I looked up from making my coffee and looked over at him. He was smirking. "Why are you smirking like you know something I don't?" I asked as I walked over to the Lazy Boy next to him.

"Yet?" He sipped his coffee, staring at me over his cup. "Damn, this nigga messy." I groaned and waved him off as I adjusted in my seat.

I guess subconsciously, I was thinking about when and how I would make a move on her if the opportunity presented itself. I shrugged my shoulders before responding. "I haven't thought that hard about it. Hazel is attractive but seems busy and likes to keep to herself. I don't know, man. If I see her again, I might make a move. She's attractive, and I've never had a challenge; maybe it'll be fun." I flashed him a smile before I sipped my own coffee. Earlier this morning, we talked about wanting a simpler woman and not wanting so much stress when dating." He laughed and just shook his head. I guess we shall see then."

...

We spent the rest of the shift reviewing the witnesses and discussing what happened. The suspect fled the scene after the shooting; the patrol units couldn't find him, so it would be our job, too. After several hours of waiting for the victim and an update on his status, we were told he was officially stable but resting. We decided to come back tomorrow and go from there.

When I finally got off work, it was nearly 7 a.m. I headed straight to the store; it was the only time I could go shopping for the kickback I was having at my place later this week. A group of my first responder friends, cops, firefighters, paramedics, nurses, and my brothers would be having a BBQ at my place. We usually link up once a month, and it was my turn to host.

I stopped at the HEB grocery store on the way home. After about twenty minutes of shopping, I nearly had everything I needed. I only needed nonalcoholic drinks, so I made my way to the drink aisle. All I needed was a few 12-packs. As I entered the aisle, I saw Hazel squatting and looking at the different varieties of fancy waters. She still had on her scrubs from earlier, so she must've just gotten off as well. As I approached her, I saw her ears covered in pink headsets. Once I was closer, I noticed she was looking at... lavender water... That sounds disgusting, I thought to myself as I approached her. I wondered what she was listening to; she still hadn't noticed my presence.

I closed the distance between us, touching the top of her bun and twirling a loose curl in my finger. I laughed internally; black people knew that touching someone's crown without permission was a no-go. She quickly stood up and shoved me pretty hard, making me take a few steps back. Her face was flustered, and she was a mix of scared and angry. When she realized it was me, she rolled her eyes and placed the bottle she had held inside her tote.

"Don't touch my hair... or me. I don't know where your nasty detective fingers have been." She said with a hasty tone. "You stalking me or what? You're showing up everywhere now," she stated matter-offactly while crossing her arms over her chest. Her head was titled, and one of her arched brows was raised. She gave me a one-over as she awaited my response.

Damn, she had a lot of attitude, I liked that. Loved a woman who didn't mind being confrontational. Since the first hello, she hasn't been scared of approaching me in any way.

"Naw, ma, all very coincidental," I relaxed and smiled at her. "You drink lavender water? I knew yo ass was fancy when I saw you in those silk PJs." I could see the smile in her eyes and the line at the edges of her lips slightly lifted. "OK, and what about it? Who's going to check me for it? I'm grown." She walked towards my basket and examined what I had. My cart was full of fruit trays, meats, beer, and chips. She lifted one of my packs of beer and looked at me in disgust. "Bud Light? Yeah, I guess I would be fancy to you."

I bit my lip and nodded my head at her; she had an attitude, was quick with the comebacks, and looked sexy while doing it, even in her scrubs after a long shift. I felt something stir deep within me. Something that others would define as attraction or lust. Her smile lines curled into a smile as she watched my facial expression. She deflected her eyes to her tote, and her hands began to move things around. I was making her nervous. Yeah, she had to be feeling me.

"Aye, chill out with all that; it gets the job done." I chuckled. "You should come; I'm having a kickback with a few coworkers and my brothers. There will be some women there as well."

I shot my shot like I said I would if the opportunity presented itself. The worst thing she could say was no, and right now, I felt like she was feeling me a bit, so I was betting on that. She looked between me and the basket, and I wondered what she was thinking, what was making her hesitate.

"What does your girlfriend think about inviting a random woman to your house?" she asked as her eyes reached mine. "Bingo," I thought to myself; this not only confirmed that she was feeling me, but she was also upset about seeing Alexis and me.

"You're thinking back to my sister's baby shower? That girl you saw is my ex were over. It was just her last effort at saving what we had." I say somewhat truthfully. Hazel's posture tightened up, and she nodded as she listened. She didn't believe me; I could see the conflict and war behind her eyes. I wanted to tap into that and figure out what happened in her past that made her not want to even chance it.

"How about I give you the address, and you can decide if you want to come or not." She was a lot more receptive to that. I noticed her body relaxing; her shoulders dropped as she searched for her phone in one of her scrubs' many pockets. She made eye contact again as she searched; I no longer saw The conflict left in her eyes, maybe because she didn't have to make an immediate decision right now.

Once she found her phone, I reached out and asked to see it. She looked at me with that "Who do you think you're talking to?" look.

She slapped my hand away, "No you give me your phone." I laughed at her as I reached for my phone. I unlocked it and handed it to her. "You're so aggressive, ma. That's the second time you've assaulted me." I joked with her. "Keep your crap up, and Imma assault you for real." She responded as she entered her number into my phone. She texted herself before she handed it back to me.

"I'll let you know if I decide to bless you with my bougie presence." She placed her phone in her front pouch and adjusted the tote on her shoulder. "You're messing with my morning routine, so I gotta go. Bye, stalker. If I see you follow me out the lot, I'm calling the police and telling them you're following me in an attempt to kidnap me while holding a gun." She jokes before leaving the aisle, not allowing me to respond.

I bit my lip and watched her as she walked away. It was starting to become my favorite thing to watch. I texted her my address before I texted Dee. "She's coming to the kickback. She's gonna be mine soon," I said to him simply. She had an attitude I wanted to check, a history and mind I wanted to indulge in and understand, and a body I wanted my hands to explore every inch of.

I felt my phone buzz as I grabbed the last of my items. "Damn, nigga what changed!? Can't wait to hear about this one." I just laughed at his message and finished my shopping before leaving.

...

The days passed, and I primarily focused on my cases, went to the gym, and repeated. I still had yet to hear from Hazel, and I had the urge to contact her and invite her out for coffee or something before the kickback, but I didn't want to come off as too eager. I decided to give her space and see if she would come to me.

On the day of the BBQ, I helped my brothers with the grill. We decided to have it at our parent's lake house rather than mine. My eldest brother Marshawn was flipping the meat while our little brother Markell and I drank beers, enjoying the view.

"So Mariah told us to get the tea on you and a girl named Hazel?" Marshawn casually mentioned while focusing on the meats. At the mention of Mariah and her request, I sighed heavily. I knew I shouldn't have called her last night to get details about Hazel. I didn't like many people in my business, especially involving a woman whom I wanted to get to know.

"It's not a big deal. I think Hazel is fine; I just want to get to know her better," I said, shrugging it off to avoid creating a fuss. Just then, Markell, in his usual wild manner, approached me and hit my back quite hard, starting to hoot excitedly ." That thick shawty in that purple dress who was at the baby shower?" I squinted at him; I didn't like that he had also noticed what I had seen. Granted, I'm sure every man there noticed as well, but regardless, it wasn't something my brother, of all people, needed to be speaking on.

"Man, watch yo mouth when talking about a woman," I say seriously. He laughed, picking up on my jealous tone. "Chill, bro, I don't want your girl..." He released a stiff laugh, shaking his head. "I saw her camera set up, and I asked her if she wanted to make some TikToks, and she agreed. Afterward, I tried shooting my shot, and she told me I was too young."

I smiled instantly at the fact she rejected him; at least I knew she didn't reject him because she was taken. "Well, I'm going to shoot my shot tonight; per usual, I'm going to keep it low-key until I'm ready to talk about it." Markell mocked me by saluting me before he went off because his phone rang.

Marshawn closed the lid to the grill, and we walked over to the rail and looked out at the lake. "I remember meeting Hazel while she and Mariah were roommates in college. Beautiful girl, intelligent from what I remembered. Not the type of girl you're used to dating." I couldn't even be offended. He was right. My type was the airhead, toxic, sexy party girls. Still, they kept things exciting when I knew I wasn't looking for anything too serious.

"Maybe I'm ready to change my type up." I meant it; I was getting older, and the toxicity in my former relationships was beginning to get to me. I was 32 now, and I wasn't getting any younger. I was craving a healthy, stable relationship; I wanted to be a dad. "Well, just be careful. That's our sister, doctor; she doesn't need any drama because of your games." I didn't want to hear all that, but he was right.

After I ensured him everything was good, I went upstairs to shower, wanting to smell fresh and good before everyone arrived, specifically before Hazel arrived. She never RSVP, but something told me she would be coming. I also sensed Hazel wouldn't let it slide if my presentation was up to par. The night before, Mariah told me how, in college, Hazel didn't play about the type of men she entertained, and presentation was essential to Hazel. That wouldw2n't be a problem for me; my hygiene was amazing. I bought the best products, kept a re-twist, trimmed my beard, and bought the best cologne.

I took a shower in the upstairs master bedroom. I lather my body in Methods Men Cypress and Cedar body wash. Once out of the shower, I change into a plain outfit. I wore a plain brown shirt with lighter brown/beige jogger pants. I stood before the mirror, making sure my locs looked good. I got a retwist and lineup earlier this morning. I had the sides lined up with the rest of my hair sitting at the top of my head. I adjust my gold chain before spraying some Tom Ford Oud wood cologne. Casual but fresh. I leaned close to the mirror to ensure my beard was neat and my face was clear of anything.

As I rubbed my jaw, a flashback came to mind of Hazel's soft hand placed on my jaw when she was looking at the cut on my face, which was now slowly fading away from the night her clinic was broken into. I shuttered at the memory; her touch had been so gentle, comparable to a feather. Her face had been visibly tired, but her eyes were intrigued by the tattoo that ran up my neck from my chest. I had a lion's mane on my chest, flowing like flames across his pectorals. The eyes of the lion are intense and fierce, embodying

strength and confidence. I felt relaxed under her touch, and watching her observe me made me feel chills. She had been a lot more soft
-spoken that night. Maybe because she was tired. Regardless, I liked both sides of her.

...

I was a few beers and two hours deep into the kickback, but there was still no sign of Hazel. I had been debating back and forth about whether I should call her or not. I didn't want to annoy her if she was just chillin', but I also wanted her to know I wanted her here. I was standing in the kitchen, and I decided to take the risk of calling her. Just as I was about to find our text messages, the front door opened, and my most crucial guest came in.

She walked in with two pretty women; one almost looked identical to Hazel, light skin and thick, and the other was tall, about 5'11/6'0", a chocolateskinned slender woman. Yet my eyes primarily focused on Hazel. The black fitted dress she wore hugged her curves in all the right places, accentuating her silhouette. The fabric clung to her waist, emphasizing her thick hourglass figure, while the neckline offered a tasteful glimpse of cleavage. The dress fell just above her knees, showcasing her shiny, shapely legs. My attention was brought to her neck, where a gold Cuban chain rested and sparkled. It matched her small diamond gold hoop earrings. She also wore several gold bracelets and a gold sparkly butterfly anklet. She was beautiful. Just that natural kind of pretty that I rarely exposed myself too.

Her girls look in my direction, and she says something about me before they all laugh and take off in the opposite directions. They go over and introduce themselves to some of my colleagues. I catch notice of Marshawn going towards her tall friend.

Hazel approached me, and I reached for a twisted tea from the cooler and handed her one. She smiled at me and accepted the drink before sitting on one of my bar stools. "So I guess you did decide to bless me with your presence." She shrugged as she opened her can. "I mean, free food and drinks. Maybe I can find a man here who knows." She laughed before she took a sip of her drink.

"What is your ideal man?" I reached my hand for hers, and she surprisingly took it. I guided her to the outdoor balcony. The sun rested over the lake, and the horizon glistened over all the mansions and large homes in the hills. It was always a beautiful view.

"Why do you want to know?" I rested my hands on the rail and continued looking over the view. "I'm just trying to get to know you, that's all."

"Well, get to know me with another line of questions, detective." Each syllable she added to my title made me look at her. I was met with a smile, which made me smile. She was being playful, and I wanted to match that energy. "Oh, you must like them hood niggas and street pharmacist then huh? The quiet, earthy, ethereal, good girls always want those types of dudes." She laughed out loud and shook her head. "Oh, so you think I'm a good girl?" She raised an eyebrow. I found it hard to believe she was anything other than what I described her. "Tell me something bad that you've done, Hazel." She pauses for a moment. I could see she was contemplating what she should reveal to me.

"When I was younger, in elementary/middle school, I always used to steal candy and magazines from the store. I also used to steal books from the public library." I shook my head and laughed. I step closer to her, closing the space between us. I noticed her eyes were brown today as she looked up at me. "You and almost every other teen girl and new moms, I wanna know what's something grown Hazel has done that was so bad." I sipped my beer but kept eye contact, waiting for that confession.

There was an energy shift. She bit the inside of her cheek and somehow made herself smaller when looking up at me before her eyes shifted. Her cheeks started to rise, and I could see them dip rapidly. She was trying to fight a blush. "You're thinking of something nasty, huh?" Her eyes went big, and she hit me in my chest, giving me the confirmation I needed. "No, I wasn't!" Her face was flustered, and I smiled.

"Once again, we grown baby, you earthy girls are freaky. I know about those herbs y'all take that increase the libido. I also didn't mean bad like that, but since we're on the topic..." She was looking down at her feet and I could see that she was looking at her sandal lace that had come undone. Was she nervous? Was I making her uncomfortable? She looks back up at me. "You're not wrong..." She says with a sly yet shy smile on her face. I put my beer down and stood before her; she stepped back before she could question me; my hands were already on her hips. She gasped, her hands wrapping around my wrist as I lifted her and sat her on the rail. "Well then?" I still wanted a response from her that wouldn't be enough.

I grabbed her lower thigh and calf. She bunches the cloth of her dress in between her thighs as I raise her leg to rest on my shoulder. Her legs were soft, and she smelled like a mix of coconut butter and lavender. I could feel her eyes on me; she was holding her breath as I worked on lacing the strings. "I'm still waiting for an answer, sweetheart." I lowered her leg and went to her other leg, lifting it the same way.

"I.. had sex with my ex in the hospital in his office. Outside of something sexual, my friends and I used to go swimming in our neighbor's pool whenever they were out of town or when we knew they were out." Her voice was soft and breathy. I looked up at her and noticed she hadn't used that tone with me yet. I liked it.

I put her leg down, and I grab her hips again. She places her arms around my shoulders as I lower her. "So you like sneaking around and the risk of getting caught?" She tried fighting the blush again. Her lips opened before closing again. She didn't have a response. I top my beer off before sitting it down. I grab another one from the outside cooler. I walk towards her, and I lean over the rail. The sun was now setting into the water, and the solar lights were turning on.

I decided to change the conversation. I didn't want to make Hazel uncomfortable. "You enjoy hiking and walks?"

"Yeah, I love outdoor things and nature." Her tone tightened up a bit. I can tell she just wanted to gain control of a situation that honestly didn't even need controlling, but that is something we could work on later...if she let me.

"Tomorrow, I'm going to this place. It's about a fourmile hike to a waterfall. Are you down to come?"

"Is it just going to be us two?" she glanced tentatively at me, her tone anxious. "Is that a problem?"

She paused momentarily, and I could tell she was trying to find a reason to say no. Expecting a decline in my offer, she surprisingly said yes. "What time do you want me to pick you up?" She scoffed and laughed. "I'll meet you there."

I smile and raise my hands in defense. "OK, Ms. Independent, just being nice." She smiled before rolling her eyes. I'm going to go inside and check on my girls." She left without another word. I lean my back against the rail, and I watch her walk away.

. . .

The kickback quickly turned into game night. Hazel had relaxed after having a few twisted teas. She went from being the quiet observer to gathering everyone to make them play card games and different drinking games. Marshawn and I stood in the kitchen watching everyone play an intense game of beer bong. Markell and Hazel were very competitive, and they trash-talked each other.

Marshawn stood beside me, and I noticed him eyeing Hazel's model-like friend. "You see something you like?" I was happy to see my brother take an interest in a woman. I know it had been a minute for him since things ended with his ex. "You mind your business, and I'll handle mine." He used my own words against me, and I just laughed. He finished his drink before walking over to her. He placed his hands on her hips, and they walked off. I wasn't sure where because my eyes focused on Hazel.

We locked eyes simultaneously, and she was nothing but a smile. She waved me over, and I had no choice but to oblige. I downed my drink and made my way over to her.

First Date

I woke up feeling excessively drained. My mouth was dry; I tried creating a little moisture, forcing myself to swallow my spit as I sat up in Marquis's bed. I look over to my right and see Marquis sound asleep. He had an arm around my waist while his head was buried in his pillow. I smiled, and I gently rubbed his back. That was the first time I had ever shared a bed in a platonic matter. I can proudly say nothing happened last night...nothing besides the heated goodnight kiss we shared. I could feel my cheeks grow warm at the memories of his lips on mine. His kisses trailed down my neck onto my collarbone, leaving tingles down my spine. If the room hadn't started to spin and my stomach hadn't churned, we would've gone further. Surprisingly, I was able to remember everything that happened last night. After beating Marquis and his brothers in another round of beer pong, I dismissed myself to use the bathroom. I wanted to ensure my makeup was intact, check my appearance, and get some space from Marquis.

I take a deep breath immediately as I lock the bathroom door. Happy to have a moment to myself finally. It was indisputable that Marquis and I had an intense electrical energy charge between us despite our childish banter, which I mainly initiated. I knew he could see the smile in my eyes despite the frown on my face. I don't know why I opted to be mean to him rather than show my soft side.

Throughout the night, when we weren't bantering, we would make random eye contact and not say anything; I would roll my eyes, not wanting him to read my expression, and in return, he would just smirk and bite his bottom lip as if he knew I was only rolling my eyes because I was nervous. While playing various party games, every time it was my turn, I felt his eyes lingering on the curves of my body. It wasn't just a casual glance like when we made eye contact, but a look filled with desire. His gaze made me panic, and it wasn't because he was making me uncomfortable but because I liked his attention. It was never hard to tell when a man was lusting after you and feeling you. Whenever Marquis needed to get around me, he HAD to place his hand on my lower back, which was one indicator that I knew he was feeling me. Did I also mention how he continued complimenting me throughout the night despite how mean I'd been acting? Men did not care about an attitude when they wanted what they wanted.

I stared at myself in the mirror, examining the remains of the various creams and liquids left on my face. The pink and brown lip combo that was on my lips had completely come off due to my drinking. My foundation definitely needed a touch-up, and my eyelashes were starting to lift. I wasn't feeling as confident as when I first arrived. As I removed the melting makeup from my face, my mind drifted to Marquis. It's been a long time since I have been attracted to anyone. I honestly didn't know how to respond to that besides proving that I wasn't a woman who could be walked all over. I don't know if that was my default, but maybe it was my mind's way of avoiding another broken heart. Regardless, I knew I needed to dial back on the attitude and see where the vibes could take us if I were ever going to tap into that attraction. I could see his attraction for me exuding from him like heat waves from an object producing warm air during the summer.

I threw all of my used makeup wipes into the trash bin. I grabbed some moisturizer from my purse and hydrated my face. I then proceeded to reapply some deodorant and perfume. I still didn't feel as confident as earlier, but I felt clean. I exited the bathroom and returned to the living room, finding Marquis alone and scrolling on his phone.

"Where is everyone?" I looked around before I turned to look out the window facing the back deck. Everyone was sitting around the fire pit; some people formed couples, and the women, including my two friends, sat in a man's lap. I turned to look at Marquis. Even the way he leaned against the wall, he had such a casual confidence in himself, and for me, that only added to the attraction I was developing for him.

I tore my gaze away from him and started rummaging through my purse for my keys. I knew it was risky to linger any longer; I didn't want to give in to my attraction to him. "I should go," I say softly as I pull my keys out. I hadn't planned on driving anywhere. I was very tipsy; I was just going to lay in my backseat, call my friends, and see who was sober enough to drive me home. He pushed himself from the wall and made his way towards me, once in front of me, and with no hesitation, he took my keys. "Ain't no way I'm letting you drive after you just had three glasses of liquor. You can wait it out or spend the night here. I have a guest room you can stay in."

I crossed my arms, frustrated with being told what to do. Although he had a point, I was not in the mood to argue with an officer about something like that, nor did I want to tell him my actual plan. I decided to comply but wouldn't make it an easy surrender. "I'm not staying in the guest room; I want the best space in the house, not just the guest room. This is your parents' lake house, right? Which means every bedroom should be open."

He laughed and nodded his head. "Yeah, you can stay in the master bedroom, shawty. I don't have a problem with that." He shrugged his shoulders, and I scoffed. "Fine." I huffed out. "Show me the way then." He walked past me and started to go upstairs. I followed him. I was so proud of myself. I began to text my friends while walking up the stairs to inform them of what being stern just earned me, and everything was going great until the third step. I missed my step and had to grip the stair railing. I landed on my knee and groaned as I turned to sit on my bottom. I rubbed my knee aggressively in hopes of dissipating the pain.

Marquis came down the steps and knelt in front of me. I was expecting him to laugh, but he didn't. He moved my hand from my knee and examined the area I was rubbing. He squeezed my kneecap and asked me if it hurt. I shook my head, no, and that's when he smiled. He stood back up and offered me his hand. I grabbed it, and he pulled me into him. Everything happened so fast that I didn't even have time to protest. Once he pulled me into him, he squatted, lifted me up, and I was over his shoulder. He made it up the rest of the stairs before we presumably entered the master bedroom, as I requested. I didn't fight him or tell him to put me down. I had always wanted to be carried this way.

He laid me down on the bed, lingering above me. One of his locs got caught in my earring. As he tried removing his loc from my jewelry, in my euphoric state, I started to run my hands over his arms. I would lie if I said I didn't know what I was doing. He was an attractive man who was clearly feeling me, and I was feeling him. He smelled good, too. He had that clean, earthy smell to him that drew me into him.

My fingers traced over the tattoos on his bicep. His hand came down to my chin, making me face him; when our eyes locked, I saw the lust in his eyes. He wanted to kiss me. I raised my head slightly and pushed my lips into his. My fingers sneaked their way to the bottom of his shirt before slowly sliding inside, rubbing his warm, thick chest. His motions were fluid. His hands simultaneously ran down both of my thighs. He hooked his hands around the back of my thighs before spreading them apart so he could settle in between them. He pulled his lips from mine, kissed my cheek, down my neck, across my collarbone, and up to my ear. "Grip my sides with those soft ass legs." He muttered into my ear as he patted my thighs, so I knew what he meant. I did as he asked, and he rolled us over, putting me on top of him. I grinded into his lap, and I smiled as I felt him get hard.

In the midst of our humping and kissing. I felt a wave of nausea hit me, and I stopped once I felt like I was going to throw up.

...

I was pulled from my flashback as that familiar watery feeling in my mouth started to occur. It was the body's natural response to prepare you for the next stage, vomiting. I remained still and took slow swallows. I shivered as the feeling passed over me. Marquis must've felt my movement; he wrapped his arm around me tighter, bringing me into his chest. "You good?" He asked in a deep, sleepy voice. I whimpered when he tightened his grip on me. I felt it coming as soon as he squeezed me. I shove him off of me very harshly. I rush to the attached bathroom, going for his toilet. Grateful that it was clean because there was no stopping the contents from leaving my mouth. I hated throwing up; I always sounded like I was being assaulted or, as my friends would tell me, a dying cat.

After a few minutes of hurling my stomach up, nothing but acid was coming out. Eventually, I was able to stand up; I looked for a spare toothbrush through the drawers. I felt so cold and wanted to drink ginger ale and lie down. I finally find one and freshen up for the next few minutes. I looked in the mirror as I self-exam myself. I was surprised that I didn't look like crap. My hair was in a messy yet cute bun. Little hairs were sticking out, shaping and framing my face in a way that brought out my facial features. The sandy brown curly strand that fell next to my eye brought out more green in my hazel eyes.

Despite feeling sick, I couldn't help but admire myself a bit more. Maybe it was the lighting, but my skin was pale yet clear. I just needed to wash my face and knew the color would return. I examine my face a bit more before finally taking a step back and fully viewing myself. "I'm beautiful. You need to get
more sun, but other than that, you're stunning." I
thought to myself as I smiled at my reflection. I grabbed one of the folded face towels from the shelf above the toilet. I turn the water on to a nice warm setting. I drench the towel for a few seconds before ringing the excess water. I buried my face into the now steamy towel. I felt so much relief

from the steam alone; if I were home, I would have a drop of lavender oil, which would relax me.

I dried my face and placed the towel down. I smiled again as I saw my warm yellow undertone return, and my face appeared even prettier. When I exited the bathroom, the curtains had been drawn, and Marquis was not in the room. I was still wearing the dress that I had arrived in yesterday. I decided to go into the closet. I knew his mother was petite, so I went to his dad's side. I go for a plain black hoodie. His father was a big man, 6'5" and 360lbs. His hoodie fit me like a dress. Once changed, I grabbed my purse from the nightstand. I dug for my lip balm and headed to the kitchen to find Marquis.

His bare back was to me as I entered the room. He was pouring a glass of water. He had also poured a glass of orange juice and had a can of Sprite. On the stove, bacon was sizzling, and eggs were slowly cooking. I sat down on the island, placed my purse down, and searched for my lip balm, applying it to my lips once I found it. Marquis finally turns around with a smile plastered on his face. He scoots all three drinks towards me before handing me a plate of food. "Thank you..." I mumbled before saying a small prayer over my food.

I grabbed the fork, going for the eggs. I take a hesitant small bite. He turned around again, watching me take a bite as he drank an energy drink. "How do they taste?" He asks curiously, anticipating my review of his breakfast.

"The eggs are actually good. I know men usually season their eggs like a piece of chicken." I laughed at my joke as I ate the food; my stomach didn't seem to have an issue. "But the seasoning is just right and the perfect amount of scrambled. I'm a fan," I say truthfully, yet in a sarcastic tone. In a way that would have him questioning my sincerity.

He sucked his teeth before waving his hand off in my direction. "I'm not worried about my cooking. I know I can cook a little something." He passionately patted his chest as he defended himself. I just continued to eat my food, waiting for him to get to his point." I'm laughing at the fact Ms. "I can drink like a man." In fact, can't even hold her liquor." My smile deepened. He was quoting me from last night. He saw me pouring myself a glass of whiskey and coke. He was unable to fathom that a woman like myself would drink something so heavy. He was on my behind all night about that. I found the entire thing funny; as a way to add fuel to his fire, I told him I could drink just like a man, if not better. I knew I was cappin, but having all the guys hype me up was fun. I was definitely a fruity and sweet type of woman, but I just wanted to have the more masculine drink for no particular reason; it was just what my taste buds wanted at that moment.

"Yeah, yeah, everyone knows first responders, especially night shifters, are a bunch of alcoholics. I was never going to be able to compete with y'all." He grabbed his heart and clinched his chest as if what I said pained him. "Yeah, well, everyone knows PAs are nothing more than thieves." He pointed to his dad's hoodie that I was wearing. "And he won't be getting it back." I shrugged my shoulders in an exaggerated way and continued to eat my eggs. This hoodie felt like rich people material, it was way to comfortable to return. I made eye contact with him as I sipped the orange juice. "Thank you for the breakfast." He waved me off as he walked around the island to sit next to me.

"Not a big deal. Are you feeling better? I almost pulled my Draco on you, girl. Sounded like someone was attacking you in there." He stated in between bites. I rolled my eyes and shook my head, denying the accusations. "You're so dramatic. I didn't sound like that." He paused between his bites and stared at me before laughing again and eating.

"Yeah, okay. Anyways, are you still down to go hiking with me?" He questioned as I stood up and threw my uneaten scraps in the trash before going to the sink and cleaning my plate off. Before I could respond to his question, my mouth became watery again. "Ugh, no, not again." I thought to myself as I grabbed my items and the sprite he left out. "We can still hang out later this evening, but I don't think I can handle a rigorous activity such as hiking right now."

I tried swallowing down my nausea as I made my way to the front door. Marquis stood, making his way behind me; once at the door, I saw him put his slides on, and I shook my head no. "You don't have to walk me to my car." As soon as the words escaped my mouth, I felt the vomit coming up; I moved from the concrete and leaned my head over in the grass, bracing my knees as the contents escaped from me. I was embarrassed, but Marquis didn't seem to mind. He was standing behind me and rubbed my back as I threw up in his grass. When I was finished, he went back inside and returned with a water bottle and napkins, handing it to me. I wiped my mouth before taking a slow sip of water. "I'm never drinking again," I say softly, causing him to smile.

"You and every other person on 6th St every weekend." I weakly punch at him before sighing heavily. "I'm sorry about the grass… I'm going to go home now. I'll text you later to see about hanging out."

As I turned around, he grabbed the back of my shirt. I paused in my movements, turning to look back at him. "Let me drive you home. I don't want you getting home and then feeling sick while driving." He stated casually. "Marquis, you don't have to do all of that. I live far from you and-" He cut me off as he grabbed my hand and led me to his truck. "20-25 mins is not a long drive." He pulled the keys from his pockets, unlocking his truck; he opened the passenger door for me, grabbing my hips and helping me into my seat. Once I was settled in, he grabbed the door. "Let me grab a few items, and then we can hit the road." He didn't wait for a response; he shut the door, and I watched as he walked back into his home. Several minutes passed as I waited for him to grab what he needed. I decided to rest my eyes, opening them again when I heard his front door shut close.

He had changed into a baggy brown and white graphic t-shirt, brown fleece sweat shorts, and the Jordan 1 Travis Scott high shoes. I could see his chest piece peaking over the collar. He pulled his locs into a bun.

This man was so handsome. I watched as he walked towards his truck. He was scanning the surrounding area, making sure his environment was safe. I understood that being a man in his line of work created habits. I mourned for the subject who decided to test his faith by approaching Marquis. The man had an overall large cornbread-fed yet athletic build. Just yesterday, I remembered how effortlessly he lifted me up the stairs, sending delightful shivers through me. As he adjusted his shirt, I caught sight of his concealed gun and bit my lip, trying to suppress a smile that just wouldn't stay hidden. I loved a man who clearly meant business—it made me feel safe.

Once in the car, he glanced over at me. "Why are you laughing?" I just shook my head. I was not about to admit my attraction to him right now. "Yeah, okay. Let me find out." He stated as he handed me his phone so I could enter my address. I rolled my eyes as he gave me his phone. I input my address before handing it back to him. "Don't start with me. I don't feel good; you need to be nice to me."

"My bad, Ms. I can hold my liquor. I should be nicer." He grabbed my hand and kissed the back of it gently before putting it back down. I snatched my hand from his. "That was in the past; you need to focus on the present." He just glanced at me before looking at the map again causing me to laugh. He examined the map for a bit before ending the navigation. "I'm familiar with the area you live in." He stated that once we started to pull out, I crossed my arms over my chest and looked at him. "Not you kidnapping me. We should've taken my car; you're just trying to hold me hostage." I kept my eyes on him, awaiting an answer. I was only met with silence. I faced forward in my seat and decided to just watch the road. I expected him to take a right from the property since that was how I came in, but instead, he made a left. "You're kidnapping me," I say with a finality in my voice. "God gone get you if you do anything to me." His silent, nonchalant stance switched into him laughing so hard he swerved into the other lane a bit.

"Dang girl, you a trip." He held his stomach as he caught his breath. "You're hilarious for that." He let out a final chuckle before finally relaxing in his seat again. "I'm so serious." I raised an eyebrow at him, waiting to clap back if needed. He realized I wasn't joking and smacked his teeth. "Listen, shawty, just chill out and relax. I'm a god-fearing man myself; I wouldn't do anything to intentionally hurt one of his people, especially one of his daughters." He glanced over at me before he placed a hand on my knee. His touch felt like electricity, causing me to sit up a bit straighter, and as much as I hated to admit it, his words struck me, "Especially not one of his

daughters." echoed in my mind. He sounded so genuine, and truthfully, he hadn't done anything to offend me or make me uncomfortable. So why wouldn't I believe him?

He patted my thigh, pulling me from my thoughts and bringing my attention back to him. "So, are you going to relax and let today be?" He asked as he kept his eyes on the road. I took a moment to respond as I turned to look out of my window. We were passing over an unfamiliar bridge. I had not noticed the fantastic view of the lake we were driving over when I drove over it yesterday. I looked down into the water, watching people paddle board and on their speed boats. The sun was beaming and reflecting in the water, giving the illusion of sparkles. I smiled as I rested my head against the window, continuing to gaze. I release a deep breath. I didn't want to fight. "Yes," I say simply as I continue to gaze at nature and people watch.

He reached over his head and pressed a button, lowering his sunroof. I turned to look back at him. The wind was blowing down on me. I felt so good and relaxed. This was the cure for my hangover because, for the duration of the ride, not one ounce of nausea surfaced.

My thoughts were in Lala land during the scenic drive to my home. He was doing more than the bare minimum right now. I was reflecting on past relationships. I remember throwing up at an exhouse. He was about to walk me out, but I told him not to worry about it, just like I had earlier with Marquis. The responses were incredibly different. One man just said "okay" and shut the door on me, didn't even text me to see if I made it home safely, or asked if I felt better. The other man was driving me home because he didn't think I was fit enough to drive, and despite hearing me throw up twice, he still wanted to hang out with me.

"So you've never hurt one of God's daughters?" I studied his face, looking for him to choke up or show some sign of guilt. I watched his throat, waiting to see if he would swallow before speaking, but he didn't. I was skeptical because he is a detective, so I could only imagine how well he has gotten at masking his emotions. He rubbed a hand through his beard, and he sighed before speaking. "I've never cheated before if that's what you're wondering. I've never put my hands on a woman, and I try to understand the woman I'm dating. I love learning why people are the way they are, especially my lover." He took a deep breath and shifted his hand placement on the steering wheel. He adjusted in his seat, and I found his movement a little stiff. I caught it, and there was something else he wanted to say. "But?" I ask him, wanting him to be fully transparent with me. "My most recent ex, we had already broken up, but after lil sis baby shower, we had sex because my mind had been on a woman who I thought was completely unattainable and out of reach."

He looked at me, meeting my eyes, assuming to gauge how I felt with this information. He refocused his attention back on the road before continuing. "After having sex, I told her that there was no going back. She just cussed me out and left. So, to answer your question, I may have hurt her, but also, the next day, she posted herself wearing a fireman's jacket and kissing a firefighter's neck; I'm sure she's okay. I do regret having sex with her. I should've kept my lust to myself. I went home, prayed about it, and moved on to something else. Not gonna lie, I ain't never done that before, and it felt sleazy." He stated with finality in his voice, concluding his answer.

"It's always the ninja saying I ain't gonna lie, who's the main one lying," I mumbled. "So you used her for sex because of me?" I knew so many things were wrong with this statement, and this very well could've been a red flag. I kept that in my mind and I turned to look back at the hill country we were driving past. He didn't respond, so I decided to keep that in my red flag category for him. No one liked a man who couldn't control his lust; I would give him a few points for honesty, but that's about it.

We made it to my loft. He really did know the area. It was a relaxing drive, and we sat in comfortable silence. Once upstairs, I gave a tour of my apartment. I was proud of my style and setup. I proceeded to take a shower. I took my time, wanting to test his patients while also still recovering from the hangover that had consumed me. My body was in a fragile state, and I would not be rushing the healing process.

Marquis Pov

I looked around her loft apartment, just walking around her ample open space. There were no walls to section off each room, but the way she decorated her home, she had created her own rooms. She used bookshelves to divide her living room from her dining area. The bookshelves lay sideways on the ground, and various types of plants and small golden statues were on top of the shelves. In her "dining room," she didn't have a table; instead, she just had three egg chairs with footstools and a large brown fluffy rug underneath them. The chairs faced the large floor-to-ceiling windows. In the distance, you can see a bridge over the water, and down below, you can see people hustling and bustling in the streets. I people-watch a bit before looking around her apartment some more. This woman had plants everywhere. She had a vine plant winding around the railing of her stairs, and every countertop was adorned with tiny snake plants, succulents, or other greenery I couldn't quite identify. So far, I have counted 35 plants in total.

I finally settled for the couch as I continued to wait for her. Even in a seated position, there was still much to observe. On her black ottoman table, she had two different Bibles and several devotional books laid out. It made me smile. I didn't know too many people who sought after the Lord, and it was clear she was in her word. There were bleed-free highlighters and pens beside her Bible, full of colorful sticky notes.

I hear her footsteps coming down the stairs. I stood and turned to face her as she passed the final step. She wore Her hair down, some of it held back by a gold butterfly clamp, and she wore a green haltered knitted top with a green meshed skirt with flowers on it. Definitely fitting that Erykah Badu and Jhene Aiko vibe we had been discussing on the car ride here. She looked moisturized, refreshed, and relaxed. My staring made her uneasy and nervous, maybe in a good way. I could see a slight blush on her face, and despite the nervous energy she had about herself at that moment, I saw a smile in her eyes.

Her fingers reached for her hair, and she began to play with the curly ends, twirling the strains around her finger. I recognize these actions when interviewing people at crime scenes and in interrogation rooms. Self-soothing was a normal reaction to calm oneself, but I wanted to make her comfortable, so I stepped up. She stiffened up a bit but didn't drop contact. "Do you like what you see or what?" she asked defensively as she walked past me towards her kitchen counter. She grabbed her brown/gold shades before placing them inside her tan bucket purse. "Avoidant." She used her hands and busied herself to break tension and redirect her focus. Noted.

"Naw." I approached her, standing directly in front of her. I could see the worry in her eyes, yet also a roast she was about to cook up. "I don't like. I love what I see; you look good," Her pupils dilated, and her eyes avoided me again. I reach for her hand and smile, raising her arm above her head. "Give me a little spin, mamas." Her face reddened, but she did as I asked, adding a little whine to it. She was relaxed and smiling now. I rubbed both sides of her shoulders to get her more comfortable as I spoke. "So I was thinking we could just walk around South Congress; it's a nice sunny day. You got this pretty dress on; we can freestyle once there and see what we can get into."

Her lips were curled in a smile, but it didn't reach her eyes. She shrugged my hands off her and headed for her door. "What? Do you not like South Congress?" I asked, following her out the door. I turn my back to her as she locks up her place, looking up and down her halls; I never knew these days, even in an area like this, what kind of dangers may be lurking around the corner. After locking her door, She led the way to the parking garage, where I parked my truck. "I've never been to that part of town." she finally answered.

I opened the passenger door for her. Before going to the driver's side. "And how long have you lived here?" She rolled her eyes at me as she adjusted in her seat. "I know I've been here for seven years." She held her hands up in defense. "Listen, in those seven years, I've never had the time to make it to that part of town." she was defensive, and I didn't know why. She crossed her arms over her chest, looking out the window as I pulled out of the garage. I glanced over at her, and her head rested on my window. She seemed agitated yet relaxed. The sun was hitting her pretty light caramel skin. She was chilling now; I would not ruin the vibe by addressing her little mood shift. Maybe she just didn't like physical touch, and perhaps she thought I was about to chastise her for not exploring the city more.

I turn on some 2000s RNB as I think of the first place I could take her. South Congress was the first thing that came to mind. It was a street full of different varieties of foods, unique, expensive shops, superb hotels, several murals, and, of course, bars. There was a bit of something for everyone, so I had a chance to do well on this date. I also wanted to avoid complete control of the date. I wanted her to be able to pick out where she wanted to go next on the strip. It would be fun to figure out what she liked and didn't like without asking her; I wanted things to naturally unfold. But in the meantime, I needed to figure out where to take her first. We just ate, so I knew she wouldn't be hungry. I was

thinking long and hard. I glanced at her again, and she was still glancing out the window. At that moment, I decided to take the longest but most scenic route I could. Her apartment was only 17 minutes from South Congress, just straight down 1st St.

The route I decided to take was Mopac to Capital, TX hwy. It would add about 20 minutes to our eta, but it would give me time to think of our first place, and she could enjoy the views of the lake and hill country a bit more. We sat in a comfortable silence as early 2000s Chris Brown played. I take notice of Hazel filming the greenery we drove past. "So you like nature? You've mentioned hiking, and I saw all the plants in your house." She stops filming before putting her phone down. "Yeah, I work a lot of hours. Being inside a building all day, even with my nice decorations, can feel so...."

She looked up at the ceiling, playing with the rings on her fingers, as she tried to find the right word to express herself. "Suffocating..." she says, followed by a deep sigh. "The plants, decor, and air diffusers make my clinic bearable, but to actually be in nature?" She looked at me, and I could see the passion on her face. "Nothing beats fresh, crisp air and the sounds of a flowing creek or river." She sighed heavily before slouching in her seat. "My plants are so pretty; they brighten the space. They have needs that must be met and are a great distraction, making the workspace not so bad. Just nothing replaces the real thing." She smiled before looking back out the window. "Every time I go hiking, I get emotional. I'm so grateful to God for his design on this earth, and I'm always overjoyed by what I'm surrounded by."

Not because I thought she was shallow or anything. I had just cheated myself out of women like her by surrounding myself with "baddies" and going to places women like herself didn't frequent. The women I had previously involved myself with only talked about social media and influencer drama, sex, irrelevant shit that wouldn't even matter in a few years. Or even a few days. Being around these women was fun at one point in my early to mid-20s. They were always lit and down for a good time, whether that be bar hopping, having sex, or traveling to do the same thing in someone else city. At that time, I was focused on achieving my goals and wasn't serious about any woman. Looking back, I can admit that the toxicity was somewhat entertaining—those arguments often led to passionate makeup sex, and it was amusing to see some of my exes get riled up. But now, I longed for a genuine, healthy romantic relationship. I had no energy for pointless disputes or worrying about a woman spending her time in shady hookah lounges and clubs.

Thinking about my exes brought me to mind where I could take her. One of my exes was an "austinite influencer." She vlogged everything and anything Austin-related. Once, she asked me to buy her flowers at this one shop on South Congress because it was trending, and she wanted to film everything.

About five minutes later, we found parking, and a few blocks later, we were standing outside a gray shop that wasn't much to look at from the outside. I opened the door for her, and once inside, immediately, she was the most expressive I had ever seen her in the short time I've known her. I tried hiding my smile; I knew I picked the right location. We were inside of Flor Keeps flower shop. It was a flower shop that had its flowers shipped from many places in Europe, such as Italy and France. Their flowers were dry-preserved, allowing them to live for up to a year.

Hiding inside the small shop were white walls; each of the five sections of the wall had a paintbrush pointed down. Below each paintbrush was an arrangement of hundreds of flowers going in rainbow order across all five sections. In the middle of the store was a table with several vases on display filled with different arrangements. On the ground were herbs ranging from lavender to eucalyptus. On another wall, there was nothing but bouquets. The flowers were color-coordinated as well, and Hazel did not hesitate to smell each one. After about 30 minutes, she decided on the "Butterfly with Pink" Assortment. The bouquet was filled with a variety of different light shades of pink flowers, and some hints of white were amongst the flowers.

After I paid, we stepped outside, and she hugged the flowers tightly to her chest. Her smile was bright, reaching her eyes as she looked up at me. I could feel her happiness as we made our way back to my truck, and a group of women passed by us. Hazel glanced at them as we crossed paths; one girl, in particular, wore a dress similar to the one she wore yesterday, though the other sported boots instead of Hazel's golden sandals. Hazel turned to watch the girl walk away and nodded in approval.

"She makes me want to get a pair. Her outfit ate." I nodded, knowing exactly where the next destination was because just before she said that, I had no idea what our next sting to be. "I got you," I said simply as we walked to my truck. I was surprised by her lack of pushback. I expected her to tell me not to buy her anything else, but there was never any pushback.

I drove further down S Congress to Allen Boot Store. She picked out a tan-colored boot that matched her accessories. She did a little two-step in the mirror and consistently clicked her heels together. She looked at me beaming; once outside, she gave me a big frontal hug. She wrapped her arms tight around me, and I instinctively wrapped my arms around her waist, lifting her from the ground a bit before sitting her back down. We pulled apart, and her face was glowing. She didn't look tired or deep in thought like earlier today. 'Imma keep that smile on her face all day.'

"I always wanted a pair of boots. I feel like a true Texan now." She grabbed my hand, and we started to walk south down South Congress. I was surprised. This girl was giving me mixed signals. Earlier, she shoved my touch, but now she was holding my hand and rubbing her thumb across the back of my hand. Now I was really curious a to what her mood swing was all about earlier. One minute, she didn't like me giving her affection, and now she was holding my hand. I was still weighing all the reasons; I didn't expect it to be too long before I found out why.

About five minutes into our walk, we discovered a place called Vespaio It was an authentic Italian restaurant. After eating, she suggested a movie. We then take my truck to Alamo Draft house, deciding on a thriller movie. We ate cookies and shared a shake. By the time the movie was out, it was already dark outside. Hazel's hair had shrunk, so she pulled into a bun on top of her head. She pulled out her phone and appeared to be looking for something. She paced in a circle as she searched for whatever she was looking for, "The night is still young..." She said openly in a singing tone as she searched through her phone. "I wanna dance. There's a bar called Busy Signal. It's supposed to be a new and upcoming black spot; wanna check it out?" I grabbed her hand as a response and nodded my head.

It was about 10 minutes from where we were. Once we arrived, the street was packed with cars, but I was able to find a decent spot.

Once parked, we entered the bar and ordered a few specialty drinks, which were highlighted on the menu. The inside of the bar was dark but had battery-lit candles everywhere. The bar was two stories. The first floor had two hookah sections and smaller intimate areas. The first floor had two sections: the bar, a dance floor, and a stage for the DJ. We grabbed our drinks and decided to peoplewatch from the second floor. They were currently playing Afro beats. Which wasn't my taste, but I could vibe with it. Hazel sipped her drink quickly, so I got her a second one before just sitting and relaxing. "How would you say our first date is going?" I asked her before taking a sip of my drink.

She looked at me and gave me a soft, appreciative smile. "I've always wanted this—a date that started in the morning and ended at night—just an entire day of enjoying another person's company." She nodded her head appreciatively. She glanced down at her outstretched legs before clicking her boots together. Thanks for the boots and for taking care of me today." I noticed her eyes glistened with tears as she turned away from me, focusing instead on the dance floor and the groups of friends dancing.

I rubbed her lower back as a way to soothe her. I wasn't sure why she was about to cry. Regardless I didn't want her feeling sad. Once my hand maid contact with her skin, she almost instantly scooted away from me. I shook my head. I wrapped my arm around her waist before pulling her back into me. She whipped her head towards me, and her eyebrows furrowed. "You've been hot and cold with me all day regarding this touching thing. What's up with that? Am I making you uncomfortable...or?" I asked her, wanting some clarity on why she was acting this way. So I would know how to move accordingly and not make her uncomfortable.

She put her drink down and reached for her collarbone, where her hair typically fell but was currently pulled up. Once she realized that she looked down at her hands, hyper-fixating on the many rings she wore before she began to shuffle the rings on her fingers, taking them on and off, shifting different rings on different fingers. She was trying to self-soothe herself from the anxiety I knew she was feeling. I observed her while my hand on her hip rubbed her gently. I was hoping after a moment, she would warm up to it.

She remained silent, so I grabbed her chin and brought her fixation back to me. I could see in her eyes that her mind was at war with herself. Deciding whether or not she should open up to me, trying to dissect every possible outcome. "I'm going to need you to open those pretty ass lips of yours and talk to me. How can I be better than the last nigga if you're just silent? Talk to me." She just frowned at me before snatching her chin from me. She goes for her drink, topping it off before handing it back to me. "Do you mind getting me another?" I looked at her for a moment. I didn't want to be too controlling or stern, whatever this tension was between us needed to be broken so I stood, grabbing the glass from her, lingering there momentarily. "This conversation isn't over. I want you to be comfortable enough to open up to me." I say before walking away without another word.

I watched her from the bar as she let her wild hair from its bun. She was stretching her shruken curls. It was entertaining to watch the shrinkage be pulled from her mid neck down to her elbow. I bet she could feel my eyes on her because she never once looked in my direction. Instead, she kept her eyes on the dance floor. I grabbed her another cocktail before bringing it up to her. She thanked me for the drink before taking a long sip. She continued to look at the dance floor, hiding her face from me with herpuffy hair. I sighed, about to say something, but she spoke up first. "It's not you; I'm just not used to intimacy outside of sex. I didn't grow up in a touchyfeely family either. It leaves me feeling tingles whenever you touch me, and those tingles can be intense." She takes a sip of her drink before continuing. "I hate when a man rubs my thigh, grabs my chin, or caresses me as a way to comfort me or get me to focus on him...it just feels disingenuous normally when that happens. He is just trying to calm me down enough for sex, not because he cares."

She bit her lip, still hiding her face from me, but she continued to speak. "What's the saying? 'I can show you better than I could tell you.' I prefer that because talk is cheap, and actions outside physical touch speak volumes to me." She finally turned to face me, her eyes searching mine as if trying to gauge my reaction to what she had just said. Then, she glanced away again, watching the dance floor. The DJ began to play RNB music, she stood on wobbled feet, but I caught her arm to steady her. I was still seated, and she was standing between my legs.

"All of my relationships have been sex-based, and you know what happened to the one nigga I did manage to cuff?, who was actually a really nice man." She dramatically lifted her hands, and her eyebrows raised; she leaned down close to me. She was still standing but she was bent over her hands rested on my knees and she leaned in close to my ear so I could hear her over the women singing in the crowd. " One day, Captain -that's his name- gets a call from his ex saying she was pregnant and that he was the father. He didn't even stop me when I tired to leave. He made sure we had sex one last time before sharing the news with me." She dropped her hands and shook her head as she stood back up.

I downed my drink before standing up placing my hands on her hips. "The nigga after him just used me for my body and the things I could do for him." Her speech was a bit animated and slightly slurred. She laughed, but it wasn't genuine. Last night, I made her laugh so hard that she snorted and giggled uncontrollably; this was a forced, dry laugh. I knew she was drunk because I had never heard her cuss, much less say nigga; her go too was "ninja." I watched her top off her drink and thought about our future momentarily. I knew women with similar backgrounds as her, and they usually needed so much reassurance and were highly needy. I wasn't sure if I could be that for her.

The silence grew between us, and I knew I needed to say something. I just wasn't sure what to say or how to react. She clearly had a wounded past. I wasn't certain how healed she was, but she seemed stable for the most part. I didn't want to say or do the wrong thing. She clearly felt vulnerable from opening up, and I just wanted to say and do the right thing. I needed to think fast as she looked at me; her eyes were a mixture of regret and embarrassment. I was about to open my mouth to say something, but she grabbed my hand, pulling me downstairs to the dance floor. "Sorry, I wasn't trying to trauma dump, I'm pretty tipsy, and I just wanna dance before we leave." She was being avoidant again, but I was grateful for the distraction. I had no idea what to say to any of that. In cases like this, saying the wrong thing could ruin the relationship, but I also learned that not saying anything would stick with her for a while. Fuck I messed up.

Currently, the DJ was playing Love in this club by Usher and Hazel whining her hips, her back was to me and she was dancing into me.My hands rubbed down her sides but, my mind was still on what was said. As she danced and I contemplated us moving forward. The Usher song transition into Love songs by Kaash Paige. Hazel was still whining and grinding until realization hit her as the floor cleared of women dancing to couples slow dancing and grinding among each other. She turned around, moving a step back from me. "Are you ready to go?" She looked up at me, and I could tell she felt awkward. I knew allowing the night to end on that note was not the right decision. I didn't say anything; I grabbed her hand and pulled her close, wrapping one arm around her waist and the other caressing her mid-back. Surprisingly, she wrapped her hands around my neck, and her cheek was pressed into my chest as we began to sway.

I wasn't sure how to respond to what she had said earlier, but in that moment, I realized I wanted to explore the possibility of a future with her. She seemed a bit anxious and carried some unhealed wounds from past relationships, but despite that, I had noticed in the short time I'd known her that she was compassionate, intelligent, selfless, kind, and genuinely funny. I didn't want her to think that her past would stop me from wanting to get to know her better.

"Yesterday, you asked me what my type is," she said, her voice soft, barely audible over the music. "I want a man who can pray with me—that's the most important thing. I need someone who makes me feel safe, who accepts me completely, flaws and all, without judging my past or who I am now. That's all I really want." She kept her head pressed against my chest as she spoke, and I listened thoughtfully.

I drew her closer, resting my chin on the top of her head. She nestled into me, encouraging me to tighten my embrace. Words escaped me, but her earlier reminder that actions speak louder than words lingered in my mind. Despite my struggle to respond to her vulnerability, the way she held onto me reassured me that staying and not cutting the night short was the right decision.

The Keke

I didn't arrive home until around 6 a.m. We got canes after dancing at the bar before returning to his family's lake house around 3 a.m. I had to go back to his place to get my Jeep. By the time we arrived, I had sobered up and drank plenty of water, ready to go home. As I tried leaving his property, he had to remind me how pretty my lips looked. What should've ended in us making out on his driveway led to his couch, the kitchen counter, and the staircase. I pulled away from him; things were getting too heated, and I just wasn't ready to have sex with him. We hadn't known each other that long, and I didn't want to taint our relationship by having sex and then things being weird. So we just ended up talking and cuddling until about 6 a.m, that's when he got a call from someone telling him about the where abouts of a suspect. That was my que to leave.

I left because I knew we would have spent another entire day together if I had stayed. This wasn't a bad thing, but this would make day 2 of me not being in my bed, and truthfully, my social battery needed to be reset, and I needed some me time. I enjoyed spending time with Marquis, but I also knew space would keep things exciting,

Despite me going home I was happy that we spoke and stayed up as long as we did. I didn't expect him to have a response to the load I dumped on him but, at least he was sticking around and that was more than what other men had done in the past. I did expect him to be better with his words because of his career but, I would see what time revealed about him.

After a hot shower, I climbed into bed, turned on my movie projector, and opened YouTube. I set a timer for an hour and selected some random background rain sounds. It didn't take long for me to drift off to sleep. I wasn't sure how long I had been asleep, but I awoke to my phone ringing. I groaned, sitting up. I didn't want to sleep my day away, so I wasn't too annoyed with whoever interrupted my sleep. I lazily placed the phone next to my ear. "Hello?" I let out a groggy whisper as I waited for the person to respond.

I jumped when my friend, Alameda, yelled through the phone. "Girl are you asleep? If you don't get up, I will come to your house and drag you out of bed. I called you to see what you would wear to dinner."

"Dinner?" I was still discombobulated and confused. I sat up in bed, groaning as I stretched.

"Hazel, don't piss me off. We are supposed to all be meeting for dinner in two hours. I called you to see what you were wearing. Glad I did because you would've just slept through dinner."

That comment sparked me to stand up. I looked at the time on my phone. It was 6:10 p.m. I groaned; it was not my intention to sleep my day away like this. "I'm wearing a hot pink corset top and a black midlength skirt," I started before standing up and going to my bathroom. "My bad girl, I didn't sleep until a little after 6 a.m. I'm getting dressed now."

"What were you doing up at 6 a.m.? You bett-" I clicked on her before she could question me and my where abouts. We had all night to interrogate me about Marquis.

It took me only a short time to get dressed. I had already showered, so I only had to worry about my hair and makeup. I decided to settle for a simple look. I filled my eyebrows, hid my blemishes with foundation and concealer, and put on some mascara and a pink sparkly lip. I knew I would be late if I stayed in the next 15 minutes. I sectioned my hair into two buns before leaving two strands out, framing my face on both sides. . I go to my closet and grab my curly half wig, which resembles my natural hair. I sprayed a little water and put some curling gel on my hair. Once satisfied, I rushed out the door.

...

I was the first to arrive at the restaurant. Traditionally, in our friend group, whoever arrived first bought the appetizer and the first round of cocktails. So we didn't have to wait for a waiter upon arrival. Alameda arrived shortly after me just as the drinks reached the table. We looked like sisters. She was also caramel-skinned, and we were about the same height and weight. She wore her hair in a long black ponytail; she wore a black tank top, ripped jeans, and black heels. and about five minutes later, Leia short for Aaliyah arrived. She was built like a model, she towered over us by at least 2-3 inches, her hair was in a short brown bob today, that complimented her smooth brown light mocha skin.

Once, the waiter brought complimentary bread and appetizers. I could see it on Alameda's face that she was dying to know why I got home so late. The waiter finally walked away, and Alameda shoved her phone in my face. She showed me screenshots she had taken of my location at various hours throughout the night."I'm grown. I'm well aware of where and what exactly I was doing." I say smugly before I take a bite of the buttery bread. "Alright, so who were you with, and what were you all doing that caused you to get home at 6 a.m. and sleep in until 6 p.m.?" Leia, who was gleefully eating her bread, looked at me wide-eyed. "Let me see the evidence?" She grabbed Alameda's phone and scrolled through the screenshots.

"Hazey... you dirty girl," Leia said with the broadest smile. "So, what were you doing?" She asked, skipping over all the other evidence. Both of them leaned forward in their seats as they sipped their martinis.

"I didn't "Do" anyone; I was just hanging out with Marquis," I say casually, not wanting to make this a big deal. The two of them looked at each other wideeyed before back at me.

"Mr.Officer? With the chest piece?" Alameda asked, Leia chiming in, "With Locs and perfect teeth?" They then looked at each other, both gasping again. "Mariah's brother?!" They both started at the same time. I continued to look at the menu, deciding to refrain from feeding into their dramatics. "Yes, The Detective, who also happens to be Mariah's brother. I decided to hang out with him yesterday." I really didn't want to make a big deal out of this. I sigh as I put the menu down and cross my arms over my chest. I was ready for the silly interrogation.

"Sooooo, how did that happen? At his kickback, I only saw y'all talk briefly?" Alameda asked as she looked up, a finger on her chin as she tried to figure out when he and I made a connection. Leia and Her were so consumed with the men they were with that they must've forgotten about me.

"I had too much to drink and when you all went outside he and I decided to stay inside and talk. I asked him if I could spend the night and he then proceeded to take me to a guest room and I fell asleep almost immediately. He slept somewhere else. The next morning we cleaned up and just ended up hanging out the rest of the day." It was half the truth so it wasn't a hard story to conjure up. It probably would've worked had I not started to giggle, I couldn't help myself as memories flooded my mind of the last two days I spent with him.

They both groaned. "Hazel, you do this every time you talk about a man. You start with that laughing stuff, when there isn't even anything funny." Alameda said annoyingly as she stuffed her mouth with bread. "Keep going. So what happened while y'all were hanging out?" Leia leaned back in her chair, looking at me with anticipation.

I don't know why, but it took me a few moments to gather myself before placing a hand on my stomach and taking a deep breath as the giggles subsided. "When we first arrived yesterday, he and I went outside to the deck to talk. My sandal strings were coming undone. You guys remember the pair I was wearing? The gold ones with the long wrap-around strings and butterflies attached? " My face started to heat up a bit, and I averted my direct eye contact with them to avoid their anticipating intense stares. "This ninja lifted me up without even asking permission and sat me on the railing, then he stood between my legs; he brought one of my legs to his shoulder and tying and wrapping the string around my leg. Mind you, he was making direct eye contact the whole time. As he put my leg down, he squeezed my calves and gave me a light massage before he switched to the other leg. Then when I tried avoiding eye contact ...." I paused dramatically as I felt myself blushing from the recap. I started to fan myself. "Yall... he asked me what I was nervous about! He knew what he was doing!"

Alameda tapped my thigh, and Aaliyah squealed a bit. "What? That's so hot! So then what?" Just as Alameda asked for more details, the waiter returned to take orders. We quickly told him what we wanted so I could finish the story.

"So, of course, I was trying to play it cool, and I told him no one was nervous. He just laughed a little bit. Once he tied the other shoe, he just stood between my legs, and I could feel the heat building up between us. He told me my lips were sexy, and then we made out." The story was filled with tiny white lies, but I didn't want to go into all the details of us laying in his bed and all the other times we kissed throughout the last two days. The kissing wasn't even the most exciting part that occurred the last two days.

They swatted at me, telling me that I was acting grown despite being 29 years old.

"I'm happy that you didn't have sex; you always end up feeling conviction and sad every time you have sex," Aaliyah said knowingly "I agree, and we all know how sex can ruin a relationship." Alameda chimed in. "So what happened the next day?"

"We just spent the day together; he started off by making breakfast, he took me on a scenic drive, then he got me some flowers that will live to up a year, and after that, he bought me my first pair of boots." I paused for a moment. That was such a fond moment. I looked at my friends, and my eyes watered a bit. "He got them for me because this random girl was on the street. She had a similar outfit, so I complimented her, and he suggested buying me a pair." I made sure to look directly at Alameda. "AND I didn't fight him on it." She always chastised me for not letting a man spoil me. It didn't feel right having a man, or anyone for that matter, spend so much money on me, but Alameda was constantly reminding me that it was okay to let a man spend money on me and that I should accept it as long as he wasn't trying to pay for sex.

"And how did that make you feel?" She had the most giant smirk, with that knowing look. "It honestly made me feel very seen...all I've ever wanted from a man was someone to do something without me having to ask or pick up on when I liked something without me having to do or say too much." I looked over to Aaliyah, who was just a hopeless romantic, and she was patting the corner of her eyes to stop the tears from falling. "Hazel, that's so sweet. I'm glad he's treating you well. You deserve it, honestly."

The waiter brought us our meals, and we thanked him before I continued my recap of my night with Marquis.

"After the boots, we got dinner, and the vibes between us were immaculate. Neither wanted the night to end, so we went to Busy Signal and stayed until the last call. After that, we got canes, talked some more, and shared some kisses, and then I went home."

I looked at Alameda and could tell she was contemplating and thinking about everything I said. "So what are the red flags here? You don't seem to be in the delusional stage; you haven't called him your husband yet." I laughed at her comment but didn't have much to retort.

"He's cool, I think he's attractive, I like how he analyzes me, and I enjoy our conversations, but he'll ask me a question, I'll open up and express myself, and then I was met with silence, and maybe he just isn't the best with his words, most men aren't." I sigh as I try to carefully pick my words. I knew that whatever I said now could be used against me later. One lesson I've learned over the years is to be careful with how much you reveal and share with your friends. Whatever you tell them, they will never forget and bring it up again, even if it's something you've changed your mind about or decided to overlook. They would never let it go.

"I'm just going to take this thing daily with him. I'm still getting to know him, so we shall see where this goes." I say with a finality in my voice before digging into my pasta.

"That's growth because, at this point, your eyes would've been glossed over in delusion, and you would've been telling us your plan to lock him down." Alameda wasn't wrong, but I was no longer in the business of fantasizing about the future. It would save me a lot of heartbreak, making letting go easier when necessary.

I didn't want to get too excited just to have him disappoint me. This time, I planned on going with the flow.

Death

I groaned as I sat up in bed. I was on call today, and naturally, these days always seemed to leave me feeling the most on edge. Being an officer was already anxiety-inducing, but being on call always amped it up for me. I could be lying in bed in a deep sleep, and then suddenly, I was responding to a call at two in the morning. Neighbors reported that they heard women and children in distress; officers arrived on the scene and forced entry, only to discover that the husband had just murdered his entire family on a quiet Tuesday morning and was now on the run, or it could be the couple having sex but the woman sounded like she was being murdered. Another possible scenario would be me responding to a call at five in the morning. A jogger on their morning jog around Lady Bird Lake discovers a face-down floating body, and now I'm dealing with the press about a serial killer in Austin.

Despite the anxiety, I loved what I do for a living and wouldn't change it. At least not right now. I head to the kitchen, go for my pre-workout, and make myself some oatmeal and bacon while I sip my powdery water. I looked out my window, watching the kids head to the school bus and people jogging and walking their dogs. My people-watching was interrupted by the crackle of my radio. Instinctively, I grabbed it from my counter, my heart racing as I walked to my closet to go and change into my uniform, which was business casual. I usually wore an APD polo shirt and slacks.

"Do you need me to log you on Homicide 11?" dispatch asked as I was putting on my pants. I stopped midway and laughed as I shook my head. I queued up on the radio and responded before going back to my kitchen to finish my breakfast. I was relieved I didn't have to start my day off with adrenaline.

I was already half-dressed and decided to skip the gym today. As I finished getting ready, I called Hazel, surprised when it went straight to voicemail. That woman always had her phone on Do Not Disturb; every time I called, it seemed to go directly to voicemail. Still, she checked her phone frequently, so I knew it wouldn't be long before she called me back—unless she was still feeling down about yesterday. The day before had been tough for her at the clinic; one of her patients lost her babies in the first trimester. I was all too familiar with the heartwrenching cries of a grieving mother, and Hazel had shared with me that it was one of her triggers.

Being in this field, we all develop triggers. For some of us, it's abused, harmed, or neglected elderly/children; for others, it can be the odor of someone who has been decaying for a while, or it was the distinct scream a woman released after losing the child she either didn't get to birth or the mother who carried and raised her child just for it to all be taken away from her once you hear it you never forget it.

I had sent her flowers and food to her home as a sign of comfort and support. I knew she would be working in the ER today, so I would bring her something. I had strongly encouraged her not to work today, but she insisted on wanting to distract her mind. I wasn't going to say anything else over the phone and just wait until I saw her in person.

As I thought about what I could get her, my phone rang. "Hey Jorden, what's up, man?" I asked as I scrolled through TikTok shop to figure out what I could buy her. "Our suspect's girlfriend Kayla from the downtown case wants to meet up. She advises that she has compelling evidence now. We should head that way. I'll text you the address."

"Say less," I stated before I hung up. I grabbed my gun, badge, work phone, and lunch.

While en route to Kayla's home, dispatch keyed up on the radio. "HOM 11, code 3 response needed to 10100 Lake Creek Blvd. The mother of your subject reported the subject has been assaulted with a weapon as well as stabbed."

"Damn." I mumbled as I flipped the lights on and turned the sirens on. I get onto the highway, going 20 over the speed limit. I already knew it was her crocked boyfriend. Dude probably found out she was going to snitch and retaliated.

What was a 25-minute drive turned into 12 minutes with my driving. I switched the channel on my radio, and I could hear the traffic related to my call. Officers were checking the area for the vehicle description the mother had provided, and other officers were securing the scene. When I arrived, an ambulance and several officers were on the scene. I briefly saw my witness-turned-victim body being moved to the ambulance via stretcher. The young 22 -year-old female was unrecognizable. Her face had been obviously bashed in with a blunt object; she had been repeatedly stabbed and was also suffering from several lower body injuries.

Her boyfriend was gang-affiliated and was a suspect in the murder of two young men after witnesses stated he was last seen with the victims at a bar arguing before the homicide. The victims of my case had also been stabbed repeatedly and suffered severe lower body injuries and deformities.

Jorden arrived on the scene before me, and he was inside interviewing the mother. While he did that, I conducted interviews with the neighbors who heard the arguing and the woman crying out for help. The mother had just come home from a workout when she saw the suspect assaulting her daughter. The damage had been done by the time she arrived. Currently, the mother was too distraught and sobbing to interview. No one saw the assault take place. They only heard the disturbance before he exited the home and drove off fast.

We knew that it could take hours before the hospital would allow us to see her, so we took advantage of our free time. We had all the evidence sent to the labs and began writing reports from our witnesses.

...

A couple of hours had passed, and we still hadn't received any updates on the witness who had become a victim. Jorden and I decided to head over to the hospital and wait there while we typed up whatever we could for our reports. I struggled to write anything; I felt a deep sympathy for our victim. There was always an internal conflict about how tough to be on someone to elicit the information we needed. We understood that her safety was at risk if she chose to cooperate with us. On the night of the murders, she had been completely uncooperative, refusing to answer any of our questions. Now, I wished she had engaged with us that night or at least come to the police station so we could have taken the necessary steps to ensure her protection.

I hate what happened to her, but I couldn't allow the guilt to weigh me down. She was a young girl who came from a middle-class family who chose to be with a low-life thug, and those were the facts despite knowing that I still didn't feel any better.

"Aye, man, let's go flirt with the nurses. They're not doing anything, and you need a distraction," Jorden said as he walked beside me and gave me a pat on the back. I knew he was keen to talk to a nurse named Michelle, whom he had been courting for about a month. I felt a bit uneasy as we headed toward the nurses' station. Since my date with Hazel, I wasn't interested in pursuing other women, but I had just come out of a relationship and didn't want to rush into anything. Now I found myself in a different kind of struggle. On one hand, I didn't want to upset Hazel, but on the other hand, I was a single man and free to do as I pleased. Yet, doing as I pleased didn't feel right.

Hazel had many qualities I appreciated; she was selfless, always helping others even when she was tired; she knew how to cook; she had a clean, aesthetically pleasing apartment; she was hilarious and didn't even try to be. She sought after the things she wanted. Most importantly, she loved our lord and savior. I was very attracted to her, but the idea of being tied down right now also didn't feel right. I loved how she was starting to soften her hardened exterior to me, revealing that gentle woman that I knew rested within her. She was being less snappy and more sappy. She was starting to show her dramatic side, suddenly she didn't want to be miss independent around. Lately, she would have me do things as simple as opening a jar or grabbing something from a top shelf. She was feeling me, and I was feeling her as well. I knew I should've clung to what felt right but the man in me also wanted to prowl to keep it simple. Being in another relationship meant being locked down indefinitely, and I didn't know if I was ready for something like that.

Being around men like Jorden didn't help; he was the homie, we had been friends since academy days, and ever since I've come to know him, he has been this fuck'em all and leave 'em type of dude. I think it had to do with his deep-rooted childhood trauma, abandonment issues that stemmed from the lack of a father, and his mother choosing substances and men over him. I wasn't going to tell him about Hazel; all he would encourage me to do was conquer her and move on to the next.

As we approached the station, I convinced myself that I needed the distraction, and Hazel probably wouldn't mind. I usually didn't have to flirt much; women would often start conversations with me and giggle at the things I said. Not to sound arrogant, but I knew I was the type that most women found attractive, especially in Texas. I'm tall, dark, and handsome, with several tattoos. I tend to keep to myself, and I have dreadlocks. As long as I approached women, they would usually do the rest of the work.

The usual nurses and a student were gathered around the station. Some were busy charting, while most were engaged in animated gossip about the latest happenings at work. Among them, a striking white nurse named Taylor approached me. She was the exact Instagram-perfect image—her scrubs were the latest trendy design, fitted closely to her form, accentuating her petite figure. Her hair was styled in glossy curls that bounced with every movement, and her bright, radiant smile seemed to light up the room.

"Why are you always frowning or looking mad? I bet all the criminals hate to see you coming!" she remarked, her tone playful as she lightly tapped my shoulder. I watched as she flipped her curls over her shoulder, exuding carefree confidence. While Taylor was undeniably cute, she wasn't quite my type. The core reason was her mean-girl aura; she had a knack for making you feel like she was laughing with you when, in truth, she was likely laughing at you. For the sake of needing to distract my mind, I decided to entertain her anyway.

A moment later, Hazel emerged, her white coat crisp and her expression unreadable. That changed when she noticed Taylor's hand resting on my bicep, tracing one of my tattoos—a replica of Michelangelo's painting "The Creation of Adam." Taylor had been asking about it. Hazel shot a disgusted glance between the two of us before focusing on me. Taylor smiled and gave me a hug before walking away. I couldn't quite decipher what expression Taylor wore, but Hazel eyes remained fixed on Taylor with a fierce glare until she was out of sight. That felt tense. A wave of guilt washed over me, and I almost apologized but pride reminded me that I was single and technically nothing happened.

I flashed Hazel a smile and took a step closer to her, about to ask her what was up and how her day was. She took a step back, keeping the space between us before speaking up. "Detective Marquis," she said, her tone clipped. You wanted a report on Kayla's condition?" I tensed a bit; she wasn't playing with me at all. "Yes, ma'am," I replied, determined to maintain a professional tone despite her dry demeanor. "How is she?"

"Stable. She's recovering from surgery, but she needs time. We don't want to pressure her with your—"

"My questions?" I interjected, frustration displaying from beneath my calm exterior. "She's a victim and witness. The sooner we can get her statement, the better." Hazel narrowed his eyes; she firmly laid her chart down on the counter before folding her arms. "Watch your tone with me, first and foremost, and what exactly do you think will happen if you push her? You're not the only one who needs to consider her well-being here."

I took a deep breath, trying to rein in my rising temper. "Excuse me if I'm a little irritated; I have two families wanting answers, and my key witness is just behind those doors." I pointed at the double doors behind her. "Our suspect can be in Dallas, Houston, San Antonio, or anywhere at this point. I've been waiting hours, Hazel."

Hazel's posture remained the same, and her voice was steady. "This isn't a crime scene. It's a hospital. Kayla needs care, not interrogation." She replied plainly. I felt my jaw tighten. "I'm not here to interrogate her. I'm here to help her. We both want the same thing—justice for her."

Hazel just stared at me, the tension growing thick between us. Finally, she sighed, the hardness in her expression softening just a bit. "I respect that, Marquis. But pushing her too soon could be damaging. Trauma doesn't heal under pressure."

I knew I got to her slightly since she dropped the title from my name. "I understand that, Hazel," I replied, my voice firm but controlled. "My biggest concern is, what if she forgets key details? I just really want to jump to my next lead so I can help her."

She studied me, seemingly weighing her words. "I get that, but again, I'm mostly worried about her well-being. I'll update you with any new information that I get regarding her well-being, and I'll let you know when the doctor thinks she can be interrogated."

I had no response. I knew she threw the word "interrogate" in there on purpose, but I wouldn't entertain that right now. I just nodded my head in response. "I need to speak to her mother now." she grabbed her keyboard and turned to walk away. For a brief moment, our eyes met before she walked away towards the ER waiting room. A few moments later, she brought the mother back with her to where Kayla was, who was still sobbing and in visible distress from the earlier site of her daughter.

As I watched them walk away, Jorden piped up: Michelle had to tend to a patient EMS just brought in. "Sheesh, my boy, that woman doesn't like you." He stated knowingly. Not knowing that Hazel was kissing on my tattoos less than a week ago, just before her patient's miscarriage. "Naw, she's just having a bad day," I said matter of fact. I knew her mood had to do with the recent trauma she experienced back at her clinic, but instead of resting up and taking care of her mental health, she decided to work.

"I think she's just jealous because you're feeling me and not her," Taylor stated as she walked past us and into the station. It took me a moment to realize Taylor was shooting her shot, and Jorden's eyes widened before he dramatically looked between the two of us. I just glanced between the two, not sure what to say. Just as I was about to turn Taylor down, The double doors to the OR loudly opened as the mother walked out with Hazel, and a few other associates followed behind. The mother was crying while also cursing them out; she directed most of her energy towards Hazel. "Why would you tell me she was okay to be seen when she wasn't? My baby is dying, and it's your fault, you idiot doctor, you stupid bitch!" She yelled out.

She then released a loud wail. Hazel's associates went to attend to the woman while Hazel remained stiff yet wide-eyed. Hazel appeared traumatized as the woman released a sound that only a grieving mother could let out. The woman pointed an accusing finger at Hazel while she was being dragged away. Hazel slowly approached me; her eyes still widened but now watery. "Kayla coded...she's being worked on. A doctor will be out to update you all.." Hazel walked away without saying another word, taking off her coat and probably leaving for the rest of the day.

I was about to go after her, but Jorden put a hand on my shoulder. I looked back at him, but he just shook his head no. "Let her have her space; she needs to process that." It didn't feel right in my mind to leave her like that, but maybe he was right.

"Let's call it for now. We will be back in an hour to follow up..." I needed some fresh air.

Depression

I sat in the locker room we had designated for staff. I was on break contemplating if I should go home or not. I had my hands burrowed in my face. My patient experienced a stillbirth yesterday.

No amount of schooling, prepping, or coaching can prepare you for the screams of a grieving mother. There was nothing I could say or do at that moment to make her feel good. After about an hour of her grieving, my staff and I poured into her. We prayed over her, cleaned her body, and read her scripture Matthew 5:4: Blessed are those who mourn, for they will be comforted. Psalm 34:18 The Lord is close to the brokenhearted and saves those who are crushed in spirit. and spent the entire afternoon with her. It was a very long day and for special occasions like this we did have recovery rooms, we hired overnight security to watch over the mother and my staff. I felt so awful; seeing a deceased child was never easy.

I should've called in but, I thought the adrenaline of the ER would help me. It turned out to be one of the worst shifts I had ever worked. Marquis was flirting with Taylor, who found me to be her biggest competitor, which was crazy because I was ranked above her; there was no competition. Seeing him flirt with her hurt, I thought the last few weeks we were getting much closer. I did this every time I got in a new situationship; I would lose interest in any other man and solely fixate on the man I was with at that time. Clearly, the private moments we shared didn't mean much to him. Just last night, he sent me flowers and food, and now that felt disingenuous. I felt bitterness hit my tongue as I thought about the way I was kissing his tattoos during the back message I was giving him yesterday. I knew he was single but to be flirting in the same ER room I worked in? That was actual insanity to me. I promised myself the next time I saw read flags I wouldn't indulged.

I sigh to myself I hated when feelings were involved because, he was the only person I wanted to call.

...

I laid on my furry rug in the living room. I had been reaching for my phone, it had fallen off my couch and ended up on the ground. I've been here since 1 pm. It is now 3:10 pm. I was stuck in an endless loop of the events that had taken place. Every time I tried doing something for myself, even something as simple as washing my hair and taking a shower I felt my mind resist the idea. I didn't feel like I deserved to do anything but grieve. I knew for a fact that both of those mothers were still grieving today and there was nothing I could do. I knew I wasn't God, that death was inevitable, and that everything happened for a reason.

Despite having that concept down I still couldn't help but grieve myself. This wasn't my first time seeing a stillborn, nor was that the first time I had seen a grieving mother or a dead patient, but, for some reason, it hit me hard this time. I had taken two weeks off from work and I kept my phone on DND, this was the longest I had ever isolated myself. My friends knew I was isolating, and I would message them when I wanted to be bothered. So far, it had only been 6 days into my 14-day hiatus. Someone didn't get the memo.

There was knocking at my door. Too drained I didn't move expecting them to just leave but, after 5 mins my doorbell was still being runged. My arms felt heavy as I patted around my body looking for my phone. I finally found it slightly under the couch and I checked my doorbell app to see that it was Marquis. I sighed heavily knowing he wouldn't go anywhere or even worse he would find "reasonable cause" and force entry into my home. Sitting up I slowly pulled myself from the ground,my head started to spin and I felt nauseous. I hadn't eaten anything in a while and it was starting to hit me. I think the last thing I had to eat was cheese crackers and a apple yesterday. I spoke through the app "Give me a minute". My voice sounded hoarse, I hadn't spoken in a few days so that wasn't surprising. I knew I wasn't myself because I didn't even bother to hide the fact I wasn't doing so well.

I checked myself in the mirror next to my front door; my usual defined fluffy curls were dull, lifeless, and almost matted. My face had dry tear streaks. My eyes watered up at seeing myself, I didn't even recognize myself right now. I was drawn from my thoughts by the knocking. I knew I looked like crap, but he insisted on bothering me, so this is what he was going to be met with.

When I opened the door I found him at the door holding a tote with an image of a brown skin, thick woman, a huge afro, doing yoga and smoking a joint. I loved it. I could see items peeking from the top my interest was spiked. My eyes met his. He looked at me, and I looked at him, neither of us speaking for a moment. I was overwhelmed with emotion yet I was being defensive because I didn't want to be vulnerable in front of him. I didn't want him to think I was some kind of weak woman. The more I thought about it the more it began to irritate me. I started to recall many conversations I overheard when I was a EMT. Whenever someone couldn't handle a rough call or showed emotion often that person was ridiculed. I believe statistically this is why a lot of first responders committed suicide, not having a solid support team could be rough on anyone.

On the other hand, I wanted him to wrap his strong arms around me, Tell me it would be okay, and hold me while I cried. I wrapped my arms tight around my chest and stood a little straighter. I didn't want or need the comfort of a man. He would just expect sex in exchange, or maybe he needed something from me. My mind was starting to race with theories, especially as the silence between us thickened and he continued to stare at me.

In a self-soothing matter. I began to play with the ends of my hair, running my fingers through the ends of my hair. My mind was beginning to fill with distress. "Calm down...maybe he's just being nice
don't assume anything...." I gently remind myself before clearing my throat. "What do you want?" I tried to remain poise, and nonchalant, despite the fact I knew he already analyzed me in the pregnant silence we experienced. He was a homicide detective, after all. It was his job to study his suspects and victims.

"I haven't heard from you or seen you in days, I wanted to make sure you were okay...can I come in? It's clear to me you're not doing okay." I was trying to figure out what his gain was. Why did he want to help me? I briefly had flashbacks to the night we spent together. Maybe there is no gain...maybe he could make me feel safe and secure again. He put the tote down, and he stepped up to me, and I took a step back. He grabbed the front of my shirt as I was stepping back. I was now leaning back in my shirt and he stopped me from moving with the hold he had on my shirt. He had a smile on his face as he pulled me back to him a little forcible. "Why do you always fight me?"

He took another step towards me, closing the distance between us. "Let me help you, mamas. You won't regret it, I promise." He gently placed his hands on my hips and squeezed lightly. "If I make you uncomfortable, I'll leave, but for now, let me try and help you." I didn't need any more convincing. It felt nice to have a familiar touch on me, and I didn't want him to leave me alone.

"Okay..." I say softly. I walk inside so he can follow behind me. My apartment wasn't messy. I hardly touched anything. I was the one who was mostly a mess. My "I don't care what he thinks about me. I hope it scares him off" attitude turned into, "I hope he doesn't think I'm super disgusting and leaves." He came to my living room and sat on the couch. He started to pull items out one by one from the tote. He bought 5 different candles, several sheet masks as well as peel-off masks, incense, body washes, shower steamers, and more self-care items. I just smiled. I showed him where to put everything.

When he got in my bathroom, he started running my bath. I stood up and followed him, leaning against the door, watching him. "You're about to bathe right now?" I asked him curiously. He placed a lavender bath bomb in the tub.

As he turned around, he took his shirt off, placing it on the counter before walking towards me. "Naw, this is for you. The first step to feeling better is freshening up, " he stated matter-of -factly

.

"Your going to bathe me?" My face heated up at the thought, and I started to feel self-conscious. He doesn't respond but only nods his head. He starts pulling out scented body washes, my shampoo, and conditioner from my shower. He sits it next to my bathtub before he walks back towards me. He squatted before wrapping his arms just beneath my butt. He picked me up and sat me on the counter. I was still amazed he could lift my thick, solid body with ease.

I was wearing a huge oversized T-shirt dress with nothing beneath it. I just watched as he maneuvered and moved things around in my space. He handed me my toothbrush, wetting it for me before putting toothpaste on it. He handed it to me, and I brushed my teeth, continuing to watch him. I spit in the sink before rinsing my toothbrush and putting it back in its holder. He grabbed a face towel rinsing under the warm water. He placed his hands beneath my knees and he scooted me to the edge and opened my legs just enough so he could fit. He stood between my legs placing the warm towel on my face. I moaned softly, leaning back against the mirror. I could still feel him shuffling through my things, but I trusted him, and I didn't care.

"How does that feel ma?"

I hadn't felt this good in days and it made me feel guilty. I tried pushing the thought back, but my eyes started to water up. Why did I deserve to feel good right now? Who was taking care of those mothers, and who made sure they were okay? I tried to change my thoughts so I wouldn't cry, but it was too late. I started to sniffle, and the sniffling turned into light sobs. Marquis stood back in between my legs and he lifted the towel from my face. I looked at him through teary eyes, and he took the towel, wiping at my fresh tears and the dried tear stains. "I know it's been rough on your mind lately, but thank you for allowing me to take care of you. It's my job to make you feel better right now."

All I could do was nod my head. He dimmed the light and he burned one of the incense he bought as well as a candle. He set my speaker on the counter and started to play some calming, lo-fi hip-hop. He stood in between my legs again. "I know you don't like people touching your hair, but will you allow me to do so?"

I had a civil war going on in my mind. Multiple voices and 1000s of thoughts racing. I was struggling with the idea of feeling good, knowing there were a lot of people grieving right now. His deep yet gentle voice silences those thoughts. I noticed that several times since he arrived. Anytime he spoke to me or came near me my focus was on him and he calmed me, I was so attracted to him. I never had anyone do something like this for me before, and I didn't have to ask...he seemingly wanted to. I was never one for physical touch. Truthfully, I had never experienced intimacy outside of sex. Any other form of intimacy made me uncomfortable, not by choice,. It's just when I needed it and/or craved it the most, it wasn't given to me. Now that

148 | P a g e

I'm an adult, I found myself rejecting it and feeling awkward.

As my friends would call it, I was in a "state of delusion." As I had been watching him maneuver and exist in my space, I found myself imagining him as my husband, and he was just taking care of me on a random day after a long shift. He was making me feel safe and secure and this man has barely even touched me yet.

I realized I hadn't responded, he was still paused looking at me awaiting an answer. I just nodded my head, and I closed my eyes, bracing myself for the foreign touch of having my curly, cloud-like texture touched. His hands were surprisingly gentle. He pulled my hair from its matted bun. He began spraying it so that it was soft enough to pull apart. He parted my hair into four sections. I felt safe enough and I placed my forehead on his chest, remaining still, something I would do as a child when my mom would do my hair. It would give him access to my full head without straining. He sprayed it with water as I instructed him to put pre-poo in it first. He combed through each section, starting at the tip to my root, until no more hair was coming out, and the brush went through smoothly. My hair stretched from just below to my ear down to my elbow. The length made me smile. He then grabbed my deep conditioner and placed it in my hair, running it root to my ends before placing the plastic bag over my hair. I finally opened my eyes and I just stared up at him.

My chin was resting on his chest and we looked at each other in silence. "You know.." I felt myself about to cry again and I didn't want that to happen. I take a moment and swallow hard. "You didn't have to do any of this, but I appreciate it." He leaned forward, kissing my forehead. Before he kissed the bridge of my nose, leading down to my lips. I didn't fight it. I lean into the kiss, wrapping my arms around his back. His hands moved to squeeze my thighs, and it sent tingles up to my inner thighs. The kisses were soft like velvet. I had never kissed a man with so much sensuality behind it. It was as if he was trying to portray a message to me, as if his lips were transmitting the feelings directly to my heart. He moved his arms behind my back, and he squeezed me.

As we kissed, his hands gently traveled down to my thighs, and I could feel the warmth of his touch as he explored. It felt pleasant until I sensed his thumb brush against my lips. I realized, a little embarrassed, that I wasn't wearing panties—something I usually skipped. With a soft nudge, I pushed him back and opened my eyes to meet his gaze. My heart raced, and I knew I needed a moment. "I just feel a bit unclean and really want to freshen up," I explained with a smile as I hopped off the counter. I began to lift my t-shirt dress, and with a respectful turn, he gave me space. As I stepped

into the shower and closed the door, I heard him say, "I made you a bath; why are you showering?"

"Because I don't want to sit in my filth; I'm just taking a quick rinse off and getting the grime off me." Several minutes later, I stepped out, and his back was still turned. He was putting away products we wouldn't need anymore and grabbing what would be needed next. I step into the bubble bath, and I moan as the warmth envelops me. He walked over to the tub, placed my bath pillow beneath my neck, and started to take the plastic bag off of my head. I close my eyes again bracing for his touch. He grabbed a cup, poured water over my hair, and rinsed the products out before he started to shampoo my hair which was quick. He was more precise once he started to condition my hair. He once again made sure it was reaching from my roots to ends and he made sure he was stimulating my scalp with deep circular motions using the padding of his fingers.

"How did you learn to take care of a BLACK woman's hair?" I made sure to emphasize black because our routine was like no others, as far as I was aware. Not something that many brothers were educated on. It also didn't make sense to me since he only had brothers so I couldn't imagine him doing what he was doing to my hair currently to them. The answer I was expecting was for him to say he learned it from a girlfriend of the past. "My mother taught me. She told me that black women can go through hair depression when their hair isn't cared for. She told me that black women carry a lot of stress in their roots and that a black man needed to know how to take care of it when his woman was unable to. She taught me that this is another form of intimacy and it would show I cared. You've been depressed, and I can just tell in general that you're not used to getting a lot of help, so I wanted to take some, if not your entire burden so you could feel some relief."

"Take my burden?" My heart started fluttering. I had never met someone who wanted to take care of me like this. I stared at him, and my heart started to yearn. I wanted this all the time, not just now.

As he continued washing my hair, my eyes started to water again. I didn't want to cry again, but I couldn't help it. The tears were falling against my will, and I could barely even get my question out. I paused, swallowing hard to keep my shaky voice at bay. "Why do you feel the need or the want to help me, comfort and care for me?" My question came out softly. If I had used any other tone, I would've only cried harder.

He moves around the tub, and he kneels beside the top so that he's positioned in front of me. I tried avoiding his eyes, but he grabbed my chin, making me look at him. Before he could speak up, I splashed a bit of water on him and snatched my face from his hands. I rub at my tears frustratingly. It was a defense mechanism...and I was overwhelmed. I sink into the tub so the bubbles can continue to cover my breast. He was staring at me and I looked away, sinking lower into the tub before grabbing a strain of my hair and deciding to hyper-fixate on the curls, twirling it around in my fingers. "You don't have to grab my face to apologize." I wasn't able to read the expression on his face, but I didn't want to stare at him and try to get a read.

"My family doesn't check up on me, my friends I love them to death but, most of the time I feel like they don't love me the way I love them. I remember telling one of them I was going through some mental stuff, and she didn't have much of a response. When I am at my weakest and lowest, all I've ever had was God, he would be my protector and healer. I've had an ex once...his name was Captain, and he made me feel secure for a bit, but then he... left me." I chuckle at the sad memory, shaking my head as I dismiss the thoughts. " Why are you suddenly showing up and doing all of this!?"

The tears were running hot as I spoke. I buried my face in my hands. Memories flashed through all the times I asked for help from others, and I was met with silence. The memories of my mother telling me she was a problem solver and didn't coddle me when I was a teenager crying and really needing comfort was something that had always stuck with me. Oftentimes, I would find myself being harder on myself or internally getting frustrated with my friends for not being able to fix their problems. Men I've dated in the past weren't much help either; they only could offer me a blunt, a drink, and or sex. The pleasurable feeling would only last a few minutes before I found myself still worried or stressed about whatever the problem was at the time.

As I grew older now and then, my mother would help financially, but when it came to my mental health, I couldn't talk to her. I knew her heart was in a good place but she's not a good listener, she would spend most of the conversation talking about her own experiences, which would then make me feel even sadder knowing my mother went through so much pain. So, instead of expressing myself, I would then become a listener for her, pushing my feelings aside.

Needless to say, I've never had anyone be here for me like this, and now that Marquis was here giving me everything I had ever wanted and more, I felt myself a little overwhelmed and scared. What was his end goal for us? Why did he want to do these things? Did he just want something from me? In my mind and based on past experiences, the only way a man could do something like this for me is if he was expecting something in return.

I felt him gently grasp my face, urging me to look into his eyes. "Look, shawty, forget your past." My tears began to slow as I met his gaze, curious to see where he was going with this. "I'm not like these other niggas, and there's nothing I can say to make you believe me. What I can do is show you through my actions, but you're going to have to trust me. I know that takes time, so are you willing to try?"

I searched his eyes for any signs of insincerity, looking for a hint of deception—any reason to push him away. I paused, digging into my feelings, but nothing surfaced; my intuition wasn't even tingling. In response, all I could do was nod. He leaned in and kissed me softly on the lips, and for several minutes, we were lost in that moment. When he pulled back, we locked eyes, and he licked his lips before rubbing my bottom lip with his thumb. "Sit back for me, mamas, so we can finish in here."

I was blushing, and I leaned back in the tub. My mind was distracted from work, and now I was focused on my feelings and future. He washed the conditioner from my hair. He stood back up, and he placed my shampoo and conditioner back in its spot in my shower. He then pulled out my leave-in conditioner, grease, moisturizer, and oil from beneath my bathroom sink. He grabbed one of my towels from my linen closet before placing it on the stool near my tub. "Let me know when you dress. I'll finish your hair, and then we can just chill."

"Thank you," I smiled at him as he nodded and left the bathroom. I stood up, partially drying off in the tub, before climbing out. After draining the water, I headed to my closet. Although I wanted to slip into my silk gowns or sexy night dresses, I felt too mentally exhausted to put in the effort. Instead, I settled for a black sports bra and an oversized Tupac shirt that fell just above my knees.

I walk to my vanity and sit on my chair, sighing with relief. For the first time in a while, I felt so good and just relieved in general. Grabbing my lotion and body oil. "You can come back in!" I yell out. A few minutes later, he was back in the bathroom. I had my leg propped up on the counter as I lotion my leg with lavender body oil. I smiled at him. "This is how I keep my skin super smooth. Oil and lotion after every bath."

"Your skin is super smooth. I'd always wonder how you got that sun-kissed moisturized look."

"Do I!?" I asked, genuinely ecstatic for that compliment. That has been one of my goals since I started to care about taking care of myself. He nodded his head in response before walking towards me.

"Let me get your other leg," he said, lifting it to his chest, which made me lean back in my chair. My shirt began to ride up, nearly exposing me, but his gaze remained locked on mine, making me blush all over again. I tucked the hem of my shirt between my legs and squeezed my thighs together. I handed him the lotion first while I held onto the oil.

His gaze remained on me as he squirted the cool contents onto my leg. He thoroughly rubbed the lotion into my skin going up my entire leg, stopping just mid-thigh. He would come back down and squeeze down my calf before massaging my foot. He reached his hand out for the oil and repeated the same motion. This was oddly erotic, and I felt good.

He kissed my calf before gently lowering my leg. "Ready to get started on this head?" He smiled at me casually as if his hands weren't just seducing me. It's been so long since I've been intimate or attracted to anyone. I almost forgot what it felt like.

"Yeah nigga… let's see what else your mama taught you," I say with a smile on my face trying to hide the arousal he sparked in me. He smirked, stood behind the chair, and began to part my hair.

He just ended up doing a medium/large 2-strand twist in my hair, which was then pulled up into a bun with two strands hanging on either side of my face.

...

At this point in the night, it was almost 10 p.m. we ended up going on a McDonald's run before coming home. I finally had a real appetite after not having hardly eaten anything the last few days.

We were back at my apartment, my legs draped over his lap as we watched TV. Honestly, the TV was just background noise; we were engrossed in conversation, talking about everything and anything. He shared childhood stories about his siblings, and we swapped wild tales from our experiences as first responders while bonding over The Office. I loved the effortless flow of our conversation, but I found myself increasingly attracted to him. The lingering traces of his touch from the bathroom were still embedded in my skin, and I craved more of him. I had expected things to progress further after our kiss, but... nothing happened. I thought that by now, we would be moving beyond just talking.

"So what's weighing on your mind right now? What's been bothering you?" He turned to look at me, but suddenly the show on TV seemed so captivating that I couldn't maintain eye contact. I grabbed the end of one of my twists and began twirling it around my finger. "As I get older and deepen my relationship with God, I find myself becoming more empathetic and emotional..." I paused, taking a breath as memories flooded back. "My patient... it's been a while since I've encountered a grieving mother, and I know you can recognize that sound—it's so distinct, unlike anything else. The wail that comes from a woman's core as she releases her grief." I finally met his gaze for a brief moment before looking down again, feeling a lump in my throat. Even in that fleeting glance, I sensed that he somehow understood my secret.

I could tell he wanted me to keep going, but I felt my breath catch in my throat. Talking about this wasn't easy. "I think back to many moons ago, almost ten years now, when I was younger. I bled heavily one time to the point of feeling lightheaded and in excruciating pain; clots were passing, and I never went to the doctor. I still don't know if I had a miscarriage, but the dreams that haunted me afterward were vivid." I shook my head as the memories washed over me. "In some dreams, I was a mother; in others, a little boy would introduce himself to me as my son." I let out a bitter laugh, feeling like I was opening up too much, but he had asked. "When I told my boyfriend at the time, he panicked and ghosted me, which I took as a blessing, and I moved on with my life. I never went to therapy or did anything to ensure my physical or mental well-being was okay." I finally made eye contact with him, my eyes welling up with tears. "The mother who lost her baby in my clinic was the same age as me. The university sends me a student every six months because I really empathize with these young women. I knew there was a possibility for her, but I... I..." I felt the familiar sting of tears and struggled to continue.

"You did everything you could, right?" He asked me, and I glanced at him, nodding my head as I wiped my tears. "I'm not saying the pain should just dissipate now, but if you did everything you were supposed to, then you released from that pain. Now, if this is because of what happened to you 10 years ago, then just know God is going to bless you in that area if that's what your heart desires. Just need to be patient and see where he takes you." He glanced back at me, and I smiled at him. I still felt awful for those women, but he had a point, and now I wanted to change the subject.

"Okay, Mr. Detective, you're asking me all these questions, so I have one for you: why haven't you kissed me again? I mean, I was so dirty earlier, and you didn't mind. Now that I'm clean, you don't want to touch me?" I felt a wave of nervousness wash over me. He chuckled, running a hand through his locs as he looked over me, his gaze lingering on my body. He shifted my right leg behind him and kept my left leg in front of him before positioning himself above me. I instinctively wrapped my arms around his neck, feeling like our bodies were meant to fit together. "I didn't want you to think I was just here for the physical... I wanted to genuinely help you." He paused looking into my eyes, searching them to see if he could gauge my emotions. "With that being said are you okay? We don't have to be physical at all if that's not something you desire."

I felt really good in this moment. He thought about me, was considerate, and unprovokedly helped me. There was a small doubt in my mind, questioning all of his motives, but I quickly dismissed them. I knew how this sounded, but I really didn't care. No one has ever done anything this nice for me, and it's been so long since I've been intimate. I just wanted to be loved on, and I had a feeling he would love me, right? I pulled him into a kiss, giving him the consent he was looking for. His hands traveled down my leg. My hands traveled across his chest, and the other ran a hand amongst his locs. I had never been so lost in a kiss before. His body felt the way my weighted blanket did. Bringing me comfort and safety.

He began kissing my neck; while most men left sloppy, wet kisses on my body, his felt electrifying. I struggled to suppress my moans as he trailed kisses from my neck down to my chest in between my breasts and along my stomach. When his mouth lowered between my thighs and his hand began to drift between my legs, I knew where this was headed. I sat up, squeezing my thighs together to redirect his attention. He looked at me, confused, and placed a hand on my knee. "I... it's just that I haven't shaved..." I couldn't meet his gaze; feeling embarrassed about something I usually told my clients was completely natural.

He placed his hands on the back of my thighs, and he gripped them before pulling me more to him, making me lay flat on my back. "Girl, that doesn't bother me. We are grown a little hair don't stop nothing." He said dismissively yet confidently. I relaxed and smiled as he lifted the ends of my dress. He didn't hesitate, and his head lowered, and he went to work.

...

We eventually made our way to my bedroom. That man was a beast; his stamina was unmatched. I had always prided myself on my ability to go multiple rounds, but no past lover had ever satisfied my insatiable appetite until I was with Marquis. It was the way he guided me through each orgasm that brought me to new heights. His hands never left my body throughout the experience—pinning my arm behind me, holding my hands above my head, rubbing my thigh, or playfully slapping my ass. The physical touch was everything. Past lovers had kept things simple with just doggy style and missionary, but this was different.

When I tried running, he only went deeper and pulled me in closer. At one point we were in missionary. I don't know if you could call it lovemaking if the two individuals aren't in love, but that's what we did. He made me whole eye contact the entire time; he spoke to me and expected a response; he stroked me at a pace that left me panting. At one point, I even cried, and he kissed away the tears before our lips met.

After I came for the final time, I collapsed onto the bed, curling up under the blanket. I felt tired, mentally drained, and now physically exhausted. I expected Marquis to leave me alone in my bed, and the thought made me a bit sad, but I didn't want to dwell on it. Just as I was about to drift into dreamland, I felt something heavy behind me, followed by a strong arm draping over my body. My eyes flew open, and a wide smile spread across my face. I decided not to question it, just enjoying the moment. I scooted back into him, and he tightened his grip around me. I kissed his arm before closing my eyes, and he kissed my cheek.

That night, my dreams were pleasant. I dreamed of my own children, and although I couldn't see the father's face, I caught a glimpse of Marquis's tattooed hand holding our child, swaddled in blankets. I couldn't make out his face, but I knew that hand was his.

...

The next morning, I woke up, and for the first time in a while, it wasn't with a heavy heart or in a dark room. The blinds were open, and I groaned happily as I arched my back and stretched my limbs before sitting up. I was mildly surprised to find Marquis wasn't in bed next to me. I felt my eyes water up, and a flood of questions entered my mind. Did he just use me for sex? Why did he leave? Why didn't he say goodbye? I turned over to the side where his body had just been lying several hours ago. I scoot over to that side, and I smiled, taking in his cedar scent. I rubbed my hand over the area where he lay. "We just opened up the door, Hazey..." I say out loud to myself.

I lay in bed a little longer, staring at the ceiling, reflecting on everything that had happened the night before. I wanted to check in with myself and see how I truly felt. To be honest, I wasn't okay. I didn't like one-night stands, and I had developed feelings for Marquis that I believed were mutual. There was no way a man would go to such lengths just for a casual encounter... But then it hit me—maybe some men would. Tears filled my eyes, but I quickly wiped them away. A sense of conviction washed over me, and I realized it was time to repent. I had no business being intimate with him, especially after promising God that I would wait for marriage.

I rolled out of bed and dropped to my knees, closing my eyes to pray. "Lord, I know that in 1 Corinthians 6:18 you ask us to flee from sexual immorality, but instead, I welcomed it. I know you've called me to be different in this walk with you, yet I have failed you... again. Every time you send me a man I believe is 'the one,' I fall into this sin." My eyes filled with tears as they began to fall. "I ask for your forgiveness, Lord, and I pray that you help remove this barrier in my life that craves physical touch. I'm grateful for the intimacy you've shown me that
exists outside of sex. I ask for forgiveness in Jesus' name, amen."

I crawled back into bed, wanting to fully embrace whatever emotions were coming my way. I felt grateful that he had come by and treated me in a way I had longed for since childhood. He nurtured me, gave me attention, was gentle, and even brought my favorite things. I was pretty sure that last night he made love to me. I remembered how he listened to my whimpers, recognizing the difference between a "that hurts a little" and a "keep going just like that" sound. He didn't rush; he wasn't just focused on his own pleasure but made sure I was okay during and after.

"What else are you feeling, Hazel? We had sex, and he really delivered, but how does it feel that he's not here now? What about the future of your relationship?" I asked myself these questions to ground myself in reality. I knew I had a tendency to overthink. First, I would replay the entire night in my mind, analyzing every moment to gauge how much he liked me. Then I'd start imagining a future together, telling my friends he was my husband and envisioning our kids and the life we could share. But the truth was, he had no idea how deep my feelings ran.

I didn't want to get hurt this time around. I wanted to be in tune with my feelings. Closing my eyes, I allowed myself to truly feel and reflect. After a moment, I was grateful he had come by, but I wished we hadn't slept together. I disliked how I often rushed into intimacy in the early stages of my relationships. I hoped that sex wouldn't define what we had and that we could develop something deeper. I didn't feel used or empty after being with him; instead, I felt content with how the night unfolded. Still, I knew I needed to slow things down and approach our relationship at a reasonable pace to protect myself. Most importantly, I planned to consult God about it.

With that thought in mind, I sat in bed and headed to the bathroom to shower and freshen up. I felt good for the first time in about a week, and it was refreshing. My mind wasn't racing with thoughts. After a nice, steamy shower, I applied a natural honey French green clay mask. I slipped into my pink silk robe and matching slippers before making my way to the kitchen.

To my surprise, I found Marquis watering my plants, and I smiled, shocked to see him here. "Wait, you never left?" I asked as I made my way to my kitchen. Sitting on the counter was an Oreo cheesecake cupcake from this nearby bakery I loved to go to. A birthday candle was sticking out of it. Next to the dessert was an assortment of different pink and purple flowers. I paused in my steps, and I just looked at the things on the counter. I crossed my arms under my breast in a comforting motion and blinked back, tears ready to fall. "How did you know it was my birthday?" I could hear him walk towards me, and I turned to look at him. He was smiling until he saw my eyes. "I asked you a month ago, and you told me...What's wrong, mamas?" His eyebrows arched, and I could see the mix of worry and confusion in his eyes.

"And you remembered?" I turned back around and looked at the flowers, picking up the bouquet and bringing the flowers closer to my nose to take in the scent. "Yeah...was I not supposed to?" he asked as if he had done something wrong, and I just laughed to myself. My younger self would be so gleeful, ready to think he was my boyfriend or husband and we were a forever thing.

"Nothing... This is very thoughtful. You know I love the color pink, hence the pink flowers, and you know I love this bakery...it was sweet." I smiled at him as I sat the flowers down. I wrap both of my arms around him, and I press my face into his chest. "Thank you. I really, really appreciate this." He squatted, wrapping his arms under my butt before he sat me on the counter. "What does the birthday girl wanna do?" He mumbled against my neck as he nuzzled against it. He wrapped his arms around me and pulled me into a strong hug.

I released an uncontrollable moan, and in return, I ran my fingers down his spine as my breast pressed into his chest. "I want to keep it simple. Let's walk around the lake, shop for some self care items and plants, maybe a museum." I shrug my shoulders. "I'm down for whatever." He kissed my forehead and smiled. "Alrighty then, shawty, go get ready." When he pulled back from me I laughed and pointed at his shirt. My green face mask was on his white shirt. "Damn it." He said before he lifted the shirt over his head. I saw his chest piece that went up to his neck much better in this light. My eyes lingered at his physique and I watched as he walked away to get a change of clothes from his car. "That is one beautiful man..." I say to myself as I hop off my counter and head back to my room to get ready

We spent the rest of the day exploring the city and neighboring places. We went to Mozart Coffee Shop on the lake to enjoy pastries and coffee on the lake, then to a few outdoor museums, plant shopping, and trying some food trucks.

The night ended with us sitting near my open window. He poured us a glass of that "good whiskey I knew nothing about," and we smoked a cigar. My back was leaning against the wall, and my outstretched leg rested on his lap as he massaged oil into my leg. "Did you have a good birthday?" I was so relaxed and in a heightened state of tranquility.

"Yeah...honestly, probably my best birthday ever...no drama, I didn't cry once, got to explore the city and didn't have to drive myself, didn't spend a dime today...and.." I lean forward, passing him the cigar, blowing some smoke into his face. "I'm not hanging out with some nasty eff boy. It's nice to be around a real ninja."

"Cry? And Ninja?" He laughed out loud. "Is that your way of saying nigga?"

I grabbed one of my pillows before throwing it at him. He caught it and hit me on my thigh before putting it aside. "Yeah, cry...I think most women cry on their birthday; it's part of girlhood." I shrug my shoulders before proceeding. "Your friends ruin your birthday by being selfish and not centering the day around the birthday girl, and then they make her do things that she doesn't want to be accused of being a "princess," so she just goes along with it. Then you end up spending way more money than you attended to and don't really feel special or celebrated."

"Makes sense why women fight in big gatherings then yall asses be doing too much."

I shrugged my shoulders, not denying it. " You're absolutely right...and then we either makeup immediately after having some time apart or never speak again, and there goes a 10-plus-year relationship down the drain." He stood up laughing, grabbing our wine glasses to go and refill them. I watched his movements through the window, and I sighed. As I stared out my window, looking at the bustling people. I wanted so badly to ask where his head was and how he felt. I was having an internal war with myself. One side told me to be upfront and just say what's on my mind so that I wouldn't fall down the depressive road of a man just using my body as a convenience. On the other hand, my mind told me that this was all new and fresh...just go with the flow, and when the time is right, tell him how you feel. In the meantime, get to know him.

He came back over with the glasses, and I smiled at him as he sat them down on my coasters. I placed my leg back on his lap and he began to massage my leg as he drank his wine. "What's on your mind?"

I pressed my back into the wall, and I sipped my glass, looking at him over my rim as he glanced towards me, deciding not to tell him what was actually on my mind. "I know you're a homicide detective...but how do you know something is on my mind?"

"You carry your emotions in your eyes..." He sat up a little straighter, and I smiled, knowing he was about to teach me something. "When you're disinterested in something or someone your eyes sit low almost giving the appearance as if you're high, when you're excited your eyes become glossy and big, when you're sad there is visibly watery and consistently moving as to avoid crying. When you're feeling flirtatious, your eyes smile....that one I can't explain, but I know when I see it ... and you're doing it right now. You like listening to me talk." He said matter of factly. "But when your mind is somewhere else, it's in your eyebrows, they are lowered, your mouth is shut in a tight line, and you start chewing on the inside of your cheek." I was impressed. That means he was watching me while pouring the wine.

I still didn't want to open up about my concerns for our future, so I avoided speaking about those thoughts and focused on the other things that are sat in my mind. "I have never taken a vacation this long so I'm just thinking about my patients and my staff, the work I'll have to do." I wasn't stressed about work right now; more excited to see how everything was going, but that wasn't my concern right now. I wanted to focus on this brown-skinned, tatted, tall, and strong man across from me. "I'm also wondering how long you're going to sit there and not kiss me."

"Oh, that's how you feel, ma?" He sat his glass down, and I followed suit. "Yeah, that's how I'm feeling." The leg he had been massaging, he wrapped both of his hands around my shin and dragged me towards him, pulling me into his lap. I giggle at being manhandled, and he pulls me into a soft kiss, wrapping his arms around my waist and squeezing me.

"Damn I can get use to this."

A man knows When he Knows

The last two weeks had been amazing yet frustrating. Although we spent a lot of time together, Hazel made it a point to kick me out at a certain hour, or if she was at my place, she left, never staying the night. Sometimes, she would be dry during text, but once we were together, she was super affectionate and sweet. She was so intoxicating. Every time we hung out right before we parted ways, she did this thing where she kissed all over my face and on the side of my neck. Then she would either walk away like she didn't leave my skin burning and dick hard. Or she would kick me out. Normally I wouldn't mind; I loved a woman who had her own thing going for herself outside of a man, but, damn, this was annoying. I just wanted her to spend the night in my bed for once; I wanted to talk on the phone for more than 5 minutes. The most frustrating part was that I knew she was holding back and didn't know why. Maybe she just didn't like me like that? I couldn't find any reason why my theory was wrong, nor could I cultivate any reason outside of that one idea.

Despite my frustrations, whatever hold she had on me was strong. I got annoyed at one of the firefighters for flirting with her in the ER. I remember after that encounter, we argued and had a heavy make-out session, I left kisses on her neck and love marks as well because she insisted she was too tired to do anything else. I felt like I was in highschool. We stopped kissing, and she went home. Surely she wasn't celibate? She would've told me and that first night of ours probably would've never happened. It's not that I needed sex; I just wanted to know what the boundaries were or if the first time was just that bad, and she didn't want to go round two. I was baffled. Most women would've begged me to stay, but not her. She was completely unbothered by me. In conclusion, I figured it was maybe just her way of protecting herself, and since I didn't want to hurt her, I wouldn't press her... at least not right now.

"I want you to stay the night with me this weekend," I tell Hazel. She didn't have an excuse. She wasn't on her period, she wasn't working at the hospital, and Mariah was her last client for the day. She looked at me, and I could tell she was in deep thought. Her eyes were searching mine for the right answer, but she knew that's not how things would work. "Hazel, why don't you want to stay the night?" I wrapped my hands around her waist and pulled her into me. Her lips became pouty, but she wrapped her arms around my neck. "It's not that I don't want to. It's just that..." I could see the hesitation in her eyes, but I was going to be patient with her.

We heard the toilet flushing, and Hazel sighed before pulling away from me. "Let's just talk about it tonight. Right now isn't the time or the place." She stated, her face appearing apprehensive, but I would respect it for now. I grabbed her hand and kissed it before walking over towards the wall, putting my back against it. "Fine, you win for now, but a conversation will be had." I waved a finger at her. In response, she stuck her tongue out at me, and she smiled. The way I just wanted to set the record straight. I knew a little act right would dissipate all of this, but she clearly didn't want to have sex with me again, and I wasn't sure why.

Mariah returned to the room, demanding I take her to get food. We told Hazel bye before leaving the room and heading out of the building. Hazel and I made eye contact, lingering before I walked out.

As I assisted my sister in hopping into my truck, I could feel her glaring at me; even as I walked to the driver's seat, I could still feel her eyes on me. "What's up Mariah? Why are you staring a nigga down like I did something?"

"Because what's up with you and my home girl? Why are y'all keeping secrets from me?" she said, arms crossed over her chest, and I rolled my eyes. "What is there to tell?" I asked her casually as I put on my shades and pulled out of the parking lot. I was curious to see what her woman intuition insight would be.

"I don't know, you tell me. I felt the tension throughout the whole appointment and the little smiles she was sending you throughout the appointment. Not to mention, when I came back to the room, her neck was wet, and you were wiping your lips....so what's up? How long have y'all been hunching?"

I chuckled to myself. I did not think we were being that obvious, but I guess that wasn't something you could hide with women. "Chill, Maya. It's only been two or three weeks. We're getting to know each other and having fun in the process. It's just a little fun; it's nothing super deep." It was deeper than that, but I still needed to have this talk with Hazel before I even crossed deeper waters. Also, I wanted to make sure she and I were on the same page before I went spewing my feelings to my sister.

"Mhmm, if you say so." She pulled her phone out, indicating she was done with this conversation and didn't believe me.

"What, Ma? You don't believe me? It's the truth."

"Then why did you bring her food? You don't get food for a woman you're just messing around with, and I told you that you didn't have to come to my appointments, and you insisted. I'm not mad at yall for messing around but, I'm going to be upset if you break her heart, that shit isn't fair to my girl. Men always do her wrong and I don't want my noncommittal having ass brother doing the same thing to her, if sex is all you want then leave her alone she deserves better."

I was silent as she spoke. I knew what she was saying was right. I didn't know much about Hazel's past, but I could only imagine though. She was kind and considerate, the "spread herself thin" type to please others. Women like her were usually dogged out because they were quick to forgive and to be kind for their own good. On the other hand, when I first met Hazel, she was not the nicest; women who were defensive, specifically towards men, always came with a past. Regardless I didn't want my sister to be the one to tell me, I wanted to be the one to ask and find out.

That raises another question: why did I want to know? Just last night, I was telling Jorden that I might be done trying to pry Hazel open—not just physically but emotionally, too. I found myself being the talkative one, which was unusual for me; I had always been the quiet one in relationships. Ever since our first time together, Hazel had seemed closed off.

I was a suitable bachelor—young, handsome, fit, with my own place, career, and savings. Many women were interested in me, and I usually didn't have to chase after anyone. Yet, this woman captivated me for some reason, and I didn't want to meet anyone else...right?

I looked at my sister once we were at a red light. "Listen, I don't want to hurt her, but I don't know if I'm ready for a full-on relationship right now."

I didn't expect that to trigger her, so she slammed her phone down on her lap and started to speak with her hands. "Then what the hell do you want? What's stopping you? She's a career woman, has her own everything, a woman of god, thick and beautiful. Everything you could want in a woman, so what's the dilemma? Your career? Yourself? What nigga? That's why I dated outside of my race because I swear black men never want to settle down. Yall niggas love to play house and have babies, thinking that's less of a commitment than marriage. You All can be so trifling. To make matters worse, you know better! Because you are a man of God, and you were raised in a two-parent household." She tsked her tongue before picking her phone up again. "You might as well should cut her off now if you're going to act like this."

A car behind us honked, and I looked at the light, noticing it was green. I focused on the road before I continued driving. "It's just been so little time... the last woman I just hopped on thinking she was the one was disastrous, and you're right, Hazel is something special, but I just want to make sure I take my time with her. I don't want to mess things up, and I can handle her correctly."

Maya scoffed again before letting out a dry laugh. "Okay, Nigga. Whatever you say."

"Damn, Maya, what do you want a nigga to say or do?"

"You've seen this woman completely naked, had your mouth on her most intimate parts—probably vice versa. Sex means nothing to you both, but when it comes to a relationship, that's where you draw the line?" She looked at me incredulously, and I let out a heavy sigh.

She raised her hand defensively and scoffed. "Oh wait, am I going too far? Is it too much to say that for men, as long as I walk away having only caught a curable STD and getting her pregnant to carry on my seed, that's all that matters?" The car fell silent as she spoke, and I decided to let her have her moment while I processed what she was saying. Thankfully, she finally wrapped up.

"Anyway, Marquis, do what you want, but if you're going to ruin this relationship, just wait until after she delivers your nephew." She returned to her phone, controlling my

Bluetooth and turning up the music, signaling that this conversation was over.

I would be lying if I said her words didn't affect me. Part of me wanted to claim Hazel—not just sexually, but in a deeper way. I wanted to break down her walls, show her what a healthy relationship looked like, and treat her well. The one time she spent the night, I loved holding her, listening to her soft snores, and having her close. I enjoyed catering to her; she never asked for much, so I took the initiative, and she seemed happy that I did.

I turned down the radio and decided to speak up. "I guess my biggest dilemma is facing that difficult stage in a relationship where communication starts to break down, and you see the other person growing out of love. My first girlfriend and I went through that, and I never wanted to fall in love again just to watch it fade or see the other person lose interest. With my ex and every woman before her, the initial stage is sweet, but it always turns sour. They end up using me for my money and posting pictures of me in my uniform. I don't want to be in a toxic situation. I like Hazel; I just want to spend time with her and see where things go. Something tells me she might run at the idea of a relationship right now anyway." This was the first time I had admitted any of this out loud.

Maya looked at me with a smile, her eyes welling up with tears. "Aww, so you just want to be loved on." I rolled my eyes, but she continued. "Aww, big brother, that's so sweet!" She wiped her tears and leaned back in her seat, still focused on me.

"Well, the women you've chosen in the past had no ambition, no real personalities, and aimed for nothing. Women who live for material things and nightlife aren't going to be healthy for you. Surely, you can see that Hazel is different. They say it takes three months to truly see a person's personality, right? If what you're saying is true, give her time. I'm sure you'll find she's a good woman."

I smiled; that was the reassurance I needed. In the meantime, I would focus on getting to know her better. We pulled into the drive-thru of a pizza shop my sister loved, and she ordered a mountain of food.

As she ate, my mind drifted back to that woman whose name matched her captivating eyes. I pulled out my phone and messaged Hazel:

"Date night? Rooftop wine bar? tomorrow 6 PM? So we can watch the sunset?"

I set my phone down, knowing Hazel kept hers on Do Not Disturb and was a slow texter. To my surprise, I heard the ding almost immediately. I quickly checked my phone.

"Oh yesss! That sounds soooo fun! Absolutely, I'm down. Can you pick me up? I don't like parking downtown."

I smiled to myself and simply hearted her message. "Yeah ma, I got you." In response, she hearted my message too. I felt like I'd won the lottery. I couldn't wait to see her tomorrow.

Situationship

I had been drinking a glass of high-priced wine delivered straight from an Italian vineyard that's been sitting since 1938, gifted to me by one of my investors. I was sipping this sweet wine about to watch Real Housewives when I received a notification. Partially annoyed because I kept my phone on DND. That means whoever was trying to reach me hit the "deliver anyways" button. Every time this happened, it was either one of my best friends trying to tell me something that was "important" or one of my employees, and I was not trying to end my self-care night.

To my surprise, it was neither. It was a name that I thought I would never see again. I mean, we all knew men come back eventually for whatever reasons, whether that be for sex, intimacy, money, food, to get on your nerves, or for whatever reason. I just wasn't expecting Captain's name to appear on my phone. Without further hesitation, I clicked on the message.

"What up baby girl!? How you've been? I see that you've been in Austin for a minute according to your socials, I'll be in town for about a week. I wanted to see if you wanted to link up, shoot the shits and just overall catch up. When are you free, and what side of town is close to you?"

I just stared at the message for a while. My intuition told me he must've broken up with his baby mama. Otherwise, I don't see why else he would have business in Austin or any other reason for him to hit me up. The longer I stared at the message, the heavier my heart grew. It wasn't long before my mind went down memory lane, but it wasn't the good memories. Instead, I found myself reliving that night I stormed out of his house. He didn't even care enough to stop me; he didn't even try to fight for our relationship; we had just suddenly stopped being us... and while he had the comfort of his baby's mother and the adventure of fatherhood to look forward to. I was grieving; I missed how he made me feel and the time we had spent. Now I've healed and moved on; suddenly, he was intruding on my life.

I put my phone down as I begin to feel my eyes swell with tears. I sighed heavily as I placed my glass of wine down and covered my face with both hands. I slowly begin to knead my forehead, being gentle with myself. "Jesus, my lord and savior, please let all

of my actions guide me closer to you. I ask that you soften Captain's heart the way you did the Egyptian pharaohs and reveal his truth as well as intentions to me. I ask that if he means any ill intentions towards me, knowingly or unknowingly, you remove him from my life to save me from the heartbreak that will surely follow. Thank you for being my protector, in your name I pray amen."

I open my eyes and slowly sit up. I wasn't going to make a decision right now. To begin with, he didn't deserve an immediate response. I stand up grabbing my wine and snacks, deciding I needed fresh air. I sat near my window seal and I people watched. I heard a siren in the distance and immediately thought of Marquis. I wanted to text him to come over, but I had promised myself I wouldn't get to attach myself to him. Until he decided to solidify the status of our relationship, I refused to let him know how much I liked him.

I didn't want to get attached just for him to decide he didn't want me and to reveal to me that all of my feelings were one-sided. I hated that empty feeling that would take several days to weeks to fade. I wanted to be chased this time, and I wanted the man to admit his feelings first.

My phone dings again, and I stand up, annoyed. "His tail must be really lonely and thirsty right now." I grab my phone, plopping back on the couch before looking at the notification. I immediately smiled cheesing ear from ear. It was Marquis's fine self asking me out on a date. I responded to him immediately. Listen... who was I to say no to the man if he wanted to see me? It showed he was interested. I stand up, going to my closet to find an outfit for tomorrow. I wanted to be grown and sexy looking for him.

...

The date was amazing. We had a few cocktails and appetizers and watched the sunset as we caught each other up on our week. At one point during the date, we witnessed a two-vehicle collision, and I listened to him call 911. Oddly enough, I found it attractive that he spoke in 10 codes and used phonetics.

Neither of us was ready to end the night early, so we decided to go back to my home and relax some more. We sat on my balcony and sipped on another gifted bottle of wine. I was nervous as I sat there. As good as today felt, I knew it was time to talk about our relationship, a "go with the flow" type of woman. I needed the very least to see where his head was so I knew how things would go. We didn't have to jump into a relationship immediately, but I wanted to make sure he wanted what I wanted, at the very least. I knew this contradicted my earlier mindset, but I couldn't help myself...

I continued to people-watch as I worked up the courage to ask the question that was tickling my mind. "So..." I took a sip of wine, and I continued to watch the people passing by, not wanting to face him. "So what are you looking for...what do you want? Please don't say "vibe" or "see where things go." Be fully honest with me; I just wanna know where your head is." I wanted to say more, but I didn't want to over-reveal what was going on in my head. I didn't want him to tell me what I wanted to hear. I felt his eyes on me, and I began to blush, but I didn't break my eyes away from the window.

"Hazel, look at me." I nervously chewed the inside of my cheek, but I complied. Once I made eye contact, he continued to speak. He sipped his wine as he analyzed my face. I attempted to keep a poker face, stopping myself from chewing on the inside of my mouth, remembering how he told me he knew that was a sign of my thinking. I sipped my wine, taking my time. If the glass covered my face, he wouldn't be able to read it so well.

He smiled at my antics before continuing. "Well, I know right now I'm not ready to fully commit to a relationship...I think I have a lot on my plate careerwise and ending things in the last relationship. I want to spend time with you and get to know you better. Plus, I'm enjoying what we have right now." He took a sip of his drink again and didn't say anything else. My eyes moved back to the window. I was trying to blink back tears. My old self would've found hope in the "right now." part of his statement. I would've been optimistic for the future and allowing that small statement to have high hopes for the "what if" I was trying to act mature and as if I was okay with the honesty but forget that. I'm tired of men who aren't ready. Men are always ready for sex, ready to act like a boyfriend but never ready to commit.

I did love the intimacy he had given me. It had been a minute since a man held me, and I enjoyed it. I could feel my mind begin to spiral into a dark mindset. Maybe I should just have sex and leave these men, maybe love isn't real and died with the previous generation. Maybe I will never find love and be forever stuck in these "what if" situations. I couldn't even hide my disappointment when I looked over at him. I take a long sigh before speaking,

"Okay."

I wanted to express myself, I wanted to tell him to never touch me again and how I wasn't going to be in some situationship where we did everything couples did minus the title. I was never a go-withthe-flow type of woman, but... admittedly, I was lonely. I wanted the physical touch,

181 | P a g e

and he made me feel so safe. The way his arms wrapped around me and the way he kissed the back of my ear, telling me everything was okay... I loved that feeling. Call me desperate, but it was the truth, and I didn't want to think about this anymore. I knew I didn't have to and shouldn't settle for what I wanted, but I would think about how I wanted to move at a different time.

"So what is it that you're looking for?" He asked me.

I looked back at him as I wiped away the tears before standing up. "I want a relationship," I said with all the bluntness I could muster. I went to my kitchen and started to pour out my wine and clean up things around me. I was so irritated. I had no idea why men never wanted what I wanted, and I was fed up.

He stood up and followed me to the kitchen, taking a seat at one of my bar stools. "Hazel, sit down and talk to me." I gripped the counter to keep my irritation in lock and turned to face him. "I appreciate the honesty. I just know what I want, and it's frustrating that you don't want what I want. Despite the fact you've been acting super into me." My eyes started to water up, and I wiped away the tears that were able to fall. I hated how I cried when I expressed myself. I was so hurt, angry, and annoyed. I sniffled, and my chest tightened in anger.

He stood up from my bar stool and walked around the island. I immediately started to walk away from him. I didn't want/need to be coddled by a nigga. I didn't need him lying to me just to make the tears stop and still get whatever it was he wanted out of me just so there wouldn't be any complications in our "relationship" moving forward. He grabbed me by my arm and pulled me back into him. He lifted my chin so I could look directly at him.

"I would want nothing more than to be in," I scoffed and started shoving at him. I was not going to let him finish that statement. "Then nigga what's the hesitation!? Why not just be with me? Because you have a to-do list you need to complete before being with me? Weren't you just dating that instahoe? What's wrong with me!" My voice cracked, and I felt small sobs releasing from me. Normally I was a girls girl and I knew no one on this earth was perfect and we all had our flaws but, I knew I was a good woman. I had no intention of hurting him or using him. I was very loyal, I had a career, I was a woman of god, I had my own everything, I was clean, I was a chef, and I knew I wasn't hard on the eyes. So what more could he want? Those traits aren't all I have to offer either.

He released me, and I sighed as I walked away from him, leaning against my counter only a few inches away from him.

"I just want to make sure all of my cards are aligned correctly, and also, I've been through so much drama with women for the last several years. I just want to enjoy my singleness for a bit before I commit to a woman."

I was silent. What he said made sense, yet it still felt unfair. I looked up at him, not saying anything as I composed myself and thought of a response rather than letting my emotions speak for me.

"I'm just tired of not feeling like an option for men...I just want someone to want me right now, and there doesn't have to be any hesitation or second-guessing. Fancy me this," I begged him. "I know this feeling isn't one-sided, right? You and I really go together so well. We have a good balance and a great time. Not to mention I'm only getting older I don't want to wait around for you to "align your cards" because who knows how long that'll take you and if you will even want me by the time you've completed that goal."

There was silence between us outside of him, taking a deep breath. My chest was pounding. What I said was a lot, but it was the absolute truth, and I was proud of myself for saying what was actually on my mind rather than later replaying this conversation in my mind and creating scenarios in my head where I said what I really wanted to say and then creating/or wondering what his response would be.

"I do want you, but I'm not going to rush into a relationship now. I don't want to commit to anyone right now. I can't, nor will I give you a time frame for when I will be ready. I like what we have right now." His response had so much finality in it, and I just scoffed, shaking my head. It was clearly up to me how we proceeded moving forward...I mean, I was the one who wasn't okay with our current situation but still didn't want all this pressure.

I grab my wine glass from the sink and pour another glass. I take a long sip, trying to calm my nerves before speaking. "I don't want us to stop seeing each other, but boundaries will have to be in place." I put my hand up as I prepare to list my boundaries.

"No sex, no sleepovers, I don't want to hear about other women. Just let me know we can't see each other anymore, and I'll get the picture, and I'm going to be going on dates and dating other men." I folded a finger after every boundary was listed.

I couldn't hide my smile when I saw his jaw tighten at the last thing on my list. "Sorry baby you can't have your cake and eat it too." I think to myself. He moved closer to me and he placed his hands on my hips. "Am I allowed to kiss you and touch you still? Why don't you want to have sex with me Hazel" He was already leaning in without waiting for an answer. I wrapped my arms around his neck and I pulled him deeper into the kiss, this kiss was more territorial and fierce. Our kisses were normally passionate and sweet. He pulled my body closer to his, and I started to run my hands under his shirt, finding that one spot on his right side that was sensitive. He released a deep groan as he lifted me on the counter. He kissed and nibbled at my neck before he began to suck hard, leaving a hickey in its place.

I pushed him away, both of us panting. Leaning in, I kissed his chest before gently nudging him back. "I want to be abstinent. I don't want to have sex. I believe we shouldn't have premarital sex, but I know I can't convince everyone.

It's something I want to practice..." I met his gaze, and he nodded in understanding. He stepped closer and wrapped me in a hug. "I've never practiced that before, but I'll try my best," he said softly before leaning down to kiss me again. I rested my hands on his chest and smiled. "You should go... we still have our pickleball date next week, right?" I said, adjusting my clothes to emphasize that I wouldn't be spending the night as we had initially planned. I glanced down and noticed he was hard, adjusting himself. "Of course... yeah," I giggled internally. He gathered his things, and I hugged him tightly before walking him to the door.

Once I locked up, cleaned, and did my night routine. I lay in bed. I go to my messages and click on Captain. I sigh heavily, pressing the phone to my chest. I didn't want him anymore...I wanted Marquis... but he wasn't ready. Captain and I used to be very close and at one point had a good connection. But what if he genuinely just wanted to catch up? "I guess we can give him the benefit of the doubt, but one thing about niggas, that doubt always ended up prevailing over the benefit." I picked up my phone again and decided to respond.

"Sure, I would love to. How does Saturday noon sound?" I picked an earlier time because a nighttime dinner date with alcohol could lead to more. The earlier, the better. He liked my message almost instantly, followed by a "see you" text.

I sighed before I put my phone on the charger. I place my eye masks over my eyes. It didn't take long for sleep to find me; with the mixture of crying, drinking wine, and the heavy mixed emotions, I was exhausted.

Deep down inside, I knew I wouldn't go on dates with other men. I only wanted Marquis.

I stormed into your room

Green Eyes

Today was one of those days. As soon as I got home, I switched off my work phone, tossed my work bag into the closet, and took a hot shower. Afterward, I poured myself a glass of whiskey, grabbed my cigar, and headed out to the patio. I settled into my black papasan chair,not exactly my style, but many exes ago, I bought them for the house after she suggested them, and once we broke up, I decided they were too comfortable to get rid of since she didn't want them. I leaned back into its embrace before bringing the cigar to my lips. I lit it and inhaled; almost instantly, I felt the stress melt away from my shoulders, and my mind lightened. I sighed and sank deeper into the chair, sipping my drink.

The beginning of my day was fantastic. I started with prayer and a devotional, which set a positive tone. After that, I hit the gym and managed to increase my reps. I also successfully avoided the lunch-hour traffic. Later, I patrolled with my best friend, focusing mainly on traffic hazards and addressing trespassing issues throughout the day. To top it all off, Hazel sent me the sweetest messages. I've been with several women in the past, and I've learned that they often appreciate physical touch and romantic gestures and typically desire most, if not all, of my attention. But with Hazel? It's different.

Hazel didn't care for sweet words; in her view, "talk is cheap," and she respected actions more than promises. She didn't need all of my time, as long as I made some time for her. I wasn't required to constantly text or call her. With her hobbies, career, and part-time job at the hospital, she was extremely busy. This was one of the things I admired most about her; the women I had dated in the past weren't as productive. They seemed more focused on their social media status and promoting weight loss teas, which didn't take up much of their time. As a result, they often spent most of their days trying to call or message me. As a detective in a major city, I didn't have endless free time.

As a busy man it dating a woman who didn't mind having our private rest days before spending time together. We both had draining jobs and the resets were a must. This often led to many fights about me loving my career more than them. I never fought them too hard on the issue. It wasn't a lie; I loved my job, and I was good at what I did. Most importantly, I was very passionate about my work. I came from a family of first responders.

My mother was a nurse, my father was ex-military and a firefighter. My older brother is a paramedic, and my youngest brother is a firefighter. I had always wanted to be on a swat team or something law enforcement-related. I used my athletic scholarship in football to earn a degree in Criminal Justice with an emphasis in psychology. After graduation, I joined the academy and later became a Law Enforcement Officer. After being on patrol for 5 years I was promoted to a detective role. I worked in the Robbery unit for 3 years before transferring to the Homicide unit. I loved the work I did, and I was good at it.

The ability to think outside of the box and use my critical thinking skills always kept me excited. I loved walking upon a crime scene, painting a picture of what took place, and then putting all the pieces together. Helping families and loved ones related to the victim find peace and justice always brought me a serenity like no other as Hazel stated in previous conversations when we spoke about our careers. I believed the work I was currently doing was the reason God put me on this earth. It feels like my calling.

I loved it when Hazel became passionate. Her normally relaxed and nonchalant posture would perk up, and her eyes would brighten and widen. She would anxiously fidget with her rings, moving them around on her fingers, and her gestures would become more animated as she spoke about her career. Thinking about this made me smile, especially considering how different she was today. She kept telling me how much she missed me. We hadn't seen each other in about four days, and her messages were extra sweet. She mentioned how she wanted to cook for me and plan an entire night just for the two of us. I just knew this day couldn't get any better—and I was wrong because it ended up getting worse.

Amber sent me a voice memo. It was right at the end of my shift, I received a message notification; I was already smiling, thinking it was Hazel telling me how excited she was that I was getting off of work. Instead, it was a new number; I clicked on the message and listened to the voice memo,

"Hey...I know you don't want anything to do with me but I found out that I'm pregnant. I did an ultrasound this week and had blood work done; I'm about 7 weeks now. When you and I separated, I did go..."

She continued to inform me that she had gone back to her ex and needed to take a paternity test the next week. I was extremely frustrated just when I found peace of mind and met a woman who could potentially be my wife. Yeah, that's not how I wanted to end my day.

There was a knock on my door, I put my cigar down and I went to my front door. I was greeted by Hazel, who had the brightest smile on her face. Her curly hair, which she normally had in a bun, was down and loose around her face and shoulders. She wore a green halter knitted top with black embroidered flowers on the edges of the shirt. It looked almost like a bikini top or a bra. I looked down, taking in her hips and thighs being contained in a tight black skirt.

She walked right past me and went straight to my kitchen. She put down her bag and pulled out a ceramic glass container before preheating my oven, and I assumed it was the seafood-stuffed shrimp pasta she had made. She pulled out a few other items before she ran towards me. She pulled me into the tightest hug and kissed my chest several times before standing on her toes; she kissed me on each cheek before pulling me into a long, sensual kiss. I wrapped my arms around her waist and lifted her into the kiss so I didn't strain my neck.

When we pulled apart, I followed her eyes as she looked me up and down. Her thumb traced my lips, and she kissed me one more time before I lowered her back down to the ground. She tilted her head sideways, and her eyebrows knitted into a frown. "What's wrong?" I could see the anxiety spark in her eyes and her brain going a mile a minute; she didn't say it, but I knew she was wondering if she had done something wrong. I spoke up before she could assume anything.

"My ex sent me a message…" I pulled out my phone and played the voice memo for her. I watched the emotions cross her face; she went from confusion, disbelief, and maybe anger to disappointment. When the message finished playing, we both sat in silence. She looked down, playing with the gold rings on her fingers. Moving them from different spots. An immense amount of guilt entered me. She walked over to my bar cart, pouring herself a glass of wine. Her eyes stared at me from over the rim as she drank the entirety of its contents. She put the glass down, still not saying anything. I watched as she dropped eye contact and proceeded to play with the rings on her finger again.

I approached her, grabbing her hands; as expected, she snatched them away before I grabbed her by the end of her top. She didn't pull any further, knowing her breast would probably slip out if she moved anymore. She glared at me as she paused before moving my hand away from her shirt. "Listen, I've been through this before and…" her voice choked for a second, and she blinked back some tears. I can see the frustration in her body language as she aggressively wiped her tears away. "Don't make this messy for me. Handle your business like a grown man, and whatever happens, just make sure you're honest with me." She goes for her wine glass again.

I sighed before speaking up. "I don't want to be with her, we can co-parent and I know this isn't ideal but, I don't want a future with her, I let her go for a reason." I watched as she sipped her wine. Trying to figure out what was going through her head. She began to run her fingers through her hair in a repeated motion. She did that often but, most noticeable when she was recalling a stressful event or when she was overthinking and trying to make sense of a situation.

"Speak to me, Hazel." I walked over to her and grabbed her hand, removing it from her hair. I grab her chin and make her look up at me. I place one of my hands behind her back and pull her in closer to me. She looked up at me, and I could see something was eating her up; it was my turn to question her, "What's wrong?" I asked as I rubbed my hand across her lower back, trying to make her feel safe and comfortable, deciding against the confrontational route.

She's shared bits and pieces of her history with me, and what I've gathered is that she's not used to men being patient or gentle with her. She's used to men being nonverbal with her, yelling, throwing/hitting things when upset, cursing, and being aggressive when communicating with her. I cared about her and wanted to know what she was feeling on the inside, but I wasn't going to force or scare it out of her.

Her eyes met mine, and her lips quivered slightly before she finally spoke. "Captain reached out to me a few days ago..." She paused, trying to gauge my reaction. I kept my expression neutral, but I found myself pulling her in closer when she mentioned his name. "He is in Austin and asked to meet with me. We haven't spoken since... well, since we were coworkers." At that moment, I understood the situation fully. Her ex, who was likely her first love, had a child with someone else and was returning just as another man, who might be her future, was potentially about to father a child of his own—one that she would not be the mother of.

"I don't think you should see him." there was no hesitation in my voice. I didn't care about my current situation. She did not need to go back to that sorry-ass nigga. The oven beeped, indicating that it was done preheating. I release her as she turns to place the food in the oven. "And why not? Why does it matter to you?" she replied as she made sure the food was secured before turning back to me. I started to walk away. She grabbed her wine glass, following me outside to my patio. She sat in the papasan chair across from me. "I'm waiting..." She said as she leaned back, leaning into her seat.

"He's trying to see if he can slide back into your life, both sexually and metaphorically. If you give him the chance, he's definitely going to take it." I looked into her eyes as I took a puff from my cigar. "Well, you're probably going back to your ex," I replied. She took a large sip of her wine and shrugged her shoulders. "Remember what you said? We're not dating, so you need to align your cards right," she reminded me, tossing my own words back at me. "I'm single, so maybe he is welcome back," she stated, her voice firm.

She scooted her chair closer to mine and grabbed the cigar from my hand. I sipped my whiskey and watched as she crossed her legs and took a puff as if she were a pro at it. "Then you're being silly," I said. She scoffed, coughing slightly before bursting into laughter. "I'm silly? That's a crazy remark coming from someone who can't commit to me despite the connection we have. If you think I'm going to sit around and wait for you to finally choose me, you're wrong. I'm not going to be your placeholder or second option."

It was my turn to scoff and sit a bit straighter in my chair. "So him coming back to you after all these years and you going on a date with him, isn't you being a backup option for him? What's crazy is that he already had you, and you just might let him do it again. You are literally his second option."

It felt good stating the true obvious nature of this man she was going to go see...but seeing the tears swell in her eyes made me wish I displayed the truth more gently. "Or maybe I just need closure..." I watched as she stood up and sighed as I stood with her. I follow her back inside to my kitchen as she grabs her purse and other items. "You know, at least he verbalized that he wanted me and took the initiative to ask me out." I felt bad. Her sweet, bright, happy demeanor diminished into something more sad and reclusive. "Enjoy the food I made...I'll be back for my items later."

As I try and grab her to pull her into a hug, she puts her hands up and heads for my door. My only comfort was knowing at least she'd be back, even if she needed space for now.

Closure

I chose a very casual seafood place right off of the lake. They served cheap margs and fried seafood and had a great view of the Colorado River. I arrived earlier than Captain to enjoy the view and to sip on a margarita before the awkwardness, the possibility of reopening wounds, and whatever else may arise.

While waiting for him, I decided to walk around the dock. I sipped my drink and leaned against the railing, watching people enjoy their water sports. The breeze was pleasant, and I was savoring the moment. As I took in the scenery, I suddenly felt a hand rub my back. When I turned around, I was met by someone from my past. Having had two margaritas, any anxiety I had felt had definitely faded away. I offered him a genuine smile as I looked up at him and pulled my old lover into a hug. As I embraced him, I felt a sense of nostalgia, remembering how I had been so excited that he was the first romantic man in my life who was actually tall enough for me to look up at him.

He looked just as handsome as the day I met him. Although his appearance was largely unchanged, the smile lines around his eyes had deepened, and he now had bags under his eyes. He was still fit, but his build was thicker, and he had a few new tattoos. As I admired him, I could tell he was checking me out too, which made me roll my eyes. I had gained some weight since he last saw me, but I had also developed into a womanly figure. Sometimes, when I looked in the mirror, I was mesmerized by my curves and fullness.

He laughed before taking a sip of his beer, which made me wonder how long he had been here before he approached me. "Your drink must've hit already because I was not expecting such a nice greeting from you."

"So you acknowledge we may have an issue?" I challenged him. I didn't want him to think everything was okay.

"Of course, we have issues we need to discuss. The last time we spoke, I told you I was going to be a father, and you left my house. That was the last time we had ever communicated." He stated matter-offactly, getting right into it.

We take a seat at a table near the guard rail so, we could be closer to the water. We ordered another round of drinks and some appetizers. Once alone I look into his eyes and his into mine. The last time I saw him we were in our early 20s and now here we were me being 30 and him 32. Something in my chest rose and tightened. I felt my eyes burning as tears made their presence known. I lean back in my chair, crossing my arms and looking out as the sun started to to slowly meet the lake. The sun, being so close to the water, cast this warm orange with hints of yellow and purple light onto the water. It brought a smile to my face, I hadn't done it in a while, but watching sunsets is my favorite thing.

"I've seen that face many times on the truck, You're upset. Talk to me, Hazel." I turn my attention back to him, no longer smiling but glaring.

"Did you make your mind up when you let me leave your house?" I asked him directly. It was one of the two things that had eaten me up all these years later. "You never once tried to stop me from leaving. You just looked at me, and you had plenty of time to talk to me about it, but we just never spoke again." I sipped my water, feeling the energy charge in me, and I didn't want to be drunk. I was no longer angry, but I was just ready to finally get all of the answers I was looking for.

He rubbed his hand through his beard, appearing tired and drained. Surely, he didn't think our meeting would just be a fun time reminiscing on good memories, such as our times in the ambulance or the mini adventures we would go on. Or perhaps he thought we could recreate a few bedroom memories. I had waited seven years to have this moment with him. Maybe had it only been two or even three years, I would've been willing to recreate some of those memories, but right now, I needed answers.

He sighed heavily, rubbing a heavy hand down his face before leaning forward and looking me directly in the eyes.

"Yes I..." I could see the guilt in his eyes as he spoke his truth. "Yeah, she was scared and had been crying about being a single mother and wanting to move back closer to her family. I was going wherever my child was."

I nodded my head as he spoke. I understood his perspective, even if I didn't like it, but I wasn't going to let him get off just that easy. His actions still hurt me, and I needed more acknowledgment of that. "So if your mind was made up, why did you have sex with me that night?" That tightness in my chest became more discomforting. I felt sobs building up as tears ran hot down my face. Knowing that he had sex with me despite his mind already being made up was sickening.

Then it hit me even harder as another thought resonated in me. "You really had sex with me even though you decided to be with another woman? So when did you make that official decision to be another woman's man?"

My anger slowly became entwined with disgust. I wanted to look away from him, but I wanted to see his face when he answered.

"We hadn't made it official. I just knew I was going to be with her once we moved in together. She knew I had to cut ties with you first and that once she and I lived together, that would be it. I didn't mean for our last night to happen the way it did. I didn't know when or how I was going to break the news to you. After we had sex, I felt guilty, and I knew I needed to tell you. So it's not like I planned goodbye sex." He stated with a finality in his tone, his posture shifted from tiredness and guilt to relief and relaxation.

I scoffed and began to play with the rings on my fingers to keep me from putting my hands on him. Was this ninja happy he got that off his chest? My hurt and anger settled into disbelief.

My eyes were still focused on my rings, unable to make direct eye contact with him since I was starting to feel homicidal. I just needed that final clarity. "So you still choose to have sex with me despite knowing we weren't going to work out, and you would have kept this thing going as long as possible had you not felt conviction?"

I finally made eye contact with him. Out of the corner of my eye, I could see our waitress coming to the table, and I stood up, gathering my items. He didn't say anything; my eyes were met with a pair of guilt-risen eyes.

Men never had anything in response when met with the full truth. I shook my head and pulled out a twenty-dollar bill. "This is her tip. You're paying for everything else," I say finally, just as the waitress comes to our table.

I wasn't ready to go home yet, so I decided to take a different path that led to the boat dock rather than the parking lot. When I last looked at the sun, it was midway in the sky, but now it was sitting perfectly on top of the water.

I wanted to watch it sink into the dark, murky water before going home.

I take a seat on the boardwalk, sitting my purse beside me. I just relaxed and allowed the sun to hit me as I sat in thought, I wanted to check in with myself before I made my next move. My feelings were fluent. I was angry, disturbed, and disgusted. Out of all of the men I have encountered, I just never expected him to do what he did. That's what I loved most about our relationship He was different than all of the men I had ever encountered. He was genuine, he was attentive to my needs on a emotional, physical and mental level.

If I even appeared a little sad or distressed while at work, he made it his duty to get me back to a happy or neutral state of mind. A thought that wasn't my own came to my mind, "For all have sinned and fall
short of the glory of God." I smiled and felt a bit of peace fall upon me. I pulled my phone out and typed that scripture in the bible app. It was Romans 3:23. No man was perfect, including Captain, who I thought was a the perfect man back then.

I was grateful that God put that on my mind. Even if he sent me a man who met all of my criteria, that man would still fall short because he was still only a human such as myself. No man is perfect or good except for Jesus.

I needed that reminder. Although his actions still hurt me, at least I wasn't angry. But as the sun finally settled into the lake, my feelings were calmed. I realized I had processed the emotions years ago; I was only so upset currently because it was fresh. Everything he had said earlier, I had already predicted that was the case; he had just confirmed it tonight.

I stood up and stretched, placing my hands on my hips before bending back. I almost did a back bend before rising back up, and I smiled. I was okay.

I make my way back up to the parking lot, feeling at peace. Captain was leaning against my car while playing on his phone. I've had the same car since college, and I wasn't going to get rid of it until I absolutely had to. I shook my head, clicking my unlock button as I got closer. He stood up straight before putting his phone away.

"I was just about to call you... I didn't want to leave on bad terms again. It's eaten me up over the last seven years, especially how we left off last time. I just wanted to say bye one more time." I stared at him, and I knew this was crazy, but... the lover girl in me thought about the future, and I just wanted to make sure this would really be goodbye.

"Besides apologizing for the past, why did you want to meet with me today? What were your other motives and intentions?"

He smiled and it was followed by a chuckle. "Ah shit, to be real with you? I was trying to see if a nigga had another chance. Me and the baby ma, she got a new dude. I told her I wanted to move back down here with our daughter to be close to my family. My family all lives in Houston now, everyone was on board. It all worked out, and so I decided that since you would only be less than 3 hours away, maybe we could make something happen."

He was feeling himself now; his daemon switched from weary to confident just like that. I searched his eyes, and I felt myself attracted to him. But was it just physical, or was there still an emotional tie? I close the distance between us, and I wrap my arms around his neck. I could tell by how he was licking his lips that he was okay with what I was about to do. I pulled him down to my height, my heart was racing, he pushed his lips into mine wrapping his arms around me. I closed my eyes, and I focused on what was happening between us. I had never been so hyper-aware of my surroundings and thoughts when making out with someone. I knew what kissing him used to feel like. We would be locked in for several minutes, and I could never let go. I always made him late for something or kept him up longer than intended with my kisses, but this time, I was grateful for the dinging of my phone.

We pulled apart slightly. "Sorry, it could be one of my patients, " I said sheepishly, trying to hide the relief I gained from no longer being connected to his lips. I pulled my phone out of my purse and checked my notifications. I smiled immediately when I saw Marquis's name pop up. He had tried calling me twice, but my phone was on DND. I saw his text message, and that made my smile even wider. That meant he pressed "notify anyway."

The text was very simple. "I'm sorry...I can't wait to see you again. Hopefully, after my trip from Colorado?" I knew he was going on a ski trip with his brothers. I had forgotten all about Captain, not realizing that he could read over my shoulder. I was just cheesing at the fact that Marquis reached out, wanted my attention, and wanted to see me. I felt Captain pull apart from me, taking me from my bliss. His face was solemn.

"So you have a man, huh? " he said knowingly, taking a step back from me and pulling his keys out of his pocket. The smile on my face didn't change. Instead, I felt my face grow a little hot, and my smile started to hurt from how big it was. "I think we're getting to that point." My blush finally dampened as realization and guilt hit me. My eyes watered, and I blinked back the tears. "I'm sorry. I just had to make sure if the feelings were still there or not." I started in a low tone. Captain pulled me into a hug, squeezing me hard. I wrapped my arms around him, but this time, I wasn't able to stop the tears. I sobbed lightly, and he pulled back, wiping the tears from my face. I hated saying goodbyes; I was never good at them.

"Don't apologize, Hazel; I came into your life disrupting the peace that you built up. You got your dream business, the loft you've always wanted, and now you're with a man who clearly must be treating you. I've never seen you smile the way you were just smiling. That nigga has to be doing something right." He kissed the top of my head and hugged me one last time. "Thank you for meeting with me today. I know you well, and that really was the most important thing to me. You continue doing big things. You hear me?" He said with a finality in his voice.

"Thank you, Jamal for being the first man to really love on me correctly, thank you for the support, your attentiveness and being genuine. Thank you for being my lover, the best partner on that ambulance and everything else." The tears kept falling as he kissed my forehead and then my cheek. "You deserved it; I've always said that about you, Hazey. Now you have Marquis, who's probably doing an even better job."

He wiped my tears, making sure no more were falling. " Are you going to be okay? I can't leave if you keep crying."

I nodded my head, laughing, the last of my tears falling out, and I wiped them away.

"Listen, if he fumbles the bag, you got my number. I'll come and scoop you up real quick. Just hit me with that "Hey big head" message, and I'll be there quickly."

I slapped his arm, and we both laughed. We hugged each other tightly until he pulled apart and walked to his truck. I watched as he walked away and smiled before something came to mind.

"Jamal!" I called out the Captain's real name. He paused in his steps and looked at me like I had committed a crime. I hardly ever said his real name.

"How did you know about my clinic and loft?" I asked curiously since we hadn't talked about it, and I didn't think I had him on social media anymore unless our old coworkers told him about it.

"I might follow Hazeynut Adventures on TikTok." I smiled at him and laughed before he got in his truck. I got in my jeep and just sat in my car for a minute. I watched as he pulled out of the parking lot, and the tears fell again. I didn't realize it until now, but he was my first love, and getting a second
round of closure was a big relief. I would miss him, but...

I looked down at my phone, and I saw Marquis' name again. I opened up my photos, going to the last picture in my camera roll, which was a video of Marquis and me. I was recording something for TikTok, and he wanted to be in the camera so badly that he took up most of the frame before grabbing the phone from me so he could get a higher angle of both of us before leaning down and kissing me all over my face.

I smiled as I watched the video repeatedly. He was my future now, and I wouldn't have it any other way.

Now this might be love

I was sitting at the bar with my brothers. We had spent a few hours going down the slopes. We now sat at a nearby bar discussing our plans for tonight. My heart wasn't really into the plans. I was not in the mood to go to a bar or a club. My mind was elsewhere, thinking of an infuriating yet beautiful hazel-eyed woman. The more I thought of her, the more agitated I became.

I don't know how much time I had spent in my mind, but I instantly felt my eyes on me. My brothers had stopped talking and took notice of my lack of words. I sighed as I chugged my beer before slamming it on the bar. "Take a picture; it'll last longer," I muttered before ordering another beer. Our youngest brother Marcell stood up, he didn't like serious conversations or being in awkward situations. He went to the other side of the bar to flirt with the group of females that walked in.

My oldest brother Marshawn patted my back, and I just relaxed as I tried to ease my irritation. "Is this about Hazel?" He asked me with a knowing tone of voice. I looked up at him and gave him a hardened stare. It wasn't directed towards him but more to myself.

"I just hate that me and Hazel haven't spoken in like two weeks and the worst part about all of this is that it's mostly my fault." I took a shaky breath as the truth stumbled from my mouth. "She wouldn't have cared about the possibility of me being a father, and she would've never met up with her ex had I cuffed her and secured her." I take another sip of my beer as I shake my head, I lean forward my head resting in both of my hands as I rethink the last several weeks. I knew I hadn't handled our conversation the right way, and I wish I had reached out sooner.

Marshawn rubbed my back the way our mom used to and still does if we go to her with a problem. "Listen, man, you gotta stop being a bitch." I scoffed and shrugged him off of me. "Man, don't call me out of my name," I grumbled as I downed my beer.

He chuckled, "Or what? Your fears are making you act like one. How are you scared to confront a woman who delivers babies for a living? But then speed race to a scene with an active shooter still armed and dangerous? You better go to your room and call her. Tell her you're sorry." He stood up and downed his beer before stretching a bit. "And don't wait for the right moment; snatch her up as soon as you can. Let her know you love her." The pain in his voice pulled me from my own sorrow. His ex left him because he couldn't commit to her, he never expressed why, he only really consolidated in our parents. I don't know if it was because he was the oldest or what exactly, but he just never talked about women with us. Regardless I knew he didn't want me to feel the pain he felt so I would take his advice.

I stood up, pulling my brother into a bear hug. We squeezed each other before releasing. We both lightened up at the sound of female laughter and our little brother sitting amongst them. Marshawn rolled his eyes. "Let's see if he warmed up at least one for me."

I shook my head laughing I headed back to my room ready to take a shower and call Hazel. I was going to take my brother's advice and reach out to her. I tap the key to my room and pause in my steps as I hear someone moving about in the kitchen. I slowly cracked the door, and I went to the coat closet. The safe was located there, and I quickly but quietly typed the code before retrieving my 9mm. I turned the safety off and kept the gun pointed to the ground as I started to maneuver to the kitchen. I started to smell cookies. Surely the burglar wasn't baking?

I turned the corner and smiled immediately at my discovery. There she was in the kitchen, wrapped in a blush pink silk gown. Her hair was pinched half up and half down, the bottom part covered in some kind of cream, elongating her curls.

"Hazel?"

She gasped as she turned around, her face was starting to turn red, and her eyes looked defeated and it showed in her voice. "I...I.." She looked around and shook her head in disappointment, yet something sparked in her. She looked back at me and smiled before she picked up her wine glass. "Come back in two hours. My surprise will be finished by then. For now, you get a sneak peek at what I have planned." She pointed a finger at my gun. "Did you think I was an intruder?" She asked as I went and put the gun in my holster.

"Absolutely, even when I smelled your cookies, some weird people out there. You could've been a big buff man with homicidal ideations and just wanted to make a snack or something like that." I knew discussing crazy scenarios would make her smile. Oftentimes, we would spend hours talking about different first responder scenarios. Like clockwork, she immediately giggled and shook her head. Seeing her laugh felt right; her being her reinstated my earlier feelings.

She turned from me, and went to check on the cookies. "Can you please leave? I want this moment to be special and set everything up as I had intended." I heard her, but I wasn't listening. I wrap my arms around her waist and kiss the top of her head. "You flew to the mountains after not speaking to each other for the last two weeks. We are alone and without distractions from work? I'm not leaving you alone for another minute." I kissed up and down her neck, in response she moaned before pushing her back against me and wiggling out from my embrace.

"Okay, go take a shower, put on some comfy clothes, and just watch me finish my set-up. Thank you, sir." She says dismissively, waving me off before grabbing her wine glass again and going back to what she was doing.

I leaned against the wall, took a step back, and just observed as she moved around. Once her eyebrows furrowed and she began to talk to herself I knew she was locked in, she did the same thing at the hospital and when doing something as simple as performing an ultrasound on my sister. I could see why she had anxious tendencies; I'd never seen her just focus on one task at once. She was always doing a million things at once. It was a controlled chaos, a chaos that I wanted every part of.

Without any prior thought, no briefing with my brothers or family. I go to lift my 14k gold cross necklace over my head. Our parents bought each of my siblings and I a cross necklace and bracelet, once working in our positions as first responders. It was something to pass down to our children once we retired from our respective positions.

I approached Hazel, her back to me. "Shouldn't you be showering?" She mumbled as she was setting up a platter of fruit. I didn't respond, but instead, I lowered the necklace around her neck. She paused what she was doing, drying her hands on a rag before turning around and facing me. She looked down at the chain and back at me. Her eyebrows knitted in confusion, "You're giving me your chain?" She looked back at the necklace, thumbing the cross before making eye contact with me again.

"I want you to be my girlfriend. I think we should be committed to each other. I know we have much to discuss, and I won't rush your response. "I'm going to take a shower and give you some space so you can think." I leaned down, kissing her forehead, before walking away and heading to the bathroom. Once in the bathroom, I began to strip off my many layers before going into the shower. I knew what I did was very forward, but it felt right. I was confident in my decision. I mean, she flew down here and did her makeup even though she hates makeup and putting together whatever it was she was trying to put together. All for what? To apologize for something that wasn't her fault? Tell me how much she missed me. I shook my head, and the smile on my face grew, reaffirming that my decision was a good one.

I took my time in the shower, knowing Hazel didn't want me rushing so she could finish up once out of the shower. I dry off before picking up all of my dirty laundry and putting it in the bin. After drying off, lotion down and spray some cologne. I go into the closet that was connected to the bathroom, I change into gray sweatpants, opting against a shirt. As I open the bathroom door, I can hear Hazel's soft voice, "I'm in the bedroom."

I make my way slowly to the bedroom, I could see candles on the dresser. Hazel lay on her side, and in front of her was the platter of cookies and a bowl of fruit and whipped cream. Her robe was still on, but her hair was being held up by a glittery gold butterfly clip. I looked down, and my chain rested about an inch under her clavicle, centering the cross right in the middle of her chest. My eyes moved to her face, and she looked defeated and disappointed.

"What's wrong?" I grabbed a cookie from the tray. "Is this that Oreo Cheesecake cookie you were telling me about?" I took a bite of it and immediately moaned; my reaction wasn't dramatized either. She perfected that recipe. She looked up at me with hopeful eyes. She sat up on her knees. "You love them? How would you rate them?" her disappointed face was now glowing, and she was smiling. "I was upset with my display. I had way more planned, and I just wanted everything to be perfect...but at least you enjoyed the cookies."

I chuckled as she expressed herself to me. She had no idea how perfect today was for me. "Hazel, I loved everything you did. I appreciate you flying down here and surprising me. Despite things not going as planned, I want you to know that everything you did today was perfect." Before she could debate and argue with me, I leaned down, kissing her pretty pink glossy lips. I hope my words gave her the reassurance she needed. She would never know how much her actions meant to me.

I pulled apart from her lips, she reached up smiling as she wiped away her gloss from my lips. "Thank you..." she was blushing, and her hand reached for the chain that lay on her chest. I removed the food from the bed, sitting it on the nightstand before, I blew out the candles as well before getting in bed next to her. . "You really wanna give this to me? I know it's a family tradition and all..." I pulled her down next to me; I wrapped my arm around her waist before pulling the throw blanket on top of us. "Let's just go to sleep and talk in the morning, okay?"

I wanted to enjoy her presence; we both had a long day and fell asleep beside each other. I knew she was tired because she hadn't fought it either. We lay in each other's embrace for the remainder of that night.

...

The following morning, my body woke up like clockwork around 7 a.m. I looked down at the natural hazel. Her makeup rubbed off in her sleep, and her clip fell from her hair. Her curls were spiraling all over her head, and I just smiled. She never looked so at ease. I didn't want to wake her up, so I lay beside her, looking at the mountains surrounding our cabin. From the window, I could see my eldest brother walking a woman to her car. She placed her hand on his cheek, and he smiled. He watched her drive off before returning to his cabin.

Hazel woke up maybe an hour later. Her eyes slowly fluttered open. The sun was hitting her face, and she looked at me with those greenish-brown eyes. She yawned and stretched, purposely hitting me in the face as she extended her arms. "I feel so nauseous." she laid back down on the pillow. She smiled at me, and I couldn't help but study her face. She wasn't trying to be seductive or persuasive; her smile wasn't mysterious. It was a smile of adoration...she adored me, maybe even loved me. I recognized this look as the same one my mother had given my father. My heart started to warm up; I never had a woman look at me the way she did. I smiled down at her and lightly bit my lip, rubbing my hand over her thigh. Her smile widened and her cheeks turned a bit red, she inched her leg away from my touch. I knew she was ticklish so I flattened my hand on her thigh and just gently kneaded it.

Her lips opened and closed lightly; I knew she had a lot of questions and didn't know where to start. So I started "For the last two weeks I've been working and doing extra overtime and you are correct, I avoided you at the hospital intentionally. I was upset about you seeing your ex, and it felt messy." I looked into her eyes, pausing to see if she had anything to say, but she just tilted her head and lifted her finger, indicating for me to continue, so I did. "Me thinking you were being messy was me projecting on you. I've been in similar situations in the past and assumed you were on the same bs." I swallowed a little hard, and I adjusted myself in the bed. I've never been this forward with a woman before when discussing my feelings, but I knew it needed to be said if I wanted to keep her. One thing I've learned about women is that they always knew when the unspoken thoughts weren't being said, and I didn't want to leave her with any doubts.

She adjusted in bed as well, sitting up. She now sat cross-legged, facing me and listening intently. I could see the anxiety in her eyes. She had no idea I was going to only say the opposite of the worst-case scenarios she was coming up with in that pretty little head of hers. "I didn't know the outcome after your encounter with that nigga. My vacation with my brothers was coming up, and fighting with you pre-vacation wasn't on my mind. I figured I would get back, and then we could talk, but this whole weekend, I've been thinking about."

She crawled on top of my lap, still thumbing the cross. I rubbed her legs in a soothing way, running the palm of my hand from her mid-thigh all the way to the back of her calf and down to her foot, and I repeated that motion. "I have to have you, Hazel...and my instincts told me to give my chain to you. I want you to be my girlfriend."

She looked down at me, her eyes swimming with hundreds of emotions. Her eyes began to tear up, and her lip quivered a bit. I sat up and pulled her into a hug, wrapping my arms around her waist. She moved her arms around the neck. I bring my lips to her ear, "Talk to me, Hazey; what's wrong?" I asked her patiently as I rubbed her back soothingly. She buried her eyes into my chest, and I could feel a bit of wetness. I push my shoulder up, forcing her to lift her head up and make eye contact with me. "These are happy tears. I've never had a man officially ask me to be his girlfriend." She began to wipe her tears, and her smile shone through. "Of course, I want to be your girlfriend."

I wiped at her tears for her before kissing her cheek, "So, will you be my girlfriend then?" I wanted her to give me a firm yes to solidify our union before the next step, which was marriage. Without hesitation, she nodded her head yes. "I will be your girlfriend, and you will be my boyfriend." She leaned in, placing her lips on me. I smiled, wrapping my arms around her waist before squeezing and flipping us over so I was on top. Before I could lean down and continue our session, she had one hand on her mouth and the other on her stomach. She got up very fast and ran to the bathroom. She leaned over the sink, throwing up, not making it to the toilet.

I held her hair and rubbed her back. When she was finished, she washed her mouth with water before going back to the bedroom to grab her toiletry bag from her luggage. "I think I had too much wine last night, " she said before brushing her teeth.

She then began to prepare for her skincare routine. "I love that you're my boyfriend, but saying boyfriend at 29 years old sounds silly. Don't you think so?" she said with a raised eyebrow before getting started on her routine but still watching me in the mirror.

"Give me a minute; let's enjoy this bliss for a while; your time is coming, mama." I give her a kiss on the neck, staring at her through the mirror, making eye contact before I smack her ass. She smiled before continuing her routine.

I walked out of the bathroom, giving her the space she needed. I texted my mother good morning, and she responded immediately with a good morning message. I responded with, "I'm going to marry her. I'm going to wait 6 months." My mom already knew Hazel because of Hazel's relationship with my sister Mariah.

My parents met Hazel several times throughout the years and mentioned her to me a few times. I always thought she was cute, but with the distance and my focus being on Instagram women, Hazel was not on my mind.

But I was grateful she was getting to meet the man I was today. I had faith in God that everything would be okay in the direction we were moving.

Self-care and Self-love

"Ugh girl I'm ready for this baby to come out of me right now," Mariah whined as I wiped the gel from her stomach. She was currently 36 weeks, at this point in her pregnancy, we performed a cervical exam, did blood work, checked on the baby, and overall discussed any new or existing symptoms she was experiencing. Once I was done wiping the gel from her, I took off my gloves. PA mode was off, and now I was in friend mode. I rubbed her belly and smiled. "Just four more weeks; it'll go by so fast. Once the baby comes it's here, so just use this time to sleep in while you can and rest up." I reminded her.

I stood up, taking off my lab coat, she was my last patient of the day, and I was super tired. I had spent all morning throwing up, my head was hurting, and I was experiencing cramping myself. Even now, I felt so nauseous.

I helped Mariah stand up and gather her things before I walked her out to her car. "You sure you can't be a foodie with me and grab dinner?" She asked as I closed her driver's door.

"No ma'am I can't, I have to finish up some stuff here." She rolled her eyes and let out an exaggerated sigh. "Fine, I guess I'll look like a big back all by myself." She let out a laugh before rolling her window up and waving goodbye before driving off.

I shook my head, laughing as I walked back inside. I head to the very back of the building; I enter through the back door that leads to our after-hours rooms. Our patients who wanted to give birth here could if they didn't want to give birth in the hospital or at home. I had three large rooms that were decorated nicely, having that modern, clean look, but instead of basic beige, white, and neutral colors, the rooms had color. We currently had two patients who were very close to labor, we had our midwives and doulas with them.

After checking on those last two patients and my staff, I went to my office to grab a chart before I headed to an exam room. I closed the door to one of the exam rooms so no one could see what I was about to do. I opened the chart I had been looking at since I came in at 5 a.m. this morning. I stared at the question on the chart: "Last menstrual cycle?"

I swallowed hard. I was supposed to get my period about four weeks ago, but it hadn't come. Marquis and I had last been intimate six weeks ago, so it would be foolish not to consider the possibility of pregnancy. I was scared; the thought of motherhood frightened me far more than I had ever admitted.

It was no secret that I wanted to be a mother. Whenever anyone asked how many children I wanted, I always answered the same way: "Three big boys so I can wrestle with them and be the sports mom, or one girl so I can spoil her and give her the world." I had even pre-planned some traditions I wanted to instill in my family, like weekly Bible studies, praying together before bed, themed movie nights, and mini-dates with each child. Yet, despite all the dreams and fantasies I had about motherhood, I often found myself worrying about becoming the worst parts of my own mother—those aspects terrified me.

Motherhood scared me because I didn't want to turn into the person my mother had been during my adolescent years. As I grew older, she transformed into the mother I had longed for. In my mid-20s, she decided to go to therapy and deepened her relationship with God. She shifted from being impatient, unsympathetic, accusatory, and judgmental—traits that had driven me away—to becoming gentle, patient, and empathetic. She now worked hard to be respectful and understanding.

Yet, despite forgiving her for her past actions, a part of me still held some resentment. I wished she had been this new version of herself throughout my life. I understood she had a tough upbringing, which explained her behavior, but it still hurt. I feared being impatient with my own children, procrastinating on important dates, or snapping at them. Although I didn't always show those traits, there were moments when those emotions could surface. I tried to quickly correct myself when that happened. One of my methods was to remind myself that it's human nature to occasionally lack empathy or be impatient and that it's okay to be a little disorganized sometimes.

Despite all the inner coaching I gave myself, I still felt an underlying fear of only showing my worst traits. I always prayed that God would bless me with a husband who was patient and could help reel me in when those traits surfaced. I often marveled at relationships where the man could calm his hyperanxious, busy-bodied wife amidst the chaos, remaining calm and smiling. A small smile crept onto my face at the thought of Marquis. I knew he would be an amazing father, and reflecting on how he treated me weeks ago filled me with peace. It reassured me that he would be the protector and partner I needed—not just in my life but in my child's life as well.

...

I drove to Alameda's office; she was well aware of the pregnancy test. I didn't want to find an obgyn, and I knew I needed a friend more than anything else right now.

When I arrived at her clinic, I walked inside, already familiar with the layout. Per her request, I met her in exam room 3. She had all of the equipment prepped, and she had the biggest smile on her face. "Go ahead and strip for me, girl. Let's hear my niece or nephew's heartbeat."

I rolled my eyes, happy that at least someone in this room was ecstatic about this pregnancy. When I was changed, I lay on the table, placing my feet on the sternals giving my friend a full view of my vagina. It wasn't odd; we were both free people, and she kept it professional as soon as I sat on the table.

I grunted as she put the probe in me but adjusted. After a few moments, I heard her voice crack as she finally spoke up. I looked at her with concern.

"Am I ectopic? What's wrong? What are you seeing?" My eyes watered up, and I started to panic.

She shook her head, a smile breaking across her face. "Everything looks good, mama. You definitely have a baby in there, and if you'll let me, I want to be part of every step of this journey." She placed her hand on my stomach, gently rubbing my womb with admiration. "I don't know what you're feeling right now, but it would be an honor to walk this path with you." We made eye contact, and I could see the passion shining in her eyes.

I nodded my head yes, and we cried together. After talking further about a follow-up appointment, she offered to take me out to dinner, but I wasn't in the mood. I needed to sit in this feeling by myself.

...

I rubbed my belly in a self-soothing circular motion as I leaned back on my couch. After a moment I was able to slow my breathing down so I could speak. The whole drive home, I felt as if I had been holding my breath. "Hi, Amber or Leo. Whoever or whatever you are, your mother is not prepared at all, but God blessed you to be in my life for a reason, and I will take on this new role and chapter in my life with pride." I look up at my high ceiling and close my eyes. "Lord, I pray that you bless me with a healthy boy or girl. I pray that you give me the emotional, mental, and physical strength to endure the next 9 months. I pray that Marquis will respond well and that we can raise these children together. I want to repent for having premarital sex and having a child out of wedlock. As parents, I pray that you guide our steps and decisions that not only bring us closer to you but bring our child to you as well. Thank you, Jesus, for this gift. In your name, I pray…amen."

After soaking everything in for a minute I finally decided to get up and pack my things up. Even though I felt slightly better after confirming the pregnancy I still felt some uneasiness in me. I knew I had a lot of planning to do and a lot of people to tell, and it was all very overwhelming.

As I was driving home, I kept debating when I should tell Marquis. I knew I wouldn't tell friends or family until I was at the 12th-week safe mark, but it didn't feel right sitting on this for six more weeks without telling Marquis. I was almost 100% certain that Marquis wouldn't react negatively, but I was still nervous to tell him.

Once I arrived home, I could feel myself moving slowly. With this newfound cargo I was carrying, I was being extra careful. Just a few days ago, I had tripped going upstairs from my living room to my bedroom. I fell down last week when standing on a stool trying to water one of my hanging plants. The thought made me wince. I had been pregnant and so reckless the last few weeks that I just wanted to be careful moving forward.

Once I had organized a few things around the house,

I went to my bathroom. I turned on my dim lights as I stared into the mirror. I looked myself up and down before landing my eyes back to my midsection. My eyes remain on that area as I slowly begin to strip my clothes off. Once naked I stared in the mirror I rubbed my belly gently. I had a little pouch anyway, so I smiled as I cupped it like it was my baby bump. I examined my body for a good while, imagining what I would look like as the months passed. I quickly changed my thoughts since the idea of the next few months started to sound stressful.

I would have to start shopping, plan a baby shower, eventually move into a more child-friendly home, and do many more things. I was also very used to doing my own thing, and now, because I had a child and a boyfriend, I would have to interact with many more people.

I shook my head, refusing to let myself spiral into an anxiety attack—not today. I decided to treat myself and focus on self-care. I emailed the staff, informing them I wouldn't be in tomorrow. After hitting send, I set my phone down, grabbed my vanilla body wash, and made my way to the kitchen.

Once in my kitchen, I gathered raw sugar, vanilla, cinnamon, and body wash. I grabbed a plastic bowl from my cabinets before making my homemade body scrub. I set that aside so it could set before grabbing the ingredients to make my comfort meal and dessert, Marry Me Salmon and Oreo cheesecake cookies.

After prepping my dinner and dessert, letting the cookies harden in the freezer, and the fish sit in the fridge, I head back upstairs. I grab a lavender heartshaped shower steamer and place it in my shower. As my shower steamed, I stared into the mirror as I undid my braid, allowing my hair to be free and do as it pleased. I rubbed my fingers through my scalp, using the pads of my fingers to massage it and stimulate some blood flow.

I stepped into my shower, allowing the waterfall shower head to wet my hair until my curls were drenched. I allowed the heat and warmth from the water to envelope me before I thought of moving. With my eyes still closed, I grabbed my bottle of heated-in shower face mask, coated my face with the sticky gel, and moaned as the heat started to come from my face.

I proceeded to bathe with my no-scent Dove body wash before doing a lavender body scrub, which I then rinsed with a scented lavender body wash once out of the shower. I put on a clay face mask before putting on coco butter lotion followed by lavender body oil. I was extra careful when massaging the contents into my stomach, and I am now extra cautious with my stomach.

When finished, I headed downstairs to prep my dinner.

...

45 minutes later, I was sitting on my couch.

Along with the fish and cookies I cooked, I grabbed my favorite snacks: frozen fruit snacks and hot Cheetos. I sat on my couch, throwing the fur blanket over myself. I turned on a reality show, waiting for Marquis to arrive.

About 20 minutes into my real housewife show, my phone rang. I aimlessly go for my phone, my eyes never leaving the screen, and I don't even check the caller ID. I bring the phone to my ear. "Hello?" I asked as I stuffed my mouth with fruit snacks. "Hey Hazey, what are you doing?" Marquis's deep, sexy voice released on the other end.

"What do you think I'm doing?" I ask teasingly as I pause my show, giving him my full attention. "The same thing as always, watching some true crime that scares you too much, so then you end up watching Adventure Time while snacking on fruit snacks and hot Cheetos." I laughed at how he just knew me so well. "Wrong, it's frozen fruit snacks, and don't forget my Arizona Green Gingseng tea. And this time, I'm watching Housewives."

He playfully let out an exaggerated long sigh before chuckling. "So don't be mad but I'm not going to make it tonight, I got two leads on my Ladybird Lake killer. I know you are busy the next few days, so I will make it up to you sometime next week." It made me smile, and I could hear the frustration in his voice. He hated missing our low-key, lowmaintenance date nights. We didn't leave the house, so we ordered in and enjoyed each other's company. Neither one of us worked, just chilled.

"You good bae, I'm just going to play sims and relax."

We chatted for a bit until Jorden called him to go. We said our byes before hanging up. I say a quick prayer, asking God to give him protection and discernment as he worked late tonight.

...

The next day, I woke up relatively early, around 9 a.m. For the first time in about two weeks, I didn't feel nauseated. I had Zofran and a can of ginger ale on my nightstand in case I felt nauseous.

I started my day by getting on my knees and praying to god. I thanked him for waking me up today and allowing me to live another day; I prayed for a few of my patients, staff, family, and friends before standing up and heading to my bathroom. After finishing up my skincare, I go to my kitchen, yawning as I put water in my glass teapot. I turned the stove on low before placing the pot down, after drinking my smoothie and finishing my daily devotional it would be ready for me to make my tea.

I go to my fridge and pantry before pulling out my blinder. I woke up with a bit of a sweet tooth. I wanted to start the day with one of my favorite smoothies.

Apple Cinnamon:

- 1 Chopped green apple or 6 pre-sliced apples
- ½ teaspoons of ground cinnamon
- 1 cup of milk (almond milk, in my case)

- ½ cup of honey Greek yogurt
- 1 tablespoon of honey
- Sometimes, for that extra crunch, I'll blindflavored granola using cinnamon or chocolate flavors.

I also needed to be healthy and didn't mind the weird taste so I also added magnesium powder, biotin drops, and black seed oil.

After blinding my smoothie, I sat down on a pillow on the ground near my window and studied the Bible using the Bible app.

After spending time with God, I people watched from my living room window, watching people enjoy there time outside in the sun. I decided to get up.

Opps

"Man tonight is soooo slow, quiet, and boring," I stated as we sat in Marquis patrol unit. He was working as a stand-by detective, we've both been quite busy, and as a way to spend time together I decided to do a ride along with him with the approval of his supervisor.

It was 11 pm on a Wednesday. We sat in an empty Home Depot parking lot, listening to the radio. Marquis had been staring off into space, my comment grabbed his attention, and he glanced at me smiling. I smiled back at him, and at that moment, I wanted to tell him about our child. It had only been two weeks since I found out I was pregnant, but I was thinking of the perfect time and way to tell Marquis. I had ordered online a newborn
-sized black shirt on the back that stated "Future APD detective. Detective Neberu," as well as a pink lab coat with bedazzle on the trimming on the righthand front side Dr. Amber.

Obviously, I knew our child could become either one regardless of gender, but I thought it would be more fun to do it this way. I also already had the names pre-picked for years, especially my boy's name. I heard Neberu in a song once and saw NASA post an article about the planet. It had no significant meaning; I just thought it was unique and cute. Ever since, I have been pretty hooked.

"Listen I'm the one who has to do the work so I'm good with slowness, besides, If I have to work that means that I will be busy trying to solve a case and not spending time with you." He rubbed my thigh a bit before smacking it. I just rolled my eyes at him before giggling. "I know I know...I still want to see some action." He sighed and rubbed his hand through his hair. "We can do another ride out; let's do it this Saturday; it should be busy, and the call volume will be high. In the meantime, let's get McDonald's; I'll buy you some chicken nuggets and a Mcflurry to make you happy." He leaned over, kissing my cheek, and I playfully shoved him off of me, but I could feel myself cheesing hard.

As we pulled onto the main street the radio keyed up. " 7 shots heard East Riverside/Oltorf about 2 mins ago, cars also heard speeding up. Marquis flashes his lights. "Show me 76." Before he took off down the road. "76?" I give him a questioning glance. "En route." He responded and I watched as he navigated through the light traffic. I had worked as a paramedic in college, so going lights and sirens didn't excite me that much, but I was curious as to what we would find.

At the intersection of Riverside and Oltorf, there were many different apartment complexes. From what I've seen on the news, the things Marquis has shown me, and just from living in Austin for the last few years, everyone knew that East Austin, especially in this area, was the hood. There were shootings every week, carjackings, a high homeless population, and many other things you would want to avoid. I had no reason to come over here, and I never did.

I began to feel a pit in my stomach, something told me this was going to be a legit call. I bowed my head and I began to pray in my mind. "Lord watch over
myself and this entire unit. I pray that you also protect any other responding unit to this call. I pray to you, Lord, that no one is seriously injured or deceased. If we are responding to someone deceased I pray that you have mercy on their soul, that they had a relationship with you, and that you bring peace to the person's loved ones. Amen."

Marquis noticed me praying, and he placed a hand on my thigh. "We're gonna be okay. These kinds of calls, we usually don't find anything, and if we do, I'm going to protect you. Aight?" I appreciated the reassuring gesture, but my intuition was tingling. Something bad was going to happen, but I wasn't going to voice that out loud.

It took us about seven minutes to get to the intersection and it was silent. Marquis had me read the message from his CAD laptop. Additional callers had reported hearing a man scream in pain. People from all of the apartment complexes had called. Once in the area, Marquis killed his siren and it didn't take long to see bullet casings on the ground near the entrance of an apartment complex. He keyed up on the radio, letting dispatch know what he discovered and where he was parking his vehicle. As we pulled in he spoke up. "Stay put, don't get out of the vehicle. You know how to get the shotgun if you need help, and I can't help you queue up on the radio, and dispatch will help out if I need more units if I am unable to do so."

No sooner than when we pulled in we found a man lying on the ground. With blood pooling around him. It took everything in me not to get out and render aid. Scene safety was more important and I didn't want Marquis to worry about me or put him in danger. He exited the vehicle and drew his gun checking the area. I heard him on the radio letting dispatch know what he was seeing. I began to rub my belly, praying for the safety of our child. Just as he crouched to the ground a black Mustang pulled up fast. My heart dropped as the window rolled down. I already knew what was coming. I was shaking. I was used to emergencies but I had never been in such a dangerous predicament.

I grabbed the radio. I couldn't see the suspect, but I saw the handgun, and several rapid shots were released. I screamed and watched as Marquis was struck. I heard Marquis groan and take cover on my side of the patrol unit. At least, he was somewhat safe. I clicked the button on the radio and I read the license plate. Able to give a direction of travel. The unit that was supposed to meet us here chased after the vehicle and shortly behind that unit, another unit pulled in behind our unit. I got out of the vehicle grabbing the first aid kit from the back.

"I'm a medically trained! Take care of the other victim! I have the officer!" I yelled out rushing to Marquis. I crouched to the ground pulling his head into my lap. He was gripping his shoulder. He was wincing in pain which was good. I didn't have to manage his airway, I was concerned with the light bleeding from his leg. I quickly cut his pants leg , he was hitting the ground with his fist. I knew he was in pain.

"I'm going to pass out Hazey." I was in the zone and more first responders were coming. "You better stay awake," I told him sternly as I applied a tourniquet a few inches about his thigh wound. He groaned out loud and my heart clenched. I knew he was in so much pain but, I knew he needed this. I then applied pressure on the wound. More and more units were coming. I heard sirens and I saw the lights of the helicopter above. I jumped when I heard more gunshots in the distance. The whole time I made sure I had one hand on Marquis I could feel his heart rate pumping. Several officers were trying to interview me and ask what happened, but I wasn't in the mindset to answer any questions at that moment. Marquis was in too much pain to respond either. In the midst of the chaos, I even yelled at them to give us space, and I pulled him in closer to me before just focusing my attention back on him, deciding to zone everything else out.

When the ambulance arrived, I broke some protocols. As they were loading him onto the stretcher I ran to the back of the ambulance. I needed to busy myself and I needed to be the one to treat him. I get a bag of lactated ringers ready and I prepare my needle. Once he was on the stretcher, the paramedic yelled at me to stop, and he handled me a bit roughly, forcing me to sit down in the captain's seat, which was right at the head of the stretcher. Marquis' eyes were closed and he seemed to be unconscious. I made a fist and began to perform sternal rubs on his chest to wake him up. He groaned, which was a good enough response for me.

The medics gave him lactated ringers, that they pushed gently into him. His skin was a bit cold, and all I could do was rub his hair as we responded code 3, lights and sirens, to the nearest hospital. At some point during the ride, I leaned forward kissing the side of his head and whispering in his ear. "I'm pregnant Marquis. You better not die from these wounds...I can't do this alone." I said softly as I could feel my eyes watering up. I lean back in my seat and rub my eyes. Now was not the time or place to be crying.

Once at the hospital, everything moved even faster. He was immediately rushed into a trauma room. I was interviewed again by the detectives who followed us to the hospital. I had to make phone calls to his family. After the interviews, being on the phone and talking to the nurses. It was almost two hours later I had a few moments to myself while his family was on the way.

I was hiding away in a private single bathroom. I had noticed during one of my interviews that my stomach was cramping. As a woman, we just knew when we were bleeding. I was so anxious to pull my pants down I didn't want to check. I gripped the edge of the sink and I could feel my body trembling. Bleeding during any trimester was cause for concern but especially in the first trimester. I was so scared and extremely stressed. "Please, God, please..." I whimpered to myself as I built the courage to move my hands to the waistband of my jeans.

I slowly unbuttoned them, and tears ran hot down my face. I pulled them down. I grabbed the waistband of my panties and pulled them down along with my jeans and there was a concerning amount of blood. It was some big spots. "No.... no... no." I released a whimpered outcry. I knew this wasn't the most hygienic thing to do, and I knew I probably should have myself admitted, but I was keeping this to myself for now. I stuffed my panties with tissues before pulling my pants up. I am about eight weeks pregnant now. If this was a miscarriage, I would just need an ultrasound to confirm if there was any remaining tissue or not. There was still a good chance this was only a threatened miscarriage.

Threatened miscarriages typically occur during the first trimester of pregnancy. Symptoms are very mild, light to medium bleeding, and light cramps that usually weren't intense or sharp. A blood count test, a pelvic exam, and an ultrasound should be performed, but I would do all of these things myself. I straightened myself up, and I finally took a look in the mirror.

This was the first time I had a good look at myself. My hair was all over my head. My eyes were bloodshot red, there was blood on my shirt, which would have only been Marquis's blood, and overall, I felt and looked like a mess. I thought I had my tears underway, but I was profusely crying again. I called out to God, asking for him to bless me with his presence and to bring me a calm that would transcend beyond all human understanding, Philippians 4:7, Despite what was happening around me, I still wanted his comfort. I never blamed God for the bad things that happened despite knowing people who would. At the end of the day, Satan still existed, and on top of that, bad things just happened sometimes. I didn't know what God's plan was at that moment, but I knew I just needed to be faithful, and it would later be revealed to me what his plan and purpose were.

I didn't want anyone to see me grieving or hurt. I turn on the faucet, throwing water on my face. I also flush my eyes to make them go back to their normal color. I grab some paper towels, lightly patting my face and forcing myself to smile in the mirror. There wasn't anything to smile about right now, but I couldn't cry if I smiled. I pulled my hair up into a bun before giving myself a final examination. The tip of my nose was red, my eyes were glassy, and my face was flushed. I looked refreshed, but you could tell I had been crying. I looked back down at my shirt, where Marquis's blood was on me. My lips quivered, and I felt myself on the verge of crying again. I quickly exit the bathroom.

As I walked back to the waiting room, I could hear his mother and sister crying. I paused, feeling a tightness in my chest. I couldn't cope with that right now; my stomach began to churn with anxiety. Turning away, I made my way to the cafeteria. Guilt washed over me—I knew I should be there for them, offering comfort. But I just couldn't do it... not at this moment. Perhaps I was being selfish, but with my child's safety weighing heavily on my mind, I simply didn't have the capacity to bear anyone else's grief right now.

While making my way to the cafeteria, I passed a break room and saw detectives, officers, and nurses talking among each other. One of those detectives was Jorden, Marquis's best friend. We made eye contact as I passed by while he was midconversation. I quickly walked away, not wanting to interact with anyone, just wanting some alone time. After a few moments, I looked behind me, and I didn't notice him or anyone else trying to follow me. I sighed with relief and slowed my pace down.

I finally made it to the cafeteria, and I went to the vending machine. It was one of those fresh fancy vending machines that offered fresh fruits, pasta, salads, and many other options that were replaced and restocked weekly. I buy a pesto salad and freshpressed lemonade. I take a seat near one of the windows that had a view of the hospital's garden courtyard, which has a beautiful fountain in the middle. I sat down, putting my feet up in the chair across from me, and I slowly picked at my pasta.

I was so deep in thought that I wasn't paying attention to my surroundings. I tensed when I felt a heavy hand on my shoulder. I turned around, fully expecting it to be Jorden so he could get the details of what happened tonight, but to my surprise, it wasn't. It was Marshawn. "The family was wondering where you went, I decided to take a walk and I passed Jorden, he told me he saw you coming in this direction. I figured I make sure you are okay." He pulled a chair up next to me, and immediately, I became apologetic. "I'm sorry…" I pulled my phone out and saw 15 missed calls, 23 messages from his family, and a few unknown numbers, presumably detectives. I put my phone back in my pocket, and I focus my eyes on my pasta again.

I took slow bites forcing myself to eat. "I just needed some space. This is just all so overwhelming…" My eyes were starting to water up again, I rapidly blinked back the tears not wanting to cry in front of Marshawn. "Trust me, I get it…my mom and sister are pretty distraught. Marquis is tough, but I know he will be okay." He took a sip of his coffee and lowered himself in his seat. I could hear the tiredness in his voice. "I know it's fresh, so if you don't want to talk about it, you don't have to, but what happened?" I could feel his stare on me, and I could feel his tears starting to fall. I pushed my pasta away, and I sat up a bit straighter in my chair.

"We got a call for shots fired, and when we arrived on scene we immediately saw a victim, Marquis was clearing the scene when a black Mustang pulled up and the dudes in the car…." I covered my face with my hands as I sniffled, trying to stifle my sobs. Marshawn scooted closer to me and rubbed my back. "He fell so fast, they…they just shot him…and he just fell so fast. He's such a big guy, and he fell so hard." I could feel a cramp again, and I tensed in my seat, taking a deep breath and releasing an intense wince as I rubbed my stomach. I stand up from my chair.

Marshawn stood when I stood. "You okay?" I averted my eyes from him. Marquis didn't even know I was pregnant. I didn't want to share this with anyone until I told him. Also, If I was having a miscarriage, I would prefer to grieve alone rather than have the whole family in my business. Despite what I was thinking, the words just slipped from my mouth. "You are going to be uncle to more than just one kid." The cramps passed, and I sat back down. "You're pregnant?" He was smiling at first, but his expression shifted to a more concerned one.

"And you're having cramps? Is that normal? Is that bad? Are you okay?" I could see the concern on his face, and I rested a reassuring hand on his shoulder. The medical professional in me seeped out. "It's not uncommon to experience cramps or slight discomfort in the first trimester. I'm also really stressed out with the current circumstances." My tears dry up, and I wipe my face before sitting down again. I put my feet back up on the chair, and I pull my pasta back to me. "I'll be okay," I state firmly before taking a bite of my food.

"Does Marquis know?" He asked as he took a sip of his drink. I could tell by his squinted eyes and overall demeanor he was not sold on me being okay. "Not yet. I planned on telling him after his shift this Saturday. We were going to ride together again, and after his shift, I was going to do this whole thing...." I told him about the shirt and lab coat I got. He smiled, nodding his head in approval. "He would love that." He had a wide grin on his face.

We enjoyed each other's company for a bit, and for the first time tonight, I felt a bit of peace. "Thank you, God, for sending Marshawn my way. I feel a little better."

He yawned as he stood up and stretched. "I'm going back to the ER to make sure everything is okay. I'll let them know detectives were interviewing you and then grab something to eat."

I smiled, I could feel my eyes watered up. He will never know how much his kindness and understanding meant to me right now. "Thank you. I'll show my face soon. I just need a few more minutes." He nodded his head and started to walk away. As he walked away, he looked over his shoulder and back at me. "Also your secret is safe with me, I'll let you and Marquis tell the family whenever you two decide to do so." The kindness was overwhelming, and I couldn't help myself.

I stood up and ran towards him. My chest connected with his back, and I wrapped my arms around him, squeezing tightly. He turned in my arms, breaking my hold on him before he wrapped his arms around me. He kissed the top of my head, squeezing me once more before we pulled apart. He offered me a reassuring smile before walking back in the direction of the ER.

I felt much better, and I finished my food. I headed back to the ER myself. I had to do one more detailed interview of the events that took place before I was able to just sit with his family and await the status of Marquis's condition. I was only worried about his thigh injury. If he was hit in his femoral artery, it would take surgical intervention and some aftercare.

It was several hours later, around 6 am, when we were given an update. Marquis had been shot in the femoral artery, and the surgery was successful. He was now in the ICU and resting. They allowed us to visit him three at a time, and I told his family to go first.

At a later time, I was finally able to see him. I was a little nervous. In the back of my mind the entire time, I wondered if he had heard what I whispered in his ear in the back of the ambulance. I entered the room by myself. It was just the two of us. I went to him, and he looked so sleepy. His smile was wide when he saw me; My eyes watered up. His right shoulder was patched, and he had an IV going on his left arm. His lower body was covered in a blanket. "If you wanted other women to see your dick, you could've just told me," I say jokingly as the tears fell from my eyes for the millionth time today. "Damn, next time, I'll just ask instead of getting shot." We both laughed, and I was relieved to see his spirits were still high.

I grabbed the pen and notepad off his room counter and pulled a chair next to him. I started writing down a list of things we would need to do once he was out of the hospital. "Tell me if I'm overwhelming you, and I'll stop." I looked at him, and he looked back at me curiously. "Once you're released from the hospital and you're no longer on bed rest, I'm going to hook you up with a physical therapist that I know. In the meantime, I'm going to have some things placed in your home to make mobility much easier since you will struggle to walk, if you can, for the first couple of weeks."

A blush appeared on my face but I held my eye contact. "I can move in for the next 3-6 months and aid you since that's about how long your recovery period is going to take." He licked his lips, and I dug in my purse, searching for my lip balm before I put some on his lips. He chuckled before he asked to see my list. He read over it briefly before throwing it across the room. "Hey!" I yelled at him, but before I could retrieve it, he grabbed my wrist and gripped it, keeping me from moving. "You moving in is a dream; you are a medical professional. I'm going to do whatever you tell me to do. I need you to sit down, stop thinking, and just be in this moment with me." He stated firmly yet only sounding concerned. He pulled me down towards him before he grabbed my chin and pulled me into a kiss. When we pulled apart, he whispered in my ear. "Now, just sit your pretty ass down and talk like a normal human being for a bit."

I blushed in embarrassment but pulled my chair up close to him again and just sat down, looking at him, unsure of what to say next. "You did a good job talking on the radio, getting descriptions, and giving directions on travel, all while rendering care to me. If you hadn't applied the tourniquet when you did and called for help, I don't know if I would still be here right now." His voice cracked for a second, and I saw his eyes water. He kissed my hand, and I leaned down, kissing his forehead. I could feel myself cheering. He was feeding that part of my brain that yearned for words of affirmation. "I just did what I knew I needed to do." I didn't know what else to say. I have always been humbled regarding my skills. Always give the glory to God for blessing me with the skills I had when it came to urgent situations.

"And you did a Damn good job." He said proudly. "Are you okay? Is that my blood on you?" He asked, pointing at my shirt. I nodded my head. I wasn't sure why the blood kept triggering my tears, but I found myself tearing up again. I was very grateful that the father of my child was here, alive and well. I knew I needed to tell him, but I wanted to now wait until I could do an ultrasound on myself again.

He read my face, and I could tell he was concerned. I pulled him into a deep kiss and stood up. "I need to take a shower, praise God, eat, and sleep. I'll be back to see you and check on you." I could tell he had more questions to ask me, but I just kissed him again before I gathered my things and left.

Birth

About three weeks passed since the night Marquis was shot. He was in somewhat discomfort but, he was able to walk with a cane and was in rehab to strengthen his core, quads . He insisted he didn't need me but, the woman in me really cared about him. I made him meals and would help him out around the house. He still wasn't aware of the fact that I was pregnant and I never mentioned it. I still hadn't been to a Alameda to confirm if the pregnancy was still viable or not. I knew it was irresponsible but, there was no major health risk, if I had a miscarriage as long as all the fetus tissue passed I would be fine.

I was terrified of what the ultrasound would reveal, and I wasn't ready to grieve at that moment. I felt extremely happy right now and didn't want to face another depressive episode, which could take me weeks or even months to overcome. I promised myself that, after delivering the baby, I would have the ultrasound performed by Alameda later.

In the meantime I would focus on Mariah who was officially 2 weeks overdue. She was an irritated mama and it didn't help that we were also friends so I was CONSTANTLY getting text updates about everything happening during the final stages of her pregnancy. I felt bad for her but, there wasn't anything I could do.

Finally, two weeks passed the expected due date she called me saying she was on her way to my clinic. Her contractions were 2-4 minutes apart every 60 seconds and her water had broken. It was a Saturday evening and I called my staff who was already there to prepare the pool and to begin setting up. After a quick shower and clothing change I was enroute.

When I arrived Mariah was already inside. My midwife and doula were with her. I smiled as I looked at my dear friend as I stepped into the softly lit room. Mariah was already undressed. We allowed the women to choose how they wanted to present during childbirth, If she wanted to wear a swimsuit that would've been perfectly fine as well, her loved ones weren't allowed to visit until after the birth. She was allowed to have two guests with her currently, she opted for her mom and husband who she was comfortable being nude around.

After we checked to make sure she was 10cm dilated. We assisted her into the birth pool, a vibrant blue, shimmered under the warm light, inviting and serene. I put my gloves on and listened as they coached her through her breathing.

I approached the pool, feeling the warmth radiate from the water. I looked at Mariah studying her face, there was a mix of anticipation and determination on her face, looked up at me. I offered her a reassuring smile, knowing how vital it was to create a safe environment. We all placed a hand on her belly and said a prayer for her.

I held my hands out in front of me, palms facing up, and I bowed my head, saying a personal prayer. "Lord please bless my hands and guide them as I assist with bringing this child into the world. None of us would be here if it weren't for you. I truly believe this is what you called me to do, Lord, and ask that these hands deliver many more of your children. Thank you Lord for being our savior."

She was kneeling while the rest of her body was pressed against the pool wall. Once she was comfortable, I rubbed her back. "Are you ready?" I asked, my voice soothing and comforting. She nodded, her eyes filled with a mixture of fear and excitement.

She breathed through another contraction, "Dang Hazel, I can't do it," She sobbed. Her husband rubbed her head in a comforting gesture. I positioned myself at the edge of the pool, "Just like we practiced, I want you to focus on breathing," I encouraged, watching her as her body tensed through each contraction. Ignoring her selfdeprecating comments.

I wanted to concentrate on the baby's delivery. It wasn't that I lacked empathy; that's why I had hired a doula who was much more skilled with her words. The doula took on that role, coaching Mariah as I watched, eager to see the baby's head appear. While the midwife assisted me, the doula remained in tune with Mariah's needs, offering gentle guidance and reassurance. "You're doing so well," she said, her tone calm and steady.

As she was coached through another breath while pushing, I could finally see the baby's head beginning to crown. "You're almost there," I whispered, my heart racing. I squatted in anticipation of the baby sliding out. She let out a loud scream, and in that moment, the baby emerged into the water—a messy yet miraculous sight. The water started to mix with other fluids, but I didn't care. I carefully lifted the baby from the water, and he immediately began to cry and gasp. It was a beautiful moment, exactly what we loved to see. Mariah's eyes widened in awe, a blend of relief and joy washing over her face. She sobbed as she turned onto her back and reached for her baby. We handed the little one to her and watched as she and her husband welcomed their new bundle of joy.

As the parents bonded with their baby, my midwife brought over the bassinet. We needed to perform a few tests on the baby. While I handled that, my midwife would ensure that the umbilical cord was cut properly and that Mariah passed her placenta. The doula would then assist Mariah in transitioning from the pool to one of our resting rooms. In that space, she could put her feet up, watch some TV, or do whatever she wanted to do while I prepared to bring the baby back to her.

Once the baby was safely back in her arms, we all held hands in the room and prayed over Mariah's healing, the child's present state, and overall safety. We all prayed over her husband, asking God to give him the strength he would need to provide, protect, and lead his family. This was my favorite part: coming together and giving the Lord his glory and thanking him.

After the prayer and making sure Mariah was okay, I went up front to where her family had been waiting...excluding Marquis. I looked at Marshawn and Marcell with a questioning glance as I escorted them to their sister. "He's coming from the north side. He said he would be here in about an hour," Marshawn stated before entering Mariah's room. I nodded my head before I took off to my office.

I logged into my computer to monitor the cameras while I was on the phone. I didn't want anyone to hear my

247 | P a g e

conversation. Alameda answered the face time after a few rings, and I laughed as she positioned her camera so I could have a full view of her body as she twerked. She was in her office and it was clear she had all her things gathered so she could leave the office. I checked the time it was 6:12 pm. She was supposed to leave out of her office a little over 2 hrs ago. She opened up at 7 a.m. and left at 4 p.m..

"Don't get too excited. I need you to work a little bit more..." I say sheepishly. She stops mid-twerk before groaning and sitting in her chair.

"Chile what do you need from me? Our appointment is for Friday, I'm trying to go home, take my wig off and drink some wine. You are acting just like these niggas trying to inconvenience me when I'm already stressed." She dug in her purse and dramatically popped a piece of gum in her mouth, before leaning forward. Exaggerating each pop and chew she took her gum. "What's up?"

"I know I know! But..." I hesitated and I sighed before I leaned back in my own chair. My eyes immediately watered up and I sniffled away the sob that was trying to leave my throat. I told her what happened at the hospital three weeks ago.

"Please don't lecture me, were both medical professionals and I've been beating myself up enough already...I'm scared and I need my sister and Obgyn right now." She sighed and she stopped popping her gum. I could tell a snarky remark was on the tip of her tongue, but she rarely ever saw me cry, so instead of opting for her usual clapbacks, she instead decided to joke. "If you wanted me to see your coochie sooner you should've just said that, I'm on my way." I smiled at her in relief before we both disconnected.

I left my office and let everyone know I was going to do paperwork, emphasizing in the nicest way possible that I didn't want to be bothered. It was a nice cover-up for what I was actually going to be doing.

"What are you doing? Where are you?" I texted Marquis before going to the Find My App to look at his location. He was on the east side, about 15 minutes from my clinic. He looked like he was on a random street corner.

It took him a few minutes to respond, " I'm Getting Mariah her favorite tacos and snacks. There's a line, and they're taking forever. Why? Is everything okay?"

I smiled giggling as I typed my next message. "Oh okay... next time I need you to respond in one minute or less. I thought you were selling penis, looks like your on a street corner. Also your not gonna ask me if I wanna taco?"

He did respond fast all he sent was the unamused emoji followed by, Your child like palate doesn't want a taco. I'm ordering you a chicken quesadilla with cheese and chicken only."

He completely ignored my comment about him prostituting. I hearted is message before typing up another response. "So you are selling penis?" before attaching a broken heart emoji.

"Yes." He responded followed by a heart hands.

I emphazised his message before putting my phone down. Alameda had just pulled into my driveway. I could tell because, you could hear her loud bass coming from the parking lot. I call my overnight security who I hired a few months ago after my place had an attempted burglary. I wanted to make sure my guest were safe when they stayed over night. My clinic has only been open for a little over a year so I had alot of kinks to work out.

I let security know to let Alameda in as I took off my scrub bottoms as well as my panties, folding them neatly and placing them on the chair besides the examination table. I giggled to myself knowing she was going to have something to say. I place a sheet over my lower half before placing my feet on the sternals.

It took her a few minutes but, when she finally walked in she smiled looking at me. "That's what I like mamas," She deepened her voice and slithered her way into the room. She washed her hands in the sink before drying them and putting her gloves on. She rubbed her hands together, raised her eyebrows, squinted her eyes and bit her lip before rubbing her imaginary beard. "Love a woman with no yap or back talk and you already in position. Next time though make sure your face down and booty up. You hear me mama?"

She dropped the act and we both laughed hard. I hit her a bit and sighed deeply as I tried catching my breath. She sat down on the stool before positioning herself in front of me before preparing my machine. "Hey girl, how are you feeling?" She asked as she grabbed the wand, before placing a hand on my womb. "Have you had anymore bleeding? Or other symptoms?"

She asked me as she continued to prep her tools and gather the things she would need. "No not really...No symptoms at all..." My eyes started to water up and my lip quivered as I looked up at the ceiling.

"I'm sorry for not saying anything sooner...I just..this may be the second one if it's a miscarriage. What if I'm infertile? I don't want fertility issues. I want to be a mother so badly. I know there's other options but, I want to carry the child naturally without any assistance, to the full term and I.... I just" I shook my head and covered my face to shield her view of me crying.

I heard her stand up and she wrapped both her arms around me, pulling me into her bosom as she soothingly rubbed my back. "Listen to me, we will have that discussion next if it's needed but for now let's just start with the basics." She pulled back a bit, grabbing both of my wrist, making me bring my hands down to my lap before she grabbed my face, squeezing my cheeks, squashing my face in her palm. "Okay

251 | P a g e

bright eyed girl? Yo mama ate with naming you after your eye color."

"okay" I responded sounding like a toddler since she was squishing my cheeks. She smiled before releasing my face from her hands, she then kissed me on the forehead before proceeding.

She grabbed the doppler, a small device placed on my lower abdomen so that we would be able to hear a heart beat. I played with the ends of my hair anxiously waiting to hear the heart beat. My eyes were shut tight. It normally takes around 1-3 minutes to detect a heart rate using the doppler. But, 1-3 minutes felt like an eternity as I waited. When we finally heard it, my eyes opened and widen immediately. Alameda had a few tears dripping down her face and we just sat in that moment as we listened to the heart beating.

Guilt entered me, Marquis should've been apart of this moment with me. Right then and there I decided I would tell him as soon as I saw him.

After putting away the doppler, she proceeded with the ultrasound. During the 12 week appointment I knew she would be checking for several things. One would be the baby's development specifically she would check the babys brain, head, face, organs, etc. It was important to make sure the baby was also growing exactly where they were suppose too. Normally during the 12th week, blood work would be performed and testing of defective chromosomes would take place to ensure my child didn't have anything such as Patau or down syndrome. We would do that testing back at her office later in the week.

She stepped out once she was finished, ensuring me everything was okay before stepping out.

I sighed happily to myself taking my time in this moment. "Thank you God, thank you Jehovah. Thank you thank you thank you." I say repeatedly as I cleaned myself up and dress myself again. The tears were streaming but I wipe them. I clean the examining table before exiting the room.

Alameda was in the room across from the examining room. She was checking my thermal printer for the ultrasound pictures. I placed my head on her shoulder feeling my softer and gentler side coming out. She placed a hand gently on my head before going back to the pictures. We awed at the pictures and shuffled through them.

"Your gonna be expecting your little boy or girl possible that last week of April, first week of May." She smiled at me before kissing my forehead. "I'm gonna go home now, I'm very tired but I love you friend. We will discuss more at your next appointment." She grabbed my hand and for once I didn't snatch it away.

We walked hand and hand, stopping at my lobby doors. We held each other in a long embrace before we pulled back slightly. "Also, no more secrets. You are my best friend, my sister, and most importantly, I'm your doctor." She gave me a knowing look before she hugged me one last time. My security officer escorted her too her car and I watched as she flirted with him, making the handsome young black man blush a bit, I saw him hand her his phone and I laughed before shaking my head.

I turned around, deciding to check on Mariah one more time before I left for the night. I was immediately met with someone's chest and looked up to see Marquis. I didn't realize he had made it here already. I punched him rapidly but lightly a few times in the arm. "Not you bumping into me, sir," I said casually, but in reality, my heart was beating rapidly. I needed to tell him right now.

"Yes, ma'am, you're right. I apologize for not being more cognizant of my surroundings." He said politely yet sarcastically. What's the tea? What secrets did you not tell her?" My heart paused for a moment, and I took a heavy yet excited sigh. "Not you in my business. You'll find out soon enough, " I said suggestively as I flipped my hair over my shoulder and walked past him.

Despite his injuries, he was still strong. He grabbed the back of my shirt before pulling me back into his chest. He wrapped an arm around my waist, instinctively I placed my hands on top of his forearm, but that just made him squeeze me. He leaned his head down to my ear. "You are my business." He stated before kissing me softly on the cheek. His lips moved from my cheek to my jawline. As his lips worked their way to my lips, his other hand grabbed my chin, making me look up. He kissed along my neck before coming back to my ear.

"You smell and taste good..." His hand was still cupping partially my neck and chin.

"This why your pregnant now." My thoughts flashed back to 11 weeks ago when he put it down on me. My body was heating up from all the stimulation. I wasn't sure what to say or do, so I said the first thing that came to mind. "Maybe it's your sister and nephew fluids your smelling on me." I giggled, knowing I just killed the mood.

He let out a deep chuckle, and I could feel a rumble from his belly since my back was pressed against him. "You play too much, honestly," he released me before grabbing my hand. Let's go say hi to our nephew then, " he led the way to the recovery room. I was in a daze from that comment. "OUR nephew...." echoed in my mind. Did this mean he wanted me to be part of his family?

When we entered the room, the family was surrounding Mariah while she held her son to her chest. She was obviously sleeping but enjoying the company. "Finally! We have two people to help with the vote!" her mother exclaimed as we entered the room.

"Vote?" I was clearly confused, and Mariah rolled her eyes. "Everyone in the family, whose name starts with MAR, we're trying to decide what his name should be. Right now, it's a tie between Marcellus and Marshall." Unanimously, Marquis and I instantly stated, "Marcellus." We looked at each other, and the way he was eyeing me and giving me a one-over, with the bite of his lower lip, made me nervous all over again...in a good way.

His mother, Marcy, stood up and jumped around cheering. She came towards me and pulled me down to her 5'2" height, kissing me on both cheeks. "See, I told you she's a keeper." She pointed hastily at Marquis before sitting on the bed next to her daughter.

"He talks about me to his mother? And she likes me?" I never had so many confirmations in just one moment. I watched as Marquis washed his hands in the corner sink before reaching for his nephew. I felt flutters coming from deep within my stomach. I watched as He sat down in the rocking chair. He was very gentle and held the baby with a nervous yet confident stance. He held the little boy to his chest, and he just looked down at the child with so much love. "This is the father of my child?"

As I admired him, I didn't realize someone was observing me. His mother bumped her hip into me, drawing my attention down to her. "Are you okay, sweetheart? " she asked, but something in her tone just told me she knew what I was hiding. Words were not exchanged, but we had an entire conversation just through our stares. I avert my eyes from her and focus back on Marquis. It was so strange to me how moms always just knew.

I was past the point of trying to come up with a special way to tell him I was carrying his child. I had the custom shirts in my car right now, and now would be the best time. Before my brain could process what my lips were saying, the words already escaped from me: "Marquis, Can you help me with something when you're done meeting your nephew?" His brothers immediately made kissing sounds and fake moans.

"Hey guys! Cut the shit!" their mother Marcy, slapped them each on the back of their heads before she went to grab the baby from him. "Go help your woman. Little Marcellus will be waiting right here when you get back." Marquis gentle handed her over the baby before standing up. As we walked out, he punched his brothers in the shoulder, who playfully groaned in pain.

The walk to my car felt like an eternity. My heart was racing, I was sweating and felt my breath become short. Despite what I just saw I was still very much worried and insecurities were starting to plague my mind. What if he was an amazing uncle but, didn't want to be a father? What if he decided he didn't want to be with me? What if he abandoned me and my child because, fatherhood became too much or I was too much?

I was trying to fight back tears as we made our way to my car. I unlocked the door and in my backseat was a plain tan book with a single blue and a single pink bow at the top left corner.. I handed it too him and he looked slightly confused.

"You needed help with this? Is it for my sister?" He handled the box, shaking it slightly as he tried to guess what was inside. My mood had dampened by my insecurities, and my tone came out soft. I was afraid of his reaction and was starting to feel unwell. My head felt light, so I leaned against my car. "It's for you... just open it."

He looked over at me, studying my face. His eyebrows furrowed, and concern filled his eyes as he scanned me, trying to figure out what was wrong. "I just suddenly don't feel good, Marquis... I'm lightheaded because I haven't really eaten today," I said quickly, hoping to divert his attention. My efforts fell short; he continued to stare, clearly unconvinced by my excuse, but he nodded anyway. He set the box down and prepared to squat, likely to lift me and sit me on the car.

"Your thigh stitches! Don't do that!" I exclaimed, and that's when I realized he didn't have his cane. "Marquis, you shouldn't be putting so much weight on one leg." I crossed my arms over my chest and took a deep breath, feeling irritation bubbling up. I was scared, anxious, overwhelmed, and now lightheaded. I could sense my frustration growing.

"Calm down, mamas, I'll be okay. I have a small limp, but it's nothing serious. I'm not walking around with a cane.

This isn't about me; it's about you." He stepped out of the doorway. "Sit down. I'll open the present; just take a seat; you look as if you're about to faint." My anxiety began to rise, and I moved sharply to my back seat, flopping down. I needed to see his reaction right now.

"Your upset...but you waited 6 weeks too tell him." I sigh taking a deep breathe and trying to calm my anxiety. "Marquis please open the box." He looked at me and smirk. He knew I really wanted him to open the box and now he was taking his sweet time. I glare at him and watched as he moved painfully slow to remove the lid.

Once the lid was removed, the lab coat and the tshirt were on perfect display; the box was also custom, so the shirts fit perfectly into the cutouts made for the items. Marquis set the box down on top of my jeep before grabbing the pink lab coat first. "Dr. Amber ...." He mumbled to himself before putting it back in the book and grabbing the black tshirt. "Future APD detective?" He looked at me and then back at the shirt. Then his eyes widen. He held the shirt out in front of him. He was taking way to long to say anything. He was paused for at least a solid two minutes and that was one too many minutes for me. He just stood in shell shock staring at the shirt.

I got out of my back seat, slamming the door before going to the driver's side and getting inside the car.

This was my worst nightmare. I always prided myself making it to 31 years of age without becoming someones baby mother. Now, here I was, possibly about to turn into a single mother. The tears I had been blinking back spilled over. He just stood there, still staring at the shirt, before looking back at me. He stood very stiff, and I scoffed. I needed him to say anything! Anything would've helped, but he wasn't saying anything.

Suddenly I was brought back to over five years ago when Captain let me leave and didn't try to stop me once. The memory made me release a sob. I pulled out of the parking spot. I heard something hit the ground as I pulled out; I checked the rearview mirror and noticed it was the box; the lab coat was sitting on the ground as well. His mother, who must've been watching from the lobby, stepped out, and she was rubbing his back. I saw her squat to the ground, picking up the tiny lab coat. She was staring at it as well and there was a smile on her face, she looked in between my car, the coat and Marquis...who was still staring at the tiny t-shirt.

I didn't want to wait around any longer. I pulled out onto the main street heading home immediately.

...

I wasn't sure how I made it home safely. My eyes were blurry the whole time from the tears that were falling nonstop. My heart was so heavy I didn't know what my next move should be. I couldn't call anyone because this was not how I wanted to announce my pregnancy to my friends or family. I didn't want to call Alameda; I knew she was tired from work, and I didn't want to be a burden.

I started to contemplate while trying to soothe myself, gently rubbing my neck, moving down to my forearms, and then crossing my arms over my stomach to rub my sides. I've always been grateful to God. One thing I often think but rarely vocalize is how thankful I am for my blessings. Just to name a few:

1. My good health, abled, strong body that hardly ever experienced illness.
2. My beautiful face, specifically my eyes.
3. Despite our iffy relationship, havingna strong mother who raised a strong, intelligent daughter.
4. The many scholarships I was blessed with despite others surrounding me not being nearly as fortunate.
5. I received continuous protection even when I put myself in dangerous situations, especially in my younger years when I met strange men at all hours of the night.

6. My gifts include leadership, critical thinking, an optimistic and empathic personality, and a genuine spirit.
7. Being picked for jobs, I was told I wasn't qualified for or extremely choosy when picking candidates.
8. My life transitions being smooth,

9. My clinic
10. My home

Just to name a few of my blessings, there was one thing that always felt like it slipped through my fingers, never lasting more than a few fleeting moments. It left me disappointed, heartbroken, heavy-hearted, and often feeling ill and depressed: love. I never seemed to be able to hold onto a man. They never saw me for anything beyond lust; it was always just my body they wanted.

It didn't matter how blunt I was about my intentions, how I carried or presented myself. It didn't matter how successful I was, how much weight I lost or how good I had became at doing my hair and make up. It didn't matter the age or race. All men from different backgrounds ended up treating me the same and I've been with all sorts of men. Slightly younger rocker white boy, 15 year age difference black therapist, asian engineer, african tech bro, country white boy, blue collared hispanic, and many others. That all ended the same regardless of how much I changed and worked on myself. As I grew older the men became worst. A situationship that would normally last at least 3 months, now only lasted about 2 weeks or less before a man's true colors were shown.

When I met Marquis I had no interest in men. I decided I would just focus on myself, pursue God with all of my heart and elevate my clinic. But what could I say? The man was a little bit of everything I liked from my previous favorite Situationship. He was gentle yet was a dominating athletic giant like Bryce, was able to read me like a book and revealed things about me that I only knew about myself like Isaiah, had a cool smooth relaxed swag about him like Darnell, A man of God who was still a work in progress like Zion. Made me laugh nonstop like Carter, and was confident about his craft like Onyx. He was everything I ever wanted and as a bonus trait he made me feel safe. No man had ever made me feel 100% safe, he was very patient with me and went out of his way too show me a good time. No man did that.

With all of that being said how did I end up here? Laying on my living room rug crying until I was choking on my own snot and tears, begging God to remove the pain. I wouldn't dare trade in my current, past and future blessings just to experience love but, I was human and I was a woman. I desired to be a wife and a mother. I didn't have a two parent household and always dreamed about raising my kids in the environment I had always wanted. I already had out my future kids routine planned. We would pray together in the mornings before they went to school, I would cook themed meals weekly, One week would be Asian cuisine, the next week would be french food and then the following would be Mexican. Then once a week based off the theme we would go to a authentic restaurant to experience it. I was going to be the best PTA mom who competed with the other moms whether they knew it was a competition or not. I was also looking forward to weekly bible study sessions with my kids discussing very topics and teaching them how to build that relationship with God.

Of course, I would be able to do all of these things but, perhaps just as a single mother. That thought alone pained my heart. Children needed their fathers. I knew that a lot of the pain I experienced while dating in my younger years could've been avoided if I could've just called my daddy and sought his comfort rather than ended up in another man's arms yearning for that comfort and protection that I knew I could only gain from a caring father. Suddenly I was 24 years old, crying after getting my heart broken again wishing my dad was there to show me how I should be treated properly. I remember very vividly sitting in my car leaving a mans house sitting in the parking lot of his apartment complex. I didn't even want to have sex but, I didn't know any other way to receive intimacy or comfort at that time.

Sex was very fleeting, I learned that lesson the hard way, It felt good for five minutes and then it left me feeling empty. Men don't care about aftercare or at least that's what I learned in my own experience. I also learned that men would resort to extensive lengths just to get some coochie. They would disguise themselves as one person just to get what they wanted. Once they achieved their goal, they would leave and mistreat you. Men who were once fast responders, gift givers, kind and amazing listeners were now, very busy, lacked money, were impatient, and were too occupied by their phones to pay me any mind.

The rapid thoughts I was having made me weary. My tears put me in a deep trance and I fell asleep on my floor.

...

I wasn't sure how long I had been out when I was jolted awake by Alexa announcing that someone was at my door. I sat up quickly, clutching my chest as my heart raced from the disruption. My apartment was dark, and I felt disoriented as I scrambled to find my phone while the knocking grew more persistent.

I finally found it on my counter it was approximately 12:48 am. I don't even remember what time I got home, but I had to have been asleep for several hours. I walked towards my door, and I checked the peephole. To my surprise, it was Marquis.

I unlocked my door and opened it, unaware of how I looked but not caring at all. I stood there with my arms folded, waiting for him to speak. He didn't meet my gaze; his eyes were baggy and puffy. Had he been crying too? He held a shirt and lab coat in his hands, and for the first time I'd known him, he looked weary. "Hazel, can I please come in? We need to talk."

I walked away from the door, leaving it cracked open, and turned on my lamp before sitting back down on the floor. Still in my scrubs, I didn't want to sit on the couch. He settled onto my sectional, staring down at the baby shirts in his hand before placing them on the ottoman coffee table in front of him. "How long have you known?" he asked, leaning back into the couch and fixing his gaze on me. I could tell he was preparing to analyze everything I said.

I swallowed hard knowing he wouldn't like my answer. "Six weeks..." I stated softly, averting my eyes and becoming very interested in my nails.

His scoffing caused me to look up at him. He was biting the inside of his cheek, and I tensed up. I was prepared for him to chew me out but he didn't. Instead, he took a deep breath, running a hand through his locs. "Why did you wait so long to say anything."

"Well, at first, our schedules didn't align. I knew we had planned that rideout together, so I ordered the shirts. The morning after our rideout, I intended to place the box on the bed while you were in the shower... I had this whole surprise planned in my head." I tried to read his expression, but it was difficult in that moment. "Then you got shot, and I just..." I struggled to find the right words, but nothing came to me. "I don't have an excuse, Marquis. The truth is, I was trying to find the perfect moment, and today, after seeing you with your nephew and everything else, I felt the urge to tell you." I shrugged defensively. He could be upset all he wanted; I didn't care.

In my mind, my attitude and actions were now justified by his lack of response. I stood up and went to the kitchen to get some water, my throat feeling dry. "And just so you know, I'm keeping this baby whether you want me to or not. We don't need you, and we will have a good life."

Marquis stood up, and I could tell I pushed a button. "Damn Hazel can a nigga not process anything?? You've had six entire weeks to come to terms with this shit! You expect me to have an answer right then and there? Am I supposed to just be overjoyous?"

I didn't typically respond well to being yelled at, especially by a man, but I was determined to stand my ground. "Yes, Marquis! In your own words, you told me you thought I was—" I raised my fingers to mimic air quotations. "A woman you thought was unattainable. So yes, I expected that since you won over the woman you wanted, you'd be extremely happy! Earlier today, you said, 'Let's go meet OUR nephew.' You made it sound like you wanted me to be part of the family." I felt fresh, hot tears streaming down my face—tears of anger. I didn't want to be called delusional or be gaslighted.

He groaned and sat back down on the couch. "Hazel, you're already part of the family since you became friends with Moriah. We're dating now... I... I..." For the first time since I met him, he seemed at a loss for words.

I felt embarrassed. Clearly, I had overthought the situation. "Well, I guess I'm delusional then." My eyes filled with tears, and I let out sobs, feeling utterly humiliated. I rushed upstairs to the bathroom, slamming the door and locking it. I paced around the small space, avoiding the mirror, knowing I wouldn't like what I saw. I heard footsteps coming up the stairs, and Marquis spoke through the door.

"Hazel, I was just shot. I do dangerous work, and that's what was running through my mind when you shared this news with me. I don't want something to happen to me and then leave you as a single mother. I was worried about

266 | P a g e

whether I'd be a good father. I know many of my coworkers who are depressed because they wish they could be more present in their children's lives. I understand you're upset, but my feelings are valid, too, and I apologize if my response made you doubt that I wanted to be a part of the baby's life. I just didn't know what to say in that moment. When I saw the future detective shirt, I started thinking about our future and the risks of my job. It wasn't about not wanting to be a father."

I listened to every single word he said. As he continued to speak, my tears were still falling—this time, happy tears. I opened my door and smiled. Marquis looked distressed, and his eyes were pleading with me. It finally dawned on me that I was being a bit self-centered. I was disappointed in myself. I had always prided myself on being able to put myself in other people's shoes, but I mistook his silence for abandonment and not contemplation.

"I spent the last several hours talking to my parents about this. It wasn't their words of encouragement that brought me to you, but it was just looking at them. They had four children, and both of them worked hard and dangerous jobs. Not just that..." He pointed towards his thigh, where his femoral artery had been injured. "I'm covered in the blood of Jesus; yeah, I work in a dangerous field, but I feel like this is my calling, and God is going to cover me regardless of what happens."

I stared at him in shock, his words striking at my very core. I took his hand and began to massage it. "I'm so sorry, Marquis, for being so hasty. One of my biggest fears is becoming a single mother, and your expression in that moment made it seem like you wanted to run." I laughed and shook my head. "Or maybe I can now admit that I was just projecting my worries and fears onto you."

He pulled my hand toward him, drawing me into his chest and wrapping his strong arms around me. I buried my face against him, finding comfort and peace in his embrace. "I could tell your mind was racing before I even opened the box," he said, pulling back to look at me. "Next time I ask what's wrong, you need to open those pretty lips and tell me. I'll admit, I probably wouldn't have been able to comfort or reassure you right then, which is why I let you drive away. I needed a moment to think and process this for myself." I could see the disappointment in his eyes. I reached up to cup his cheek, rubbing my thumb in a soothing motion. I didn't want him to beat himself up over it. "But moving forward, we need to communicate how we feel. If we can't do it at the moment, we should take a few minutes to gather ourselves and talk. It's going to take practice, and I'm sure we'll have our fair share of failures, but we have to get this right for our child. Agreed?"

I had no push back; I simply nodded my head. I smiled as he provided me with all the reassurance I needed. I thought about my prayer wall in my closet, and he was gradually checking off many of the qualities I desired in a husband. "In return, I promise not to be so quick to make assumptions

and shut the door on communication," I promised him.

He stepped back and began to dig in his pocket. He pulled out a small light pink velvet ring case. I clutched my chest and watched him. I could see him trying to get down on a knee, but he grimaced, and I quickly pulled him up. "Don't tear your stitches!" I lectured as fresh tears began to adjourn my face.

He smiled, and he opened the box before me. It was a gold banded ring with a pink pear-shaped diamond in the middle of several carats surrounding it. He grabbed my left hand, and my heart was pounding. Merely hours ago, my mind was spinning. I didn't think I was worthy of love, and now here I was being proposed to.

I pulled away from him, and I decided to look in the mirror. One side of my hair was extremely flat from where I had been lying down. There were crusty tear strikes on both sides of my eyes, and my nose was red, and had snot coming out. I looked back over at him, and the sobs were coming out again. "Are you seriously choosing me right now?!" I didn't get it. I truly didn't, especially after the way I acted today.

He stepped inside the bathroom and faced us both towards the mirror. "How could I pass up the girl who loves God and tries to devote her life to him? How could I miss out on a woman who will stop what she's doing to help a stranger? Prefers pickleball to clubs and enjoys sunsets and nature over a 5-star restaurant. The woman who cooked me an entire dinner and meal prepped me meals despite being tired from a long week of work, so I wouldn't have to worry about that for the next week. The woman who is a self-proclaimed chef and can actually back up what she can cook?"

I rolled my eyes, but I was still smiling. "Okay, so you like that I'm a cheap date, that I'm kind, and that I'm a chef as well as a Christian?" I needed more affirmation right now.

He smiled. "Yeah, that's exactly what I'm saying. He grabbed my face while staring at me through the mirror, and we made eye contact. "I also need to see that wild hair sticking up, followed by those gorgeous eyes of yours making eye contact with me on a daily." He turned my face to look back up at him. "Listen, God aligned you in my life for a reason, and now we're going to be parents. I love you. I knew that when I came over after you were depressed. My plan wasn't to take care of you the way I did; I just wanted to hang out for a bit and drop the gifts off. Something in my spirit moved me to take care of you, and when I was doing it, I realized I wouldn't mind doing it for a very long time."

My jaw dropped, and the waterworks came for the millionth time today. "I love you..." my heart fluttered. I had never been in love before, but there were several times I almost said it to him. I stopped myself every single time because I was scared of rejection. So, I suppressed the feelings and focused on how good he made me feel.

"I love you too Marquis."

He pulled the ring from his pocket again and grabbed my left hand. "Will you allow me to put this ring on you?" I nodded my head and watched as he slipped it on my finger. He pulled me into a kiss, and I felt his hard-on push into me. and I laughed as I gave us space. "We're gonna have to get married fast because this Abstinence thing isn't going to last much longer." I held his chin in my hand, using the palm of my fingers to massage his beard.

"Fo sho, but we can talk about that later you always get me hard, I'm just better at hiding it at different times." I laughed, hitting his chest. "You're disgusting."

"Shoot, you're about to be Mrs. Disgusting, then." He pulled me into a deep kiss before I could respond.

I wrapped my arms around his neck and relaxed into the kiss. "Oh, to be loved....Thank you, Lord, for blessing me with this experience." We pulled apart, and I smiled at him, and he looked down at me. "I just unlocked something new. Your eyes are glistening right now, and I've never seen them this green before." He stated as he admired my orbs. I felt something new wash over me. I now knew we were locked in. He was everything I had ever prayed for, and I knew he was crazy about me just as I was about him. I was in love, that's what it was. I had never been in love before, but now that I was, there was no taking this feeling away from me.

...

I took a shower before changing into a sports bra and shorts. Marquis stood behind me, cupping my belly as I did my skincare routine. I always had a bit of stomach, so there was no significant difference for me at three months of pregnancy.

"Can I ask you something? Promise you won't get mad first." I looked at him through the mirror, and he had the biggest grin on his face. I knew he was either about to really piss me off or make me laugh. "Tread lightly," I answered as I applied toner to my face, anticipating whatever he was going to ask me.

"What is a Neberu? And why are we naming our son that? The names in our family, ESPECIALLY for the boys, a non-negotiable has to start with "MAR." I just smiled at him. Five years ago, even a year ago, if someone had told me, I would be arguing with my fiance over baby names. I would laugh in their face and go on about my day. I shook my head in disbelief. I truly was living in many answered prayers. I turned my head and gave Marquis a slow, sensual kiss. When I pulled back, his eyes were filled with love for me.

"Thank you, Lord, for your grace, mercy, and patience towards me. I'm thankful for all that you are and all that you do. Thank you for answering my prayers. I owe it all to you In Jesus Christ's name, we pray"

AMEN.

Recipes

Oreo Cream Cheese Cake Cookies:

- 10 tbl of salted butter
- 2 tbl of cream cheese
- 1 cup of brown sugar
- 1/2 of granulated sugar
- Mix those ingredients
- 1 large egg
- 2 tps of vanilla
- Mix together again
- 2 cups and 2 tbl Flour
- half a tps of baking soda
- Mix Again
- crush oreos into the mix.
- Place in the freezer for a few hours.
- Bake at 400 for 10 minutes

Marry Me Salmon:

Season your Salmon with paprika, all-purpose seasoning salt, garlic powder, and olive oil

Air fry your salmon for about 20-25 mins at 400

In a pan, add olive oil

Once heated, add garlic and onions Once brown,

add sun-dried tomatoes add in 2 cups of double

cream or heavy cream Once the cream is

colored, add spinach.

Season the sauce with black pepper and all-purpose seasoning salt Add Parmesan cheese

Then add your salmon.

About the Author

At the time of publishing this book I am a 25 year old female. I currently live in North Austin, living my best life. I spend my free time going to the lake almost everyday to either watch the sunset or rise. I am a daughter of God and wish live a Christ driven life. I'm also very much single at the time of writing this. https://www.hazelnutbooks.com
https://www.tiktok.com/@hazelnutlc
https://www.tiktok.com/@marquis.and.hazel
https://www.instagram.com/hazelnutpublication
https://www.hazelnutbooks.com/Contact

Made in the USA
Columbia, SC
12 December 2024

48075741R00150